Praise for
WHAT NORA KNEW

"Linda Yellin's feisty heroine Molly Hallberg is sassy, cynical, irreverent, and hysterically funny. With a wounded heart and gimlet eye, Molly delivers razor-sharp observations on love and fear that have us completely identifying with her, and crackling, witty dialogue that's so damn entertaining I wish Yellin would start writing screenplays."
—Claire Fontaine, author of *Come Back*

"Linda Yellin has given us a tart, funny, totally lovable heroine whose path to true love is hilarious and heartwarming. Nora Ephron would have loved this book."
—Jenny Allen, essayist, *The New Yorker's Disquiet, Please!*

"Could someone please apologize to my husband and children for ignoring them all weekend as I gobbled up this delicious book? I loved every minute of it."
—Karen Bergreen, author of *Perfect Is Overrated*

"Linda's lively story sparkles and dances off the page."
—Tracey Jackson, author of *Between a Rock and a Hot Place*

"Linda Yellin has written an irresistibly funny, authentic novel about the two-steps-forward-one-step-back pursuit of life, love, and career in New York City. She writes for all of us with Molly Hallberg's laugh-out-loud, poignant inability to accept she's met her equal, while everyone around her takes the plunge. Yellin is a Nora Ephron–inspired humorist with a voice of her own."
—Kathryn Leigh Scott, author of *Down and Out in Beverly Heels*

"I laughed my way through Linda Yellin's *What Nora Knew*—when I wasn't nodding in recognition. Witty, wise, insightful, and altogether charming."

—Emily Listfield, author of *Best Intentions*

"Linda Yellin's novel is by turns touching and funny, and her heroine has charm and chutzpah to spare."

—Christina Haag, author of
Come to the Edge: A Love Story

Praise for
THE LAST BLIND DATE

"*The Last Blind Date* is a laugh-out-loud funny, nakedly revealing, kooky look at romance told with sweetness and soul. From the minute our hero Randy picks up our heroine Linda at the airport with his fly accidentally unzipped, and takes her to his friend's son's bar mitzvah, where he mistakenly calls her by the name of his ex-wife, it's impossible not to root for their love."

—Susan Shapiro, author of
Five Men Who Broke My Heart

"*The Last Blind Date* is a valentine for optimism, risk-taking, and love itself. With self-deprecating charm, Yellin takes her reader on a journey from Chicago to Manhattan, eviscerating New York City folkways with gentle yet biting wit."

—Sally Koslow, author of *The Widow Waltz*

"Yellin's story is not only a delight to read but an inspiring example of the good that can come from taking risks."

—*Publishers Weekly*

"*The Last Blind Date* is a candid and charmingly funny account of love. Linda Yellin's sympathy, wit, and nerve make her determined forging of a family a success, and this book about it completely winning."

—Hilma Wolitzer, author of *An Available Man*

"Filled with lots of girl-talk, this memoir will appeal to readers who just can't get enough of the beginning, middle, and sweet endings of love stories."

—*Kirkus Reviews*

"Linda Yellin's modern love story will leave you laughing 'til it hurts."

—Sam Apple, author of *American Parent*

"I keep on trying to think who I can compare this to, but you really can't. I can say Erma Bombeck but younger, Chelsea Handler but kinder, but that doesn't do the book justice. It's a voice that is unique and compelling."

—Amazon Review by Total Stranger

Praise for
SUCH A LOVELY COUPLE

"Yellin has a gift for moving the plot along and imbuing a familiar tale with freshness and humor. A good read from a writer with the wit and verve of Susan Isaacs."

—*Publishers Weekly*

"Such a rare, ringing clarity of tone and vision. The emotions, the dialogue, the scenery are just dead on."

—Susan Kenney, author of *In Another Country*

"Warm and funny and honest."

—Ann Hood, author of *The Obituary Writer*

Also by Linda Yellin

Such a Lovely Couple

The Last Blind Date

WHAT NORA KNEW

Linda Yellin

G

Gallery Books

New York   London   Toronto   Sydney   New Delhi

G

Gallery Books
A Division of Simon & Schuster, Inc.
1230 Avenue of the Americas
New York, NY 10020

First Gallery Books trade paperback edition January 2014

GALLERY BOOKS and colophon are registered trademarks of Simon & Schuster, Inc.

For information about special discounts for bulk purchases, please contact Simon & Schuster Special Sales at 1-866-506-1949 or business@simonandschuster.com.

The Simon & Schuster Speakers Bureau can bring authors to your live event. For more information or to book an event contact the Simon & Schuster Speakers Bureau at 1-866-248-3049 or visit our website at www.simonspeakers.com.

Designed by Jill Putorti

Manufactured in the United States of America

10 9 8 7 6 5 4 3 2 1

Library of Congress Cataloging-in-Publication Data is available.

ISBN 978-1-4767-3006-6
ISBN 978-1-4767-3008-0 (ebook)

For Randy Arthur—

I love you so much it's ridiculous.

There's no one who's more romantic than a cynic.

—Nora Ephron, *Rolling Stone* magazine

WHAT
NORA
KNEW

Prologue

Ten minutes after saying "I do" at the Garden City Hotel in Long Island, I was already having my doubts. But how do you say "I don't" to a man who's considered *quite the catch.* Everyone was constantly telling me—even strangers—that Evan Naboshek, of the firm Naboshek, Halla, and Weiss, was a fabulous hell of a prize.

In answer to the question, should anyone ask, "So how'd you two lovebirds meet?"—it started when lovebird #1 stepped out of a cab into a puddle. I was trying to open my umbrella at the same time I was juggling my grocery bags, spilling tomatoes, peppers, onions, three frozen-lemonade cans, and a dozen eggs onto the sidewalk. A dashing stranger went dashing after my produce, holding his umbrella aloft like Don Quixote.

That's all it took. I fell in love.

Evan has all the tall, dark, and gorgeous attributes that add up to trouble. The deep-set eyes. The Roman nose. The square jaw that I later wanted to slug. Despite the rain, his custom-made suit looked perfectly pressed, and when he handed over a runaway onion, I noticed his French cuffs with the gold links and that he wasn't wearing a wedding band. Not that a bare finger's any indication of a man's availability, but at least you've got a fifty-fifty shot.

Balancing his umbrella over both our heads, Evan helped me restuff my plastic grocery bags and escorted me to the corner garbage can, where I ceremoniously dumped the sticky egg carton. The tomatoes, peppers, and onions also met their maker. The dented lemonade cans survived, but my dignity was a goner. *Rain will wash away the mess,* my knight in shiny tailoring assured me, his words sounding like a song lyric. I pictured droplets dancing around Audrey Hepburn and George Peppard; rain cascading over Hugh Grant and Andie MacDowell. I wanted to sing: *The sun will come out tomorrow!*

Back then, I was still capable of dreams.

"Next on your agenda?" my rescuer asked, his smile revealing the best set of veneers this side of a TV anchorman.

I opened my umbrella. "Home," I said, nodding at my apartment building, your basic white-brick Upper East Side building. "I splurged on a cab so I wouldn't get my groceries wet."

"Well, that didn't go well." He laughed. But not an at-me laugh, more of an at-the-situation laugh.

Beneath our now-adjoining umbrellas, he told me he was a partner in a law firm and would be happy to help me sue

Mother Nature should my grocery debacle result in whiplash, adding, though, that he didn't usually specialize in curbside accidents. His expertise was divorce.

If only I'd listened.

I thanked him for pursuing my salad ingredients and said I could probably manage the last twenty steps without requiring legal aid. He invited me for coffee to help me de-chill from the rain.

"You aren't a married divorce lawyer, are you?" I asked.

"No," he said. "I'm a happily divorced divorce lawyer."

Like I said, trouble, trouble, trouble.

He waited in my lobby while I hurried upstairs, jammed my lemonade cans into my freezer, googled him, changed out of my wet shoes and shirt, spent three minutes blow-drying my hair into a semblance of presentable, and returned downstairs.

Evan was talking into his cell phone and held up two fingers to indicate he'd only be two minutes. Except he was still on the phone fifteen minutes later, so maybe what he was really doing was making a peace sign. While I sat in the chair opposite his, I waved hello to my neighbor, Mrs. McBriarty, who was passing by on her walker. I went and checked my mailbox, then came back and sat down again across from my future husband.

On the phone Evan sounded like a real hardnose, demanding this, outraged at that, saying things like *This matter is not closed! If you want to go to court, my client's happy to go to court!* He insisted on the house in the Berkshires and the

3

condo in Aspen, and that the lease be paid off on the Lexus immediately. But when he did look up at me, he had this warm smile on his face. He mouthed, *Just one second,* then went back to being Mr. Kick-Ass Tough Guy. In the early stages of our courtship, his ability to switch personalities on a dime seemed powerful and sexy, a masterful manipulation of mood and emotions, the key to his success in a courtroom. I later found myself bemoaning that nobody warned me I'd be married to Dr. Jekyll.

Warnings? Warnings? There were a million warnings, all of which I chose to ignore. I preferred to focus on the late-night dinners at Del Posto, Evan's car-service Lincolns versus my subway MetroCard, his three-bedroom Park Avenue apartment (*so much nicer* than my crowded studio apartment), the barrage of red roses, and the juicy gossip about his clients' nasty divorces. We'd call it lawyer-girlfriend privilege when he'd tell me off-the-record stories.

"Promise you'll pretend I never told you this?" he'd say.

"Scout's honor," I'd say.

My Girl Scout leader Mrs. Tuke would have been ashamed of me.

Evan liked blabbing scuttlebutt as much as I liked hearing it. The man couldn't keep his mouth shut. Or his zipper. That little tidbit he did keep quiet.

I loved his smooth life. He loved my curvy butt. I loved the way he looked at me. He loved that I looked up to him. I didn't question when Mr. Spill the Beans excused himself to take calls in private. I didn't question his nonstop honeyed words. I allowed myself to believe that I was so clever, so witty, that I was his one-woman sideshow.

And, oh, how he won over my family! He admired my mother's arts and crafts, heaped flattery on my youngest sister Lisa's punch recipe, complimented my sister Jocelyn's insightful observations about the ailing euro, and volunteered to play Ping-Pong with my father. Twenty minutes after meeting the guy, my parents were wanting to book the caterers. I was almost thirty-one years old; it was time, they said, and I suppose I felt so, too.

When it came to track records for romance, I wasn't what you'd call a gold medalist. My ability to find relationships hurtling nowhere was worthy of a Hubble telescope. Sophomore year at SUNY Albany, I fell head over boots (there's lots of snow in Albany) for Glenn-with-two-*n*'s Crosse-with-an-*e* when we got into a debate in our Great American Writers class on the subject of Ernest Hemingway and Virginia Woolf and geniuses committing suicide. Glenn argued on the side of genius leads to suicide. I argued on the side of that's ridiculous. We dated for two years, most of it spent arguing. Last I heard, Glenn was a magician living in Colorado and selling hallucinogenic mushrooms.

After moving to Manhattan postcollege, I often suggested to my first New York City boyfriend, Clive the Actuary, that we buy tickets for a Broadway show, hear some tunes, see some stars, although his idea of great theater was the Knicks at Madison Square Garden. To be fair, he tried. We turned down a Memorial Day–weekend invitation to Fire Island so I could see *The Producers*. ("The beach!" he said. "Nathan Lane!" I said.) As soon as I opened the program, twenty little sheets of white paper fluttered out, each saying that for that night's performance, understudy so-and-so would be substituting for regular so-and-so. Clive shook his head. "Even Matthew Broderick would rather be out of town."

Three weeks later we split up. Clive got custody of the Knicks. I got custody of Times Square.

I dated Vince, then Bobby, then Sean. I broke up with Vince, then Bobby, then Sean. I seemed to be on a six-month plan with each guy. We'd be moving along fine, and right about that six-month point I'd ask, "So, how do you think things are going with us?" and that would lead to a discussion and the discussion would lead to a realization and that'd be that. Just to be safe, I didn't ask my next boyfriend, Brett the Paramedic, how things were going after six months. He asked me. And that was that.

I had no idea how other women did it, how'd they know what they were getting and love what they were getting. I just kept stumbling my way from one romance to the next. Of course, the relationships started out well. I wasn't a masochist. But before long the initial fascination would wear off; the guy with the six-pack abs was never around because he was always at the gym; the man who made me feel needed was too needy; the guy who taught me the difference between Syrah and Shiraz was a closet alcoholic. By the time Evan showed up I didn't trust myself to know what I was supposed to want. And what with everyone I ever met in my entire life, including me, in awe of his charm and seduced by his magnetism, and saying I'd be out of my freaking mind if I let this one get away, well—suddenly I was registering at Bloomingdale's.

Oh. And we were fabulous in the sack together. The dynamic duo. Scarlett and Rhett. Antony and Cleopatra. Tarzan and Jane. I'm sure I wasn't the first woman to find herself wearing lace and tulle and standing with an armful of white lilies because of sex. Love may be blind, but great sex is the ultimate blindfold. I wanted Evan to be perfect, so I assumed he was. He gave me excuses; I'd give him the benefit of the doubt. He was my fiend with benefits.

After everything unraveled, I'd rerun the *Evan and Molly Show* in my head, searching for the missed signals. With the genius of hindsight I'd write lists filled with signals galore.

Five things about Evan Naboshek under the heading "I Should Have Known Better":

1. Just because a man buys his socks at Barneys does not mean he won't wear them *twice*.

2. Cheap tipper when no one else is around. If he's entertaining a client in a fancy-schmancy restaurant, he'll be sure to lay on the 20 percent. But if some poor guy delivers spring rolls and moo shu pork on a freeze-your-ass-off night, Mr. Big Shot hands the guy a quarter.

3. Baby talk. There are some women in this world who are not comfortable being called Poopsum or Daddy's Little Girl. I am one of them. "How'd you like the appellate judges of New York State to hear you talking like that?" I'd say, not that it did Poopsum any good.

4. Farts on cue. I suppose some people might consider this an admirable ability, people who are still in fraternities or under ten years old. "Pull my finger" is one of Evan's favorite jokes. He can also wait an entire evening, getting through a cocktail party, dinner party, and after-dinner cocktails, saving all his best stuff until he gets home and lets her rip, often driving me out of our bedroom screaming into the night.

5. Always asks for a better restaurant table. *Always.* We were seated at the head table at our wedding and I was waiting for Evan to request a better table.

None of these are major enough reasons for breaking up, but all constitute possible lifetime annoyances.

And then there's number six:

6. Left me for another woman.

That last one is a good reason for splitting up.

I found out about Evan's messing around because he didn't have the decency to shut down his home computer. E-mail messages with inappropriate subject headings from his legal secretary, Diane Forlenza—that was her name at the time, although now it's Diane Forlenza Naboshek—were just sitting there right on the open screen where I couldn't help but notice them while dusting. (I was a wife who actually cared enough to straighten out my husband's desk and dust his keyboard and mouse. Can any woman have been a bigger fool? While I was dusting Evan's pencil box, he was dusting Diane's.) But she was always so *nice* to me when I called the office. So nice that Evan would come home from work and I'd be complimenting Diane: "You're so lucky to have her."

Oh, Molly, Molly, Molly.

To amp up the cheesy quotient, when I was emptying my dresser drawers and tossing shirts and skirts into my suitcase, bellowing, "Your secretary? Your secretary? What could be triter!"—he had the nerve to correct me and tell me she preferred to be called administrative assistant. Like the real problem was that I'd demoted her. Bags in tow, I grabbed a taxi to Penn Station and a train out to my parents' house in Roslyn.

At night I'd read suicidal poems by Anne Sexton. Suicidal poems by Sylvia Plath. And cynical poems by Dorothy Parker. I'd pity myself. I'd berate myself. I'd pity myself. Back and forth in my head like a crazy woman, and when I was done with that routine, I'd cry into my pillow on the convertible couch in my former childhood bedroom that was now my mother's arts-and-crafts room, and then I'd get mad at myself for crying because crying gives you wrinkles and someday I might want to start dating again. Although not any day soon. Maybe never.

How is it some people get their hearts trampled and they bounce right back and fall in love again, no questions asked. Is it because they *don't* ask questions? I could no more easily figure out love than I could figure out the insides of a toaster. I longed to believe in romance and excitement and possibility. But deep-down love, deep-in-the-ventricles-of-your-heart love, was something that happened to other people, make-believe people in fairy tales and movies.

I'd walk past the romance sections in bookstores gazing over all those covers of women faint with lust in the arms of bare-chested pirates and sweaty slave masters, their eyes gleaming with passion. *Hey, ladies, have fun while you can.*

I imagined their six-month talks:

DAMSEL: Well, Sinbad, you've been ripping my bodice for half a year now and I was wondering just where this relationship is heading.

SINBAD: Huh? I'm a pirate. Where the hell do you think it's heading? I'm on the next ship outta town, baby.

My entire marriage lasted twelve days short of three years. It would have been our leather anniversary. I looked it up. To celebrate, I went out and bought myself a new wallet.

The divorce itself took four months to finalize, which in the State of New York with its archaic laws at the time (no no-fault, just *fault* fault) constituted some kind of legal miracle. (Unless, of course, a too-big-for-his-britches and often-not-in-his-britches lawyer pays off a few judges. Not that I'm insinuating anything.) To unload his guilty conscience along with his wife, Evan covered the security deposit and two years' rent on a one-bedroom for me. My new apartment was only a block away from the puddle-laden street where we first met. I had a better view than from my pre-Evan apartment—but a more jaundiced view of love.

1

When Deirdre Dolson left a note on my desk requesting my presence in her office at 2:00 sharp, my first thought was *What did I do wrong?* My second thought was *Hey, maybe I'm getting a raise!* But that thought didn't last as long as the first one.

You may have read about Deirdre in the gossip columns—she employs a personal publicist to make sure you read about her. Good for business, she likes to say, but really, it's just good for Deirdre. She's the editor in chief of the online newsmagazine *EyeSpy*. Gossip! News! Pop Culture and Reviews! And the reason I have dental and a 401(k).

The note was written in Deirdre's signature purple ink. Her other signature is her headache-inducing perfume. She wears it by the gallon. I couldn't tell if Deirdre personally deposited the message on my chair or if it was dropped off by her assistant, Gavin. Deirdre's assistants are always male. I've worked here four years now, since the year after my divorce, and in that time she's been through half a dozen assistants, all male.

I got to the office around eleven, having written at home that morning. One of the perks of my job is you're allowed to go off and be creative in other locales. Deirdre sees our main competitor as either *Gawker* or *Jezebel*; it's hard to tell, but someone once told her that *Gawker* writers get to work at home, so now we get to do it, too.

When I walked in, ass-kissing, backstabbing Emily Lawler was sitting in her adjacent cubicle with her nose in a book. Usually, she's poking her nose into my business. Emily has this really white skin and really dark hair and round, dark eyes. She looks like Snow White minus the dwarfs. After I stowed my purse in my file drawer, next to my backup heels and box of Lipton chicken-soup packets, Emily popped up, looming over me with that cutsie, sneery face of hers, and said, "Good thing you showed up before two," which proves she didn't have the decency to even *pretend* she didn't read my note. "Gavin was asking where you were."

"Oh, really?" I turned on my computer.

"I told him if there's something Deirdre needed, that I'd be happy to help." She smiled her fake sweet smile that's not meant to be sweet, just fake.

"You're a true pal, Emily." I feigned intense typing to make my pal go away. "Must be nice to sit around reading all day."

Emily's got the all-time cushiest of cushy jobs. She writes book reviews for *EyeSpy*. She held up a novel, *Larceny among Lovers*. The cover had a cornball illustration of a man, in a trench coat and fedora, standing in a doorway and casting a shadow across a dead woman's legs.

"This guy had to grow up with a lot of sisters," she said, pointing to the author's name. "He really understands women."

"Isn't that a crime book?"

"Criminals have sisters."

"Emily, can I *pay* you to go away?"

"You wish," she said and disappeared behind our mutual wall.

When I first started at *EyeSpy,* we all had actual offices. Now only Deirdre and the CFO have offices. About a year ago they knocked down walls, squeezed us together, and knocked off a full floor's rent. The official party line was that an open plan would foster communication and encourage rapport, but all that really happened was now everyone sits at their desk listening to iPods, blocking out any distractions and each other.

Maybe Deirdre wanted to meet to tell me what a commendable job I was doing. We'd discuss moving my office; she'd say I deserved any cubicle of my choice. Maybe she was so thrilled with me that I could request my own column again. I do that a lot. Request a column. And maybe this time she'd say yes!

Well, maybe.

Before *EyeSpy,* I was writing for *Hipp* magazine, which was anything but. *Hipp*'s readership was decent until the magazine industry went into the toilet, and even after that it was still semidecent, but their readers are aging—more interested in hip replacements than hip nightclubs, a side effect of *Hipp* not converting to an online format. The good news was, the magazine was floundering enough that they pretty much let me do whatever I wanted, which is how I got to write a piece about a powerful, well-known, unnamed New York divorce attorney who cheated on his expense account and did unflattering impersonations of his clients.

Oh, and who'd recently dumped his journalist wife.

I still don't know how Deirdre ended up reading the story—she must have been at her beauty salon or something—but she called me at *Hipp* and introduced herself. Like I wouldn't know who she was!

"Loved your piece on Evan Naboshek," she said. "You did to him what Nora Ephron did to Carl Bernstein."

"Technically that piece wasn't about my ex-husband; it was about—"

"Your ex?"

"My ex."

"Did you hear from him?"

"A cease-and-desist order, although it was too late to cease or desist because the piece was already published."

"You'd think he'd be a smarter lawyer than that."

"You'd think."

She asked me to send her my résumé. To say I hung up the phone and wanted to knock out a few cartwheels would be an understatement.

For years, my résumé was a testament to hyperbole, exaggeration, and creative fiction. Two days after graduating college I moved to the city to be a famous writer, vowing to never end up in my family's Long Island upholstery business. (Four generations of upholsterers—if you count my sister—a solid, successful business, and my worst nightmare.) Appalled to discover my journalism degree did not lead to offers to run the *New York Times* or write cover stories for *Time* magazine, I re-aimed my career goal to *paying the rent*.

I started with a job at Starbucks that came with a cute title but lousy pay. To compensate for the gaping hole in my budget, *Barista Molly* spent the next two years posing nude three nights a week at a SoHo art studio. I developed a talent for holding still without shifting or wobbling or needing to pee. During breaks I'd slip on my robe and walk from easel to easel to see how I'd turned out. Despite my lifelong desire to look mysterious and exotic, I am incorrigibly fresh-faced and all-American. Like somebody whose face belongs on a box of laundry detergent. Pretty enough to be pretty, but maybe not so pretty as to stand out in a crowd. Unless, of course, I'm the only naked person in the room. Then you might notice me.

Along the way I sold ballet shoes, house-sat, cat-sat, and worked behind a Hertz rent-a-car counter, a job I left the nanosecond I got hired as an advertising writer for kids' cereals. That job lasted until the client meeting where I made an unfortunate comment involving the word crap, followed by a job as a technical writer for a mountain-biking company, until it was discovered I knew everything about lying my way through an interview, and nothing about technical writing or mountain biking. Next came a few years writing for a Weight

Watchers–type website, and one Christmas season selling Mixmasters and can openers in the appliance department at Bloomingdale's. I stumbled onto my job at *Hipp* because of someone I slept with whom I had no business sleeping with right after my divorce, but my self-esteem at the time wasn't exactly helping me make sound decisions.

Other people might have read a résumé like mine and thought, *No focus.*

Not Deirdre. She got it in her head that I was some sort of fearless daredevil who'd do anything. For my interview we met in her office "before hours," which for her meant before her 8:00 a.m. meeting, and for me meant before I was actually awake. When she offered me a cup of coffee, I didn't tell her I'd already had two.

Deirdre's office at the time was all-white laminate and chrome and glass with a white carpet. Now it's all-white laminate and chrome and glass with a gray carpet. She sat on one side of her glass-top desk; I sat on the other on a white Mies van der Rohe pavilion chair. A side benefit of a family in the upholstery business—you know your furniture styles.

"So tell me about this nude-modeling job," she said, running her gel-tipped fingernails through her spiked, blond hair. Deirdre dresses young for her age—her age at the time being forty-eight, but her wardrobe more like eighteen, with her low-cut dresses and ankle-high boots and enough bracelets to open a jewelry stand. "What did you get from the experience?"

"Fourteen dollars an hour plus tip jar," I said. "It helped pay expenses."

"Were you self-conscious?"

"It's not a good job for self-conscious people."

"It must have required a certain amount of bravado." Deirdre held out a bowl and offered me a cashew. I shook my head no; I didn't want nuts in my teeth. "I admire that," she said. "The piece about your ex demonstrated bravado."

I tried to look full of bravado while she told me she needed a writer who'd be willing to take on the more creative challenges. She emphasized the word *challenges* with an odd smirk.

"Will it involve removing my clothes?" I asked.

"No. It requires a good attitude and a sense of humor."

A good attitude and sense of humor? How tough could that be?

Deirdre told me the job specifics and benefits and gave an example of a typical assignment, something about a pit crew at a racetrack and changing tires under duress, but I was too busy getting inwardly thrilled from hearing the salary and how I could come and go as I pleased and that she didn't believe in chaining her writers to their desks. By then I couldn't get the words out of my mouth fast enough when I said, "I'll take it!"

So while Emily sits on her sweet ass reviewing books for her column, Emily Literati, I get assigned all the whack job pieces, or what used to be called human interest, but in my case is more like human sacrifice.

I reviewed my last several assignments in my head looking for ways I might have screwed up, reasons why Deirdre might have requested our 2:00 meeting.

Let's see, the aerial-yoga class where I had to swing upside down on fabric trapezes? No. Deirdre liked that piece. The shooting-range-in-New-Jersey article also went well, and I really think the gentleman from Passaic got over that little incident with the clay pigeons. And Deirdre wrote me a purple-inked memo congratulating me on my undercover bra-fitter piece. We received all sorts of comments online, most of them positive, except from that one woman who swore she'd never shop at the Brassiere Firm again. (Honest, Ms. 42D, I swear *it wasn't my fault*.)

I couldn't come up with anything, at least not anything that would get me fired. Of course, I'd been fired enough times in the past to know you never know.

"I want you to write a piece about romance," Deirdre was saying to me, the two of us sitting on opposite sides of her big-kahuna desk.

"Me? Really?" I'm the last person on the planet Earth I'd assign to write about romance. Maybe a nice dissertation about loser romance, but any other expertise on my part was highly questionable.

"Did you see that video of the guy proposing at a basketball game?" Deirdre said. "The couple on a Kiss Cam?"

"The viral one, where the girlfriend walked out and left the guy on one knee?"

We cringed in unison.

"How can anyone so totally misread his relationship?" Deirdre said.

Been there, done that, I thought.

"He's buying diamonds while she's signing on to Match. What made him think she was the one?" Deirdre paused, looked at me, and waited.

I finally said, "That was a rhetorical question, right?"

She leaned forward, all earnest and excited. "What with texting, skyping, online dating, how's anyone to know what's real? How does romance cut through the digital bullshit?" Deirdre's energy went into overdrive. "We'll make this a big article, have you question people on how they recognized their soul mates." I didn't mention that I thought soul mates were bullshit. "Did their eyes meet across a crowded bar? Did a brick land on their head? Or did they get humiliated on a Kiss Cam?"

I said I believed any circumstances leading to a Kiss Cam were humiliating.

Deirdre swept her hands in the air, her bracelets jangling. "'Cyberdate? Or Soul Mate?'" She was writing headlines in the air. "'Love at First Sight? Or First Gigabyte?'" She zoomed her attention back to me. "I'm giving you three weeks."

Boondoggle! Turnaround time on assignments is usually never more than a few days. Then Deirdre explained she wanted an extensive, well-researched piece with lots of interviews; and I'd be writing it in addition to my other assignments. A certain personality type might have thought, *What an opportunity!* I was thinking, *Dammit, extra work.*

"Sound good?" she said.

"What an opportunity!" I said.

"I want this to be sharp, witty, candid. Poignant and intimate. Written like Nora Ephron."

I gulped. An audible, embarrassing gulp. "But I'm not Nora Ephron."

"You aren't Abe Lincoln, but you can study the Civil War."

Before I could respond, Deirdre told me she was simply unable to emphasize the importance of the assignment. Then spent the next five minutes emphasizing it.

I sat there wondering what was the downside of bungling the job. Failure? Embarrassment? The disdain of my peers? Versus pissing off Deirdre if I said thanks, but no thanks. My Visa bill flashed before my eyes. "Tell me more," I said.

"Make it fun and romantic. Like Nora's movies," Deirdre said.

"Fun and romantic. Like her movies. Fine. Got that." *Holy shit.* "Do you mind me asking why you chose me for this assignment?"

Deirdre laughed. "You're not afraid to ask people personal questions."

"Can I ask you a question?"

Deirdre frowned. Sat back.

"If I do a good job on this, can we talk about me writing a column? I'd call it MyEye. Mainly the same sort of things I'm writing already, but with, you know, my picture and name on top."

"See," Deirdre said. "You've got nerve. That's why I value you." She hit her buzzer and barked into the little black intercom, "Gavin! Coffee!" She smiled at me, nodding at the same time. The smile meant *You can go now.* The nod meant *Right now.*

But on my way out of her office, she added, "Let's see how you do on your Nora piece. Then we'll talk."

As soon as I returned to my cubicle, Emily's head floated over our divider. "Hi!" she said, as if she were surprised to see me, instead of what she really was—going crazy waiting to hear what had transpired between Deirdre and me.

A crueler, unkinder Molly Hallberg might have taken serious advantage of the situation, told Emily that I was getting promoted, that I was Emily's new editor, and that my first official act was to slash her salary by 50 percent.

"Hi back," I said, not particularly enthusiastic.

"How'd things go for your meeting?"

"Great! I'm getting promoted, I'm your new editor, and for my first official act I'm slashing your salary by fifty percent."

"Hardee-har-har," Emily said. "What did Deirdre want to talk about?"

"Oh, the usual. Financial advice. Love-life advice."

"Well, I hope she didn't stick you with that soul-mate assignment. Even I dodged that land mine."

2

I met my boyfriend, Dr. Russell Edley, through a Groupon deal. You might be surprised to hear I even have a boyfriend. After all my bad-judgment romances and pathetic marriage, it's easy to assume I just hung it up, swore off men, joined a nunnery, and renounced anything with an XY chromosome. For a while there, that was the game plan. But *stay away from anything with a penis* soon turned into *one little drink can't hurt.* I like going out for drinks and I like penises. I also like back rubs.

Russell is a chiropractor with big strong hands and big strong shoulders and a flat stomach from doing forty-five push-ups every morning. His salt-and-pepper hair makes him look more like a distinguished professor than a man who knows his way around a vertebral subluxation. He has a thriving practice; he keeps two rooms going at once, running between neck cracking and massage therapy and hooking patients up to a stim machine, which is a way to zap a back and beef up the bill. I landed in his office after landing on my butt while attempting to play ice hockey. (Another Deirdre idea.) If I hadn't worn a helmet, I might be dating a brain surgeon.

On my first appointment, Russell made me walk across the room, then told me my hips needed realignment, a sexy thing for a man to say when you take it the wrong way. We chatted about my knees and shoulders and how my right leg is half an inch shorter than my left leg.

"Really?" I said, staring down at my feet. "They seem to match."

"It's not uncommon," he said. "How often do you get backaches?"

"A grand total of once. During ice hockey. But it hasn't gone away yet."

Russell said I needed at least three months' worth of treatments, starting with three times a week for the first six weeks. My Groupon deal was only good for two treatments, so by the third visit I said, yes, I'd go to a movie with him. After that I stopped going to his office, my hips were realigned, and before you knew it, he was my boyfriend.

We've been dating for eight months now, having never had the six-month discussion. I skipped right over that time bomb. Russell's steady, normal; we have an extremely pleasant relationship. I keep waiting for him to reveal he wears women's underwear or have him request a threesome with his sixty-four-year-old receptionist, Vanessa. But other than his recent addiction to Words With Friends and his confounding man-passion for Nicolas Cage, about as crazy as Russell gets is his devotion to those forty-five push-ups every morning. He can have a 105-degree fever with his head exploding and he'll still slug his way through his push-up routine. He is also an avid proponent of gargling salt water. He maintains that all Edleys are born with a weak constitution, resulting in most of his ancestors' kicking the bucket early in life and inspiring him to exercise, eat a healthy diet, and pursue a career in medicine.

And if you're one of those people who don't consider chiropractors real doctors, keep it to yourself; Russell's extremely sensitive on that point.

Is Russell my soul mate or the one? Or whatever it is Deirdre wants to call it. Beats me how to tell! I can't wait to read my article and find out. But for now I could practice on him to help me write about romance. I rolodexed through my brain for something romantic I could do that wouldn't require poetry or wearing a thong. (Thongs are ridiculous. Don't get me started.) The fact that I was dumbstruck said in big neon letters just how terrible a choice I was for Deirdre's assignment. Finally, I called Russell at his office and invited him to dinner that night.

"Great," he said. "We can watch a movie."

I didn't tell him I was planning a romantic dinner. I'd keep that a surprise. More than a surprise. Probably closer to a shock.

After work, standing in the produce section of Gristedes, I was speaking to my mother on my cell phone: "Got any fast, easy, no-sweat romantic recipes?" I asked.

"Yes," she said. "Pull out your take-out menus." My mother hates cooking. She used to love cooking, but one morning she woke up and said twenty years of chopping, slicing, broiling, and roasting for a husband and three unappreciative daughters was twenty years enough. "Why the sudden interest in recipes?" she asked.

Across the aisle from me, a woman was sniffing grapefruits. "I want to cook Russell dinner."

"Why?" she said.

"A romantic dinner."

"Cooking's not romantic."

"I'm supposed to write about people finding their soul mates and make it sound fun and romantic like a Nora Ephron movie."

"Really? Why'd they assign you?"

"Because Cupid's not available."

"Do you have to *cook* like Nora Ephron?"

"No. I don't believe so." The grapefruit lady dropped a grapefruit, picked it off the floor, stuck it back in the pile, and selected a different grapefruit. "What are you and Dad having for dinner?" I asked.

"Burgers," my mother said. "My soul mate's been lighting the coals for the past forty-five minutes."

"Burgers sound good," I said. "But not romantic."

"Order in ziti, light some candles, and toss on some Kenny G."

After thanking my mom for the maternal advice, I picked up brownies in the bakery aisle and candles in the miscellaneous-household-goods aisle and stopped for a bottle of wine on my way home.

Mr. Messick owns my neighborhood liquor shop. He looks like somebody's friendly uncle, mainly because he wears his pants too high. He's really smart with wines and I like that he knows my name. Not because I'm a lush, but because he's read it off my Visa card. (One of my goals in life is to have all the maître d's in New York's top restaurants know me by name, but I'm about five hundred restaurants away from that ever happening.) As he was ringing up my purchase, I asked, "Mr. Messick, is there a Mrs. Messick?"

"Yes," he said.

"How did you know she was the one?"

He shrugged. "You marry someone. Wait thirty years. If she's still there—she's the one."

I didn't bother to ask if I could quote him on that.

I got home, straightened the living room, and ordered two veal parmigianas and a couple of Caesar salads. Then I set the table with my good china, a souvenir from my marriage. Although what's so good about china that reminds you of your bad marriage?

I had thirty minutes left before Russell was supposed to show up. I spent several of them scowling at the contents of my closet, debating what would qualify as romantic-dinner attire. My wardrobe tends to be of the crisp and clean variety: tailored white shirts, khaki slacks in summer, black slacks in winter, jeans, jeans, and more jeans. I'm like a walking ad for the Gap. The only time in my adult life that I wore anything close to girlie was my wedding dress, and we all know how well that turned out. I opted for my black funerals-and-cocktail-parties dress and slipped on some heels. I plugged my iPod into my speaker, sorted through my DVDs, and lit the candles. About which time Russell called to say he was running late.

"Darling," I said, in my best 1950s housewife voice, "the roast will be dried to a crisp!"

"You cooked a roast?" he said. Sometimes it takes Russell a while to realize I'm making a joke.

I said, "Your pipe and slippers are also dried to a crisp. I'll serve them as a side dish."

"I'll bring extra ketchup," he said, before hanging up.

I kicked off my heels just as I heard someone pressing on the buzzer—which meant Angela.

"What's with the Steve Winwood music?" she asked as soon as she waltzed in carrying my copy of *Wuthering Heights*.

Angela Leffel lives in a studio apartment across the hall from me. We've been friends ever since the first night I moved in, when she knocked and asked to borrow a bottle of wine. Angela's a former on-air weather girl from Indiana who's now a self-declared social-media expert. She is congenitally cute, a circumstance she considers irksome for a thirty-four-year-old woman. Dimples. Freckles. Built like a perky pom-pom girl. Without makeup she looks ten years old. She once tried dying her brown hair an inky Goth black. She looked cute. Then she tried going dark red with crimson lips. She looked cute. She's back to brown now and has a tattoo of Snoopy on her shoulder. Which might also contribute to the cute perception.

Angela moved to New York soon after her meteorology career fizzled; she could never quite coordinate her arm movements with the green screen. When I first met her, she was working as an assistant to a wedding photographer, until she couldn't stand one more glowing bride or tossed bouquet or drunk toast from a best man. "I wanted to turn the flashgun on myself," she said. She's still a fan of photography, though. She works from home, and since I often do, too, we hang out a lot. When cabin fever sets in, we go eat at one of two diners on Second Avenue, my favorite being the one with the decent chef salad and Angela's being the one with the triple-decker tuna sandwich. She's a tuna sandwich fanatic. She takes pictures of everything she eats and posts them on Facebook. We'll be sitting in a restaurant and she'll start rearranging the tuna sandwich with the coleslaw, and the french fries with the mayo cup, so they all look more appealing. Her Facebook page is a study in tuna sandwich shots. Her other favorite food is Twinkies, but she never photographs those. Even Angela believes in too much transparency.

"Who died?" she asked, looking at my dress.

"It's supposed to be sexy."

"Maybe it needs a belt."

I thought about my belt collection; none of them were sexy.

"How come I've never seen this china?" Angela was walking around my holds-three-comfortably, holds-four-uncomfortably dining table.

"It's my good china," I said. "I'm having a romantic dinner with Russell."

She looked around the room. "Don't you need Russell for that?"

"He's on his way. Along with the dinner. I ordered from Zorzanello's."

"Oh! I've never tried there. Call me if you have leftovers."

"I'll leave a doggie bag outside your door."

I told Angela about having to interview people about recognizing true love, and how I was using the evening as my personal warm-up. To help *me* feel more romantic.

"Why'd they give you this assignment?" she asked.

"No clue."

"That dress definitely needs a belt."

"Thank you, fashion expert."

I don't know about the other social-media experts out there, but I've rarely seen Angela in anything other than sweats and a T-shirt ever since she bought a copy of *The Complete Idiot's Guide to Social Media* and went into the business.

"I'm returning this," she said, holding up *Wuthering Heights*. "I don't get it."

"What don't you get?"

"You call this a healthy relationship?"

"I know. They're both total head cases." For the past couple years I've been writing my own something-or-others; they're either short stories or essays, I'm not sure, but basically wise-ass commentaries about novels I was forced to read in high school. "Want to try *Ethan Frome*?" I asked, pulling it off my bookshelf.

"Is it good?"

"It's short."

"That's good. Any crazy people?"

"Not as many."

The intercom buzzed. "Food delivery," the doorman said.

"Send him up."

"If Russell doesn't show, you can invite me to dinner," Angela said.

"Keep staring through your peephole. If you don't see him in the next two hours, you can come back."

Angela left and the food arrived. Then Russell arrived. "I know I'm late, but I brought a movie," he said, striding into my apartment. Russell doesn't walk; he strides. He removed his tie and kissed me. I kissed him back. Kissing Russell is one of the best things about dating Russell. He stopped. Looked at me. Looked around. I could see that tenor of panic men get in their eyes when they think they might have forgotten something. "Why are you dressed up?" he asked. "And why the fancy table?"

"I got assigned to write about romance. I'm trying to be romantic."

"Does this mean we can't eat in front of the movie?"

Okay. So Russell's not that romantic, either. But I consider it something we have in common. His pragmatism. My abject fear.

Russell followed me into the kitchen and poured himself a glass of wine. I was already on my second glass. "We've got great veal parmigiana," I said, shoving the delivery container into the microwave. "Unless the cheese gets hard from reheating, in which case we've got lousy veal parmigiana." I closed the door, pushed the one-minute button. I never know how long anything's supposed to cook, so I only use the one-minute button and keep pushing it. "And, yes, we can watch a movie." So much for my romantic dinner. "But I need to see *You've Got Mail.* I'm doing research."

"What kind of research?"

"A big exposé on the postal system."

I transferred the salads from their take-out cartons to a bowl and drizzled on the dressing from the little plastic take-out cups. Russell hates soggy lettuce, so we always add the dressing last minute and never add too much. He hates too much dressing.

The microwave buzzed. Russell removed the veal without checking the cheese. "But you haven't seen the sequel to *National Treasure*," he said.

"Yes, I did. Nicolas Cage has to steal the Declaration of Independence."

"That's the first one. In this one he has to break into Buckingham Palace and either get elected president of the United States or kidnap the current president."

"Those are options?"

"He's got no choice." I handed Russell the plates while he scooped veal parm. "John Wilkes Booth accused Nicolas Cage's great-grandfather of murder."

"Forgive me if I don't comment on that. But I have to watch romantic movies. I'm supposed to make my article romantic like Nora Ephron."

"Then what about *Moonstruck*?"

I carried the salad bowl and Russell carried the veal into the living room, where we could sit side by side on the sofa with our dinners on the coffee table. "What is it with you and Nicolas Cage anyway?" I said. "And *Moonstruck*'s not Nora Ephron."

"How do you write like Nora Ephron?"

"Easy. You're born Nora Ephron." I reached over for *You've Got Mail*. I wish I had a camera to show you Russell's face. He looked as if somebody had just canceled Christmas. "Okay, fine," I said. "We'll watch your DVD."

We ate our salads. We ate our veal and drank wine. Russell was right. Nicolas Cage's great-grandfather was getting screwed, and who knew the real reason Calvin Coolidge carved Mount Rushmore was to hide the City of Gold? In between all the excitement Russell's phone would vibrate and he'd pull it out to check his Words With Friends games. He's a great speller with an impressive vocabulary and can keep several games going at once. So he's not as devoted to Nicolas Cage as you might think because, sometimes, instead of watching Nicholas, he's staring at his phone, and when he does that, I stare at him. He's got this pleasant, nonpartisan face. Nothing offensive. Nothing controversial. No unique features. But pleasing to the eye.

When the movie was over, Russell rubbed my shoulders, which is a great way to end a day. After all, he's a professional rubber.

3

Pammie Salus married money and now she's Pamela Bendinger. Pammie was my roommate my last two years at SUNY Albany. Back in college she had aspirations of becoming a sous-chef, which sounds sort of like *socialite,* which is what she became.

Pammie had all the prerequisites for marrying money. Long-legged. Voluptuous. Blond and tan. Her tans used to come from Jergens tanning moisturizer; now they come from winters in Palm Springs. If you asked her, she'd say she wasn't looking to fall in love with a man twenty years her senior with a big fat bank account, that's just the way things turned out. I'd say parading down the Hamptons beaches in a skinny bikini past the big mansions, the summer after college graduation, didn't hurt either.

Hello, Bruce Bendinger.

Pammie's the third Mrs. Bruce Bendinger and, oddly, friends with the first two Mrs. Bendingers. Socialites do that sort of thing, form friendships with ex-wives so they don't have to avoid each other at parties. Nobody in the Hamptons wants to miss a party, and that's where Pamela and Bruce spend their summers. And where Russell and I were invited to spend Memorial Day weekend.

June 20 may be the official start of summer on the calendar, but in New York summer starts Memorial Day weekend; that's when summer leases begin on rentals. And when the citizens of Manhattan make it their business to blow out of town. Every Friday half the city leaves the city to get away from the city and ends up spending the weekend with half the city on a beach. If you don't own a place, you rent a place, and if you don't rent a place, you do your best to get invited someplace.

Which is surprisingly easy.

Weekend-home owners are too busy stoking their barbecues and sunbathing by their own pools to go traveling around. So they invite other people to visit. Ever since Pammie became Pamela she starts booking her summer guests by the first week of March. She'll call and say, "I want you to have first dibs on the weekend of your choice."

"Can I pick according to the other guests?" I'll ask.

"I don't know the other guests yet. I called you first. But you know we only invite fascinating people."

I could name names of previous guests I've met at the Bendingers' home and be hard-pressed to consider most of them fascinating, but that would be rude and Pammie's

34

about the nicest human you'll ever meet, so I said, "How about Memorial Day?"—figuring I'd get the pressure over with early in the season.

And it is pressure. I feel competitive with the other fascinating guests to come up with a fascinating hostess gift. I've seen what sort of items are offered up: wine coolers, coffee-table books, hand towels, beach towels, guest soaps, wooden serving trays, salad servers, picture frames, and ceramic figurines with seashore motifs. I can barely keep straight which boyfriend I've shown up with from summer to summer, let alone whether I already gave Pammie a makeup bag last year or was I confusing that with the hostess gift I brought to my friend Nathalynne in the Berkshires when I was still married to Evan and still friends with Nathalynne. Evan, by the way, though he could've afforded a summer place, never purchased one. The man is a professional mooch.

Of course, any possible value one's supposed to obtain from a couple of days away ends up totally wiped out by the getting-to and getting-from parts of the weekend. You've never driven bumper to bumper until you've driven bumper to bumper on the Long Island Expressway on a summer Friday night.

"Nice digs," Russell said, as we drove up the Bendingers' stone-paved drive. He parked between a Mercedes and a Lexus. Bruce was in the front of the house playing with Victor and Mooney, the world's two luckiest schnauzers. Bruce waved us to the left, off to the side of the house. Russell started up the car again and reparked.

"I guess Bruce doesn't want a Zipcar logo sullying his front driveway," I said.

There's an entire Hamptons hierarchy of status Hamptons and so-so Hamptons, depending on whether you live on the South Shore versus the North Shore, and the South Fork versus the North Fork. Location relative to the Montauk Highway is also involved, but beyond my comprehension or interest. Pamela née Pammie lives in East Hampton, the *good* Hampton.

I introduced Bruce to Russell and Russell to Bruce, who shook hands while Mooney lifted a hind leg and peed on the hydrangeas and Victor pooped on the lawn.

"Boys! What are you doing!" I heard Pamela scold as she hurried out the front door to greet us, wiping her hands on the front of her tennis dress. By *boys* I assumed she meant Victor and Mooney, not Russell and Bruce. "No respect for my hard work." She laughed. Pamela's an avid gardener. I would be, too, if I had a twice-a-week landscape crew.

Bruce excused himself to procure a plastic baggie. He's not a handsome man; he's stout, pumpkin-faced, bald—but fastidious. Pamela once confided that he waxes his back. I could have lived a perfectly happy life without ever learning that particular nugget, but Pamela seemed to find it adorable. Bruce's family owns half the gas stations along the Eastern Seaboard. She also finds that adorable.

"About time we met!" she said to Russell. She hugged him hello and nodded at me over his shoulder, her eyes saying, *This one looks decent.* "You two get the Daisy Room. It's Molly's favorite." She gave Russell a quick tour of their sixteen-room house and told us we'd have plenty of time to change for dinner. I hadn't planned to change for dinner, but fortunately I'd brought along some extra sandals.

Russell and I unpacked in our daisy-drenched bedroom—the wallpaper, curtains, and furniture, all in the same insanely cheery pattern. It's like a drugged version of something you'd see on the cover of *Architectural Digest.* After settling in—Hamptons talk for "unpacking"—we were instructed to meet in the lanai—that's what Pammie and Bruce call their covered porch furnished with three full-size sofas and a table long enough to hit the border of Westhampton. When you own more than a seven- or eight-room house, you start making up names for the overspill rooms.

Downstairs in the lanai-porch-living-room-type room, we were subjected to nonstop food. Cocktails were offered. Snacks were offered. Bowls of steaming pasta and heavy plates of grilled vegetables were offered. That's the main activity at one of Pammie's weekends. Food. And conversations about the food. I couldn't even tell you who was staying in the Tulip Room or the Lily Room or the Pink Carnation Room. I was too busy eating.

By Sunday morning, lying together beneath our daisy-design quilt, I turned to Russell and asked, "You up?" His response was somewhere between a growl and a snore. On weekends he has a completely different morning personality from his up-and-at-'em, go-getter workday personality. He looked a mess with his hair scrambled and his sleep mask askew. I was happy for Pammie in her shiny Pamela life. My girlfriend was nice.

My boyfriend was nice. Lying with my boyfriend on my girl-friend's four-hundred-thread Frette linens was nice. On paper, my life was perfectly nice, but something felt off. Not always. But more often than I wanted to acknowledge.

It would sneak up on me, this nagging sadness, a wistful sense of longing. People were dying of cancer, blind, deaf, sick, starving, and there I was thinking I even had the right to not be happy? *Really, Molly, what's wrong with you?* I was with this lovely man who somehow considered me wonder-fully likable. *Count your blessings, Molly.*

Russell stirred and lifted his mask. Awake now, he pulled me closer, and I soon felt better.

The big event of the weekend, besides sex and indigestion, was the Sunday luncheon the Bendingers were hosting for forty of their favorite neighbors. Here's the secret about the Hamptons: devotees are willing to plop down sizable chunks of change to build mega-mortgaged homes, in what used to be a giant stretch of potato fields, because of the air. It's not normal, everyday breathe-in-breathe-out air. It's not even nor-mal ocean air. It's lighter, fresher, infused with a magical sil-ver light. The beaches sparkle, the wide green lawns sparkle, the people and their conversations about food sparkle. Air like that's worth celebrating, so everyone throws parties. Especially the Bendingers.

"Anything I can do to help?" I asked Pamela before the luncheon guests arrived. "Skim the pool? Fold napkins into swans?" I should have offered to help with valet service. I couldn't believe how many cars showed up from people who lived a few blocks away.

Cocktails were served and hors d'oeuvres passed on the patio. Harry Connick Jr. played on the built-in speakers overhead. Russell was having a marvelous weekend. I'd watched him play badminton and croquet, sunbathe and swim laps, and ask the other guests how they slept the night before. If anyone complained about a bad back, he'd promptly produce a business card. I admired his opportunistic drive, found it mortifying but admirable. As we stood together next to the crudités table, with Russell sipping a gin and tonic, me sipping a vodka tonic, he whispered, "Everything's so fancy here."

"Yeah? Well, I knew Mrs. Fancy when she was still spending Saturday nights barfing into a toilet bowl." I waved cheerily over at Pammie. She was speaking with a man wearing dubious pink pants and a polo shirt. "Let's mill about," I said to Russell. "We're at a party. Let's mingle and mill. Maybe I can get some quotes for my article."

We got three steps before bumping into a couple with matching golden tans.

"Darrin Aschbacher," the man said, holding his hand out to me, "entrepreneur."

"Molly Hallberg," I said, shaking his hand, "salaried person."

"I'm Marya," the woman said, "with a *y*."

"*Y* where?" I asked.

"Everyone thinks my name's spelled with an *i,* but it's a *y*." Her tone said, *My cross to bear.*

"I'm Dr. Russell Edley," Russell said, shaking hands with Darrin Aschbacher, entrepreneur.

"What specialty?" Marya asked.

"Chiropractic," Russell said.

"Oh, that kind of doctor." She couldn't have looked more dismissive if he'd said he delivered pizzas.

"A lot of dancers from the New York City Ballet go to Russell," I said.

"My chiropractor claims that," Marya said.

"They all claim that," Darrin said.

Then we played the "How do you know the Bendingers?" game. *Oh, really? Yes! How do you know the Bendingers!* I figured it was as good a time as any to slip in a quick interview. I said to Marya, "You seem like a happy couple. How did you know Darrin was the one?"

"The one what?" she asked.

"The one for you."

"You mean why'd I marry him?"

"Yes. I suppose I do."

"That was thirty-five years ago," Darrin said.

"Thirty-seven," Marya said.

"Who can remember these things?" Darrin said, shrugging.

Russell and the Aschbachers moved on to chatting about back pain while I noticed a couple arriving across the lawn. I recognized Heike Vogel from newspapers; she's one of the most powerful women producers in Hollywood—the grand total of women producers adding up to about five. Two years earlier she'd produced a notorious bomb, a May-December comedy starring Justin Bieber and Diane Keaton that went straight to DVD. Everyone said Heike was ruined after that, but she bounced right back with a Jennifer Aniston hit. *EyeSpy* gave the movie a half-star review but the public loved it, saving Heike Vogel's reputation.

It's easy to recognize Heike. She has bright-pink hair and wears oversize, black-frame glasses and used to be famous for sleeping with old-time Hollywood studio czars and legends, but now she's in her late sixties and most of the legends are dead. Her escort wore a Cincinnati Reds ball cap that stood out more than Heike's hair. Ball caps are rarely seen in the Hamptons, and Cincinnati Reds caps are never seen. Two women walked up and kissed him hello. Heike headed off in the direction of the bar. The man removed his cap and stuck it in his back pocket; he looked at least twenty years younger than Heike. Was he her son? Her lover? Her baseball coach? Another woman scurried up and greeted him.

"Oh! Do you know who's here!" Marya said to me.

"No."

Without saying *good-bye* or *excuse me* or *please step aside before I mow you down,* she made a beeline to Mr. Reds Fan.

Russell and Darrin had moved on to discussing financial opportunities in neck braces, and I excused myself to refill my drink and maybe get to meet Heike. A quote from her, for my soul-mate piece, would be a total coup. She was standing by herself at a cloth-covered table lined with bottles of liquor and wine, holding her phone out the distance of a neighboring state and speed-tapping with two thumbs. I can never do that—that double-thumb thing. I headed toward her, trying to act cool and journalistic.

"Damn cell service," she said, tossing her phone into a large straw tote. She picked up a glass of wine and eyed me over the top of her big frames. "Who are you?" she asked. She immediately glazed over and looked past my shoulder. "Oliver! Darling!" she cried.

I turned to see Oliver West. Oliver is a darling of the art world, at least for those who like expensive paintings of women with no faces. Oliver and Heike double-cheek air-kissed, and I said, "Hello, Oliver, nice to see you again."

"We've met?" he said.

"I believe so," I said.

His expression went from puzzled to blank. "Oh, yes, I recall. Didn't you purchase *Nude on a Window Ledge*?"

"I believe not."

"Oliver, how's your ex-wife?" Heike interrupted.

I ducked away. Bruce was shaking hands with the Cincinnati Reds guy, and Russell was giving his card to the entrepreneur guy. I waited until Pamela was done talking to a server guy, then pulled her to the side.

"Are you having fun?" she asked.

"The funnest," I said. "Who's that man talking with Bruce and Marya?"

"She spells it with a *y*, you know. Isn't that peculiar?"

"The peculiar-est. What's with that guy in the Reds cap?"

"Cameron Duncan. Heike Vogel brought him," Pammie

said. "She's optioned the rights to his last two books. Crime crap. Aimed at women. Nothing we'd read."

"We're women."

"He's got this ongoing detective character, Mike Bing, who's sensitive and caring and never kills the bad guys; he just sends them to jail."

"Crime crap," I said.

"Detective Bing falls madly in love in each book but the girlfriend always dies. One on the tower of a nuclear power plant. Another on top of the Washington Monument. The women are always in these high-up locations and he can't save them."

"You read these books, don't you?"

"Busted," Pammie said with a good-natured smile. "Hey, why'd Russell need to borrow salt this morning?"

"He's a gargler." I blew bubbles in the back of my throat, but stopped when I realized I was making fun of my boyfriend. "Pammie, how'd you know Bruce was the man for you?"

She looked around at her big, snazzy house, and out at her sweep of lush landscaping, and said, "I just knew."

I wrapped an arm around her shoulders. "You were always perceptive."

Pammie was glaring toward the far end of the lawn. "Unbelievable!" she said. Marya Aschbacher and another woman were rearranging the place cards. "I hate when people do that!" Pammie turned to me. "You should talk to Cameron. You're both writers. Time for lunch!" she announced, and circulated through the guests encouraging everyone to head down to the afternoon meal.

I found Russell and interrupted his speaking to a guy wearing madras Bermuda shorts and suspenders—not the grandfather kind of suspenders, the Wall Street kind. Russell was handing the man his business card. "This is my girl-friend, Molly," Russell said. "Molly, Thatcher Kamin."

"Mergers and acquisitions," Thatcher said to me, shaking my hand.

"Great!" I said. "Pamela wants us to acquire lunch."

"Ah," Thatcher said. "I must find my wife." He wandered off.

I linked my arm through Russell's as we promenaded with the other guests to the back forty of the lawn. "That's Oliver West, the artist," I told Russell, nodding my head in Oliver's direction. Oliver was walking with Heike, who was shaking her finger in his face. "I posed nude in front of him for over two years and he didn't recognize me."

"Maybe he doesn't recognize you in clothes," Russell said.

"Should I show him my tits?"

At which point Cameron Duncan, who must have sonic hearing, was walking past with half the couple staying in the Tulip Room—the female half—and grinned at me. For all the estrogen-laced fussing over him, he wasn't handsome. He had this high forehead and short, dark curls. I couldn't tell if his forehead was high because it was high, or if his forehead was high because his hairline was receding, but one eyebrow was straight and the other angled up as if he were constantly amused. His mouth also tilted to the right. That was what made him attractive, even though he wasn't attractive—his crooked, twinkly smile.

I leaned in closer to Russell and sped up my walk.

A white-clothed table with white china place settings was set up across the expanse of the yard. I felt like we were entering a scene out of *The Godfather*. The guests circled the table looking for their place cards, while Pamela frantically tried to rearrange them the way she'd originally wanted. "I set things up girl-boy, girl-boy!" she said, making a few quick switcheroos until two women grabbed seats musical-chairs style and another threw down her purse, staking her claim. Pamela finally gave up, snatching one last card for one last change, resulting in two groans and several complaints.

She'd seated me next to Cameron Duncan on her end of the table. Bruce was holding court at the other end. Somewhere along the free-for-all, Russell had been relocated two seats over on the opposite side, next to a lovely young woman with a Southern accent who introduced herself as Lindy Sue Michaels, interior design. Across from me, next to Lindy Sue, a woman introduced herself as Rachel Starr, horticulturist.

The woman on my non-Cameron side leaned forward to reach across me and shake his hand—actually it was more of a lingering squeeze—and said, "I'm Blair Kamin." Apparently Thatcher Kamin didn't locate his wife in time to avoid having his place card moved. Thatcher was sitting next to Bruce. "I'm thrilled," Blair said, her elbow in my face. Cameron was surrounded by a sea of female fans. Heike Vogel on his opposite side. Marya Aschbacher across from Heike. And of course, Pamela, the closet Cameron fan.

Bruce stood and made a toast welcoming his neighbors

and welcoming summer. Pamela seconded the toast, and everyone agreed and toasted each other. Cameron Duncan smiled when he clinked my glass. He smiled at Rachel Starr when he clinked her glass. He smiled for Heike and Marya and Pamela and reached his wineglass across the bread basket to Lindy Sue. Every woman got clinked.

Lindy Sue winked as he clinked. "Is that my water glass or your water glass?" I heard her ask Russell.

"Your water glass," he said.

She winked at him. She was wearing a fitted vest with a fringed scarf draped around the front of her neck and over her shoulders. No blouse. Just the scarf and vest.

Thatcher Kamin stood and made a toast, thanking Pamela and Bruce. Amid more clinking and sipping, Cameron clinked me again and said, "It's a pleasure to meet you." He wasn't content with all the drooling women, he had to win me over, too. "What do you do?"

"I'm a writer at *EyeSpy*," I said. "I cover human interest."

"Major responsibility."

"Yes. There are a lot of humans out there."

The end of the toasting signaled the onslaught of food, a parade of servers presenting platters of Spanish dried sausages and applewood-smoked meats, fresh foie gras, Portuguese cheeses, trays overflowing with sliced Scottish salmon, chèvre wrapped in fig leaves; the server poured tender cabernets and smooth merlots.

While passing the salmon, Rachel said to me, "I can't believe you've never read any Mike Bing mysteries. His heart gets broken at the end of every book when his girlfriend gets killed."

"He doesn't sound like a very good detective," I said.

"Oh, he's amazing," Lindy Sue said, winking at Cameron.

"Pamela, I love your sausages," Marya said.

"Thanks," Pamela said. "I love your earrings."

Lindy Sue turned to me. "Mike Bing's stopped a drug cartel, a nuclear bomb attack, and in book three he saved the national treasury. But the books are really about crimes of the heart."

I could see Russell perk up. "Did you see *National Treasure?*" he asked Cameron.

"Nicolas Cage is my hero," Cameron said.

"What's the name of your book?" Russell asked.

Heike halted her texting. "Books," she corrected. She picked up a fork and stabbed at a turkey meatball.

"Books," Russell repeated. I could tell he didn't want that fork stabbing *him.*

"Will there be a new love interest in your next novel?" Rachel, horticulturist, asked Cameron.

"They never survive?" I said. "Not one of them? What woman would date this guy?"

Rachel scowled at me.

"I'd date him!" Blair said. "I cried in book two when he sent Monique a white rose every Monday and then buried her with white roses. You know what women want, Cameron."

Yes, nice funeral flowers, I thought. The truth is, I was jealous of this Cameron guy. Nobody ever fawned over my writing. I never got fawning. "How'd you become such an expert on women?" I asked.

"Four sisters," he said. "All older."

"Any brothers?" Lindy Sue asked with a wink. I admire good winkers. My winks look more like a tic.

"No. Just me," Cameron said. "I'm the baby in the family."

Did he just refer to himself as the baby in the family?

"That is so sweet," Marya said.

"Adorable," Rachel said.

"No wonder you're so sensitive," Blair said. "And Mike Bing's so romantic."

Cameron did this fake aw-shucks, shy-guy thing, complete with humble shrug and sheepish smile. "I think men are much more romantic than women give them credit for," he said. "What man doesn't love *Sleepless in Seattle*?"

The women all cooed. The men all looked confused.

"Is there any more corn?" I asked.

After a short discussion praising the delicious garden-fresh zucchini, and who had Lyme disease, Rachel said, "I hated when Mike Bing couldn't save Sasha on top of the power plant. Darn arachnophobia."

"*Acrophobia*," Cameron said, smiling. "Heights. Not spiders."

"I can't wait for the movie," Blair said from one side of me across to Cameron on the other side of invisible me.

"Me, either," Cameron said. "I'll be sitting in the very front row like I'm part of the show." He turned to me. "Sylvester Stallone's making my movie." Another humble shrug. Another sheepish smile.

"Really?" I said.

"Really?" Russell piped in.

"Who's playing Sasha?" Rachel asked.

"That's up to Sylvester," Heike said. "We're hoping for Angelina."

Pamela paused mid-fig bite. "Oh, they'll be a terrific couple. Slygelina!"

"I picture Gwyneth Paltrow," Blair said. "Slytrow!"

"Gwyneth's too young," Rachel said. She was checking her lipstick in the blade of her knife. "I hate these eight-hour lipsticks. They last eight minutes."

"I wonder if they gave couples combo-names back in history," I said. "Romeo and Juliet: Julio. CathCliff or Heatherine?"

"You read romantic literature?" Cameron asked me.

"I'm just making a point." Nobody seemed too interested in exploring my theory further.

"Mike Bing's girlfriends aren't bimbos," Lindy Sue said. Why was she looking at *me*? "They're always age-appropriate."

"Did anyone watch that terrible Diane Keaton–Justin Bieber DVD?" Russell asked.

A general mumbling of *Never saw it, never saw it* followed, interrupted by Heike's barking, "It's not my fault Justin Bieber can't act!" while punching her thumbs into her BlackBerry.

I wondered if it was too late to change my seat to the Bruce side of the table.

"How old is Mike Bing?" I asked Cameron.

"Forty-two," he said.

"How old are you?"

"Forty-two."

"Sounds like this Mike fellow and you might get along. Do you like age-appropriate women?"

"I like all women."

"Really? How time-consuming."

The plates were cleared and desserts served—lemon curd cheesecake, chocolate bundts with créme anglaise, poached pears with apricot sauce, fresh watermelon slices—and the conversations broke down into smaller configurations. Pamela was talking to Marya and BlackBerry-tapping Heike. Rachel was talking with Lindy Sue. Russell was handing Blair his business card. Farther down the table Thatcher and Darrin were arm wrestling next to a plate of pastel-colored macaroons. Somehow it was just Cameron and I chatting while I ate watermelon. I love watermelon. I consider seedless watermelon the single most marvelous invention in the history of man. Right after Post-its.

"So, Cameron Duncan, if your Mike Bing's good at love, he must be good at recognizing it." I was using a knife and fork; at home I would have just picked up my watermelon rind and gnawed it. "If you were speaking on his behalf, how does Mike know when someone's the one?"

"A Magic 8 Ball comes in handy."

"Was that a serious answer?"

"Was that a serious question?"

"Maybe," I said.

"You should try salting that to bring out the taste," Cameron said. "Watermelon's really good that way."

"There's taste here. I can taste it." I continued eating sans salt.

"I guess it's a Midwest thing." Cameron sat there watching me chew. I felt more comfortable when I was posing naked.

I said, "This detective of yours must be pretty desirable if he can find a new girlfriend every book."

"He believes in love. He holds out for love. He's a romantic."

"And he's fictional."

"But not unrealistic."

I bit into a renegade seed in my seedless watermelon, doing my best to remove the little rascal while daintily covering my mouth. I didn't think Pammie would appreciate my spitting it out onto her lawn. I asked, "So, do these Mike Bing girlfriends have anything in common? Other than they all end up dead."

"Yes. They all salt their watermelon."

"Too bad. I guess I'm not his type."

"He might not agree with that."

I was about to say something on the order of *Ha!* or roll my eyes and tell Cameron I hoped his prose was as smooth as he was, when he said, "You've got watermelon dripping." He pointed toward my napkin. "May I?" I looked over at Russell. He was talking with Lindy Sue and eating a blini.

"I can manage." I wiped my face.

"You missed a spot."

"Did not."

"Trust me." Cameron leaned closer, took the napkin from me, and dabbed my chin lightly, almost tenderly, and only for a moment, but the weird thing is, after he moved his hand away I could still feel the pressure of his fingers against my skin. Warm. And confusing.

He smiled at me, as if the two of us had shared a secret while surrounded by Pammie's guests.

What the hell was that little back-and-forth? my inner Molly wondered as Pammie was cupping her hands around her mouth shouting to get everyone's attention. "Who wants to play touch football!"

A rumble of interest rose up, probably enhanced by all the bottles of wine that had been consumed, except from Heike, who said, "You're kidding, right? That's a joke?"

Russell was the surprising one. He abandoned his blini and said, "I love touch football! C'mon, everyone, it'll be fun!"

I had no idea he was such a fan. Then again, anyone who threw out their back could mean potential business.

Pammie called down the table, "Bruce, sweetheart, do you want to be one captain and I'll be the other?" and lunch was officially over. As everyone—even a reluctant Heike—pushed back their chairs and discussed choosing teams or whether they preferred volunteering for cheerleading duties, I mouthed the words *no thanks* to Russell.

"Don't you leave without me getting your autograph!" Blair said to Cameron as she raced off.

"Or me," Rachel said, turning to call out, "I want Bruce's side!"

"Have fun," I said to Cameron.

He remained seated. I remained seated. After a minute or two of our sitting in silence, I said, "Mike Bing's not an athlete?"

Cameron shook his head no.

I asked him to pass some more watermelon.

He picked a wedge off a platter and deposited it on my plate. All around us servers were removing plates and glasses and folding up chairs.

"Do you really like Nicolas Cage?" I asked.

Cameron smiled. At least he had the decency to look embarrassed.

"Why'd you claim you did?"

"I made a book sale."

"So you'll say anything?"

Cameron didn't say anything.

"I bet you don't love *Sleepless in Seattle* either." I glanced around at the empty table. "Your audience is gone now. You can fess up."

"It's a perfect movie," he said. "The last scene on the Empire State Building is one of the most romantic scenes ever. In the perfect setting."

I concentrated on my watermelon. Told Cameron, "I think you say what you think women want to hear, not what you really believe."

"That's your big assessment?" he said. "When'd you get so cynical?"

"Five years ago when I divorced a divorce lawyer." What was I going to say? That after my divorce I ended up madder at myself than at Evan because I no longer trusted my judgment? That the day I read his wedding announcement in the *New York Times* was about as bad a day as a day can feel.

"Five years is a long time to be a skeptic. Life's too short," Cameron said.

"Yeah. Especially for anyone who dates your detective." I crisscrossed my knife and fork on my plate. "Excuse me, but my boyfriend is waiting." I scanned the lawn looking for Russell. He was busy getting tackled.

Oliver West was walking up to Cameron and me. He stopped, snapped his fingers, and pointed at my chest. "I *do* remember you! Gorgeous!"

On the drive back to the city that night, sitting and not going anywhere in our Zipcar, bumper to bumper, honking horn to honking horn, Russell and I taking turns adjusting the air-conditioning level, then readjusting it, and changing the radio station from his favorite to my favorite, I said, "Can you believe that Cameron Duncan's arrogance?"

Russell drummed his fingers on the steering wheel. "I didn't notice."

I made my voice sound deep and mocking. "Sylvester Stallone is making my movie."

"That's not arrogance," Russell said. "*Ben Affleck is making my movie* is arrogance. Not Sylvester Stallone."

"Well, it sounded like bragging to me."

"He seemed like a decent guy."

"I talked to him more than you did. He's a phony. And I know one when I see one."

4

Russell kissed me good-bye and drove off in his Zipcar. Five minutes later I was exiting the elevator on my apartment floor. Lacey and Kevin Gallo, my newlywed neighbors, were pressed against each other outside the trash-chute room, making out next to a Hefty bag. What was it about tossing garbage that they found such a turn-on?

The Gallos look alike, all arms, legs, lips, and tongues. Same mussed hair and pale complexions—probably from never leaving their bedroom. They've lived next door to me for seven months now, and I have no idea what they do or where they came from; they never talk, maybe not even to each other, they just rub up against one another and play tonsil hockey.

"Have a nice holiday?" I asked as I passed them.

Inside my own four walls, I was unzipping my suitcase when somebody buzzed. I opened the front door without peeping through the peephole.

Angela held up a half-eaten Twinkie. "Want a bite?" she asked.

I shook my head no.

"How was the Hamptons?"

"How was the Shore?"

She was wearing yoga pants and a T-shirt, her hair pulled into a ponytail; she looked cute. She followed me into my bedroom, and while I unpacked, she sat on my Hallberg-upholstered reading chair, blue-and-white-striped, with perfectly matched seams. "Were there any good people there?" she asked.

"Good how?"

"Famous."

You have to watch what you say around Angela. You can't have a conversation without her tweeting. Say anything she considers halfway clever and she'll whip out her phone. Her biggest client is a gourmet grocery store, Iannuzzeli's. She tweets about sales and produce tips under the fake name of a fake customer. *Like us on Facebook and learn how to sniff a cantaloupe!* It makes her nuts that the store name takes up half her letters. The fake customer's name is Flo because it only has three letters. Angela also tweets as Angela.

I pulled out my nightgown, my sunblock, my diaphragm. "Not much in celebrity sighting," I said. "One semifamous producer and one author, only I didn't know the author was famous so he didn't count. Cameron Duncan."

"You met him?"

"Sat next to him. Major kiss-ass phony."

"I'd let him kiss my ass."

"You read his books?"

"I loaned my copies to my mom and can't get her to give them back. People say he's the Dashiell Hammett of this generation."

"Isn't James Patterson the Dashiell Hammett of this generation?"

Angela paused, smiled, pulled out her phone, and tweeted.

"He salts watermelon," I said.

"Oh, that's interesting. May I quote you on that?"

"Don't you mean may I *steal* that?"

"Until you have your own account, all your comments are public domain."

"I will never have a Twitter account. It's one more time-suck. A bunch of people talking like fortune cookies."

"Well, I think Cameron Duncan's adorable. I follow his tweets."

"He tweets?"

"Everyone tweets." She happily tapped away until her face turned into one of those uh-oh expressions. I was in the middle of deciding whether my shorts needed laundering.

"What?" I asked.

Angela held out her phone. I dropped the shorts in the laundry pile and walked around the bed to read, *Cynics are made, not born. Who's still in a bad mood 5 years after a divorce?* I read it twice.

"That'd be you, right?" Angela said.

"Who's going to see this?" I read the tweet a third time.

"His ten thousand followers. Mostly women."

"Really? Write something bad about him! Say no woman should fall for his bullshit."

"Start an account and write your own insulting tweets."

I weighed my annoyance versus the possibility of my being someone who tweeted. "Oh, forget it," I said. "I've got work to do."

"Did you get any good quotes in the Hamptons?" Angela asked.

"Nothing juicy."

"You should've interviewed Cameron. He's an expert on romance!"

After Angela left I looked up Cameron Duncan online; the press seemed to interview him every time he brushed his teeth. They sure liked reporting his social life. He was arm candy for one woman after another. How'd the guy have any time to write? I read his Wikipedia profile. Born in Hamilton, Ohio. Graduated Ohio State. Former columnist for *Ellery Queen* magazine. Three bestsellers in the last three years. Nominee for the Edgar Award. No mentions of marriages, but Wikipedia wasn't reliable. He could have a dozen ex-wives. All dead. And nowhere did it mention his rude tweets.

INTERVIEW NOTES. CENTRAL PARK. TUESDAY, MAY 31
Sheep Meadow
ME: How do you know someone's perfect for you?
GUY IN RED SHIRT: You never want to say good-bye.
WOMAN IN MATCHING RED SHIRT: Ever.

ME: Tell me more.

WOMAN: We can't. We have to go.

GUY: Good-bye.

Bethesda Fountain

ME: Have you ever thought a woman was the one for you and then realized you were wrong?

DUDE HOLDING A HOT DOG: Sure. About a million times.

ME: Why is it so difficult to recognize true love?

DUDE: Love? Oh—I thought we were talking about sex.

Boathouse

ME: Can you remember the first time you looked into each other's eyes?

YOUNG WOMAN: About twenty minutes ago. We're on a JDate.

ME: Oh. Sorry. How's it going?

BALD MAN: Great! She's prettier than her picture.

YOUNG WOMAN: (frowning) He's older than his picture.

ME: Best of luck to both of you.

Great Lawn

ME: Hi, there. I was wondering if I can interview you about love.

GUY IN SWEAT-STAINED T-SHIRT: I'm in the middle of a Frisbee game.

ME: I see, but—

GUY: Duck!

Wednesday night I filled in for Joel Mooy, *EyeSpy*'s restaurant critic. My assignment: check out a new, upscale Lower East Side delicatessen. I immediately called Kristine, who insists I immediately call her whenever I'm on expense account.

Kristine Marshall's one of my best friends, only I'm not allowed to say that. She says *best friend* is a label only seventh graders use. I love her but she's always coming up with these rules and edicts nobody else ever heard of. Kristine's forty-two, three years older than me, and recently divorced from her husband, Zach, following an eight-month trial separation during which Zach dated while Kristine waited for him to come to his senses. Zach is now engaged to a kindergarten teacher.

Kristine has since declared her brain a no-Zach zone. She's determined not to be one of those women who divorce a guy but maintain a relationship in their head, rehashing and rearguing, using up their psychic energy. And, yes, I'm her role model for a bad example. She's turned herself into the queen of moving forward, online dating with a vengeance, working her way through all of cyberspace as a determined optimist. Except she's way picky. She stopped seeing one guy when he showed up wearing a fanny pack; rejected another because he called Myanmar, Burma.

Kristine and I first met the Christmas I worked in Bloomingdale's appliance department. She was using her discount to buy a juicer for Zach's mother. Kristine works in Bloomingdale's furniture department. She calls herself an interior decorator; Bloomingdale's calls her a sales associate. Whenever she comes to my apartment, she starts rearranging my chairs and pushing around my sofa. But I don't mind. She has excellent taste.

Kristine's wide-eyed and thin-lipped, with eyeglasses that are always smudged. Honest to God, she must dredge them through a mud puddle every morning. She wears heels to make herself not just tall, but intimidating, and can outeat a military division without gaining an ounce. Her superhigh metabolism makes her the perfect companion for the occasional restaurant assignments I get when Joel's sick at home with food poisoning.

"What's with this place?" Kristine asked, surveying the restaurant's glossy walls, frosted-glass panels, and linen fixtures, its long, curved bar substituting for a deli counter. We were seated side by side on a leather banquette, ivory with gold piping. "I feel like we're eating in a spa."

Our waitress was wearing what looked like an aproned uniform and ruffled, white cap if Armani had designed an aproned uniform and ruffled, white cap. I ordered six appetizers and four entrées. Only a moron wouldn't suspect I was reviewing the place.

"Nothing else?" the waitress asked. She kept warning us the portions were big. "Any allergies?"

"Penicillin," I said.

"Fine," she said, walking off. "Stay away from the chicken soup."

While Kristine and I waited for our food, we made conversation like we were normal patrons, instead of undercover patrons. "How are your write-'em-like-Nora interviews?" she asked.

I said, "Thanks for ruining my appetite."

"That badly?"

"That slowly. How about I interview you right now?"

"Isn't it cheating to interview your friends?"

"I prefer to think of it as efficient."

"Okay. Shoot."

I used my best fake radio-announcer voice. "So, Ms. Marshall, how will you recognize your perfect man?"

"Besides his devastating good looks, animal prowess, and trust fund?"

"Yes. Besides that."

"He has to be willing to die for me. And then prove it."

"Thank you," I said. "End of interview."

"Have you been studying Nora's movies?" Kristine asked. "And I don't mean *Silkwood*; that one's depressing. The romantic ones."

"Yes, and I've read her neck book and bought her remembering-nothing book, but I can't write like her."

"This is the suckiest assignment in history," Kristine said. "When Jennifer Love Hewitt made *The Audrey Hepburn Story,* the press crucified her for not looking like Audrey Hepburn."

"What about that old senator who told that vice-president guy, 'And you, young man, are no John F. Kennedy.' I have nightmares about that."

"Lloyd Bentsen and Dan Quayle," Kristine said.

"Of course you'd know that."

Kristine shrugged. "I know stuff."

She does know stuff. She's a walking encyclopedia of trivia. She was on *It's Academic* as a kid.

Our waitress returned, plates lining her arm. "Enough appetizers for you?" she asked, after depositing our first round. We nodded our heads yes and she left.

I tasted the quinoa varnishkes and wrote a surreptitious rating in the notebook hidden on my lap. I must have looked like I was masturbating throughout the meal. "How would you rate the free-range-chicken salad?" I asked Kristine.

She wiggled her hand side to side like so-so. "I hate thinking about all the happy little chickens," she said, "free, running around the range, and the next thing you know—bam! They're salad."

"Pulled pork gets me. I picture little piggy tug-of-wars."

We shared a moment of silence. Then we shared nova mousse with cream cheese.

Over wild-halibut gefilte fish Kristine told me she was exhausted from dating. "What's the difference between a first date and an interview?" She didn't wait for me to answer. "Two glasses of wine."

I said, "That's why I'm grateful I found Russell."

Kristine groaned. "What's the difference between Russell and a heart attack?"

"What?"

"One's exciting."

Kristine is not a Russell fan. She is tolerant of Russell, not enthused. I maintain she just needs to know him better. "Russell's exciting," I said.

"Give me an example."

I thought a bit. "Russell and I have a very comfortable relationship."

Kristine shook her head. "Aren't you about thirty years too early for *comfortable*?"

"I tried excitement once. Comfortable has more long-term potential."

"You can have both, you know." Kristine peered closer at her plate. "Something's funny about this horseradish aioli."

"Clean your eyeglasses. It's fine."

Over Kobe-beef brisket she informed me that *she* was not giving up on love, her subtle implication not all that subtle. She scrunched her face at the brisket, gave it a thumbs-down. "I have four dates lined up this week. A musician, a writer, a stand-up comic, and a pharmacist. I hope one of them's decent enough to sleep with."

"My money's on the pharmacist," I said, scribbling *bad brisket* in my lap. "If the date's depressing, at least you can ask for drugs."

"Maybe I'll buy a dog. People meet people at dog parks all the time."

"Dog lovers meet other dog lovers at dog parks. You hate dogs."

Kristine sampled the organic-egg salad. I sampled the organic-egg salad. And added salt.

"Hot guys frequent rock-climbing clubs," she said. "That could be a place to meet someone."

I grinned at my optimistic friend. "Yes, sweetie. Right before you meet a paramedic." I flipped my notebook to another page and read off my lap. "How's this work as an opening for my piece? 'If you're looking for true love, don't forget to ask for an ID. Otherwise, who knows what you'll get. Heartache? Deceit? Maybe embarrassed to death on a Kiss Cam.'"

"That's meant to be funny?" Kristine said.

"It'll get funny."

"How soon?"

"Soon."

"Better be soon because so far it's not funny."

"It's honest. Honest is good."

"You want Nora Ephron. Not Charles Dickens. That sounds like an article about love written by someone who doesn't believe in love."

"So?"

"Jesus, Molly, how can you listen to those *When Harry Met Sally* couples and not believe in love?"

"Those are *actors*," I said. "And what's more unknowable than the happiness of couples? My parents seem happy, and Pammie and her rich husband seem happy, but if you knew Evan and me, you'd have thought we were happy, too. Unless, maybe, you'd run into him in a bar, in which case he probably would have offered to buy you a drink, then hit on you. Under those circumstances you might have wondered."

Kristine adjusted her eyeglasses. "What if we've already

met our soul mates, only we just haven't realized it? The hus-
bands *we'll* be sitting next to on a love seat someday, talking
about our lifelong romances." I looked around in search of
these mystery men. Kristine cupped her right hand in front
of her left and held them to her eye like a camera lens focused
on me. "*When Molly Met Whomever.* Maybe you already know
whomever."

"Maybe Russell's whomever."

Kristine snorted. "Yeah, sure."

Kristine lives in the Village in an illegal sublet. She took a
cab west to get home. I took the F train and transferred to
the 6. My fellow travelers included people sleeping, people
reading, people staring into space. I sat across from a young
couple. A tattoo on the guy's forearm said WHALE BELLY. I
assumed it was the name of a band and not his favorite side
dish. The girl had a safety pin pierced through one eyebrow.
I couldn't see her other eyebrow; her face was mashed against
Mr. Whale Belly's shoulder.

"Excuse me," I said, competing against the noise of the
subway. "I write for *EyeSpy,* the online magazine that's not
Gawker but like it, and I'm doing an article about love."

"Love?" the guy said.

"Will our names be used?" the girl said.

"I can see you two look connected."

"We do?" the guy said.

"He's my boyfriend. Not my relative," the girl said.

"How'd you two meet?"

"At a concert," the guy said.

"How sweet! What's the first thing you said to one another?"

"I don't know. I was high," the girl said.

"Me, too," the guy said.

"This sounds like a terrible article," the girl said.

5

INTERVIEW NOTES. TIFFANY'S, 5TH AVENUE. 2ND FLOOR. THURSDAY, JUNE 9

1:45 p.m.

ME: Can I ask you a question?

YOUNG MAN: I don't work here.

ME: I see you're eyeing engagement rings.

YOUNG MAN: Do you work here?

ME: No. *EyeSpy.*

YOUNG MAN: On customers? That is really rude.

1:52 p.m.

ME: Looks like you two are getting engaged.

WOMAN WITH BANGS: We're ring shopping.

ME: How do you know it will last, that two years from
now you won't be trying to resell your ring on eBay?

MAN WITH SIDEBURNS: Who sent you here?

WOMAN WITH BANGS: His mother?

ME: I'm a reporter.

WOMAN WITH BANGS: (teary-eyed) She's right! What if it
doesn't last?

1:58 p.m.

ME: So where did you two soul mates meet?

GIRL IN PONYTAIL: At a barn dance.

ME: Excuse me?

FRESH-FACED GUY: We're from Nebraska.

GIRL IN PONYTAIL: We're visiting New York because
what's more romantic than buying your engagement
ring at Tiffany's?

ME: Buying the same ring for half price on 47th St.

2:03 p.m

SECURITY GUARD: I'm sorry, ma'am. But we must ask you
to leave.

On Friday, Deirdre dropped a press kit and plastic baggie on
my desk. "A new assignment," she said. "See if they work."
She jingled and wafted off.

"If what work?" Emily called out from the other side of
my cubicle.

"Gift certificates for Bergdorf's," I called back.

I opened the baggie and pulled out panties with some kind of rubber plug, about the size of a nipple on a baby bottle, sewn into the crotch. Now I knew why Deirdre had made a Road Runner exit. According to the instructions, if I inserted the one-inch silicone extension vaginally, I'd have a focus point for performing Kegel exercises. Several bullet points on the press sheet explained why tighter is better, one of which claimed I could release stress throughout the day. A good thing, since these panties were already stressing me out.

Saturday morning I was meeting Angela and Kristine at the Met. Angela's idea. Something to do with a client of hers, a Greek restaurant. Kristine and I were waiting at the top of the stairs when Angela came bounding up, out of breath. "Sorry!" she said. She'd been with Mr. Iannuzzeli, discussing lamb-chop promotions.

"No problem," I said. "I kept busy."

"Are you wearing them?" she asked.

"Tighter is better!" I said.

Two German tourists were ahead of us in the ticket line. I apologize for any racial profiling, but you can always tell from their socks and sandals; that, plus they were speaking German. Kristine was digging out her wallet while Angela was tweeting and asking how to spell *slowpoke* in German.

On our way past the uniformed security man, Angela told us her big plan to use Greek history for her client. "How often can you tweet about moussaka?" she said.

The museum was packed. People swarming about, peering into glass cases of museum-quality dishes, bowls, and figurines, shrugging and walking away. The whole thing made me depressed, seeing the visitors zipping past artifacts that were some ancient craftsman's life's work. But nothing depresses me more than the museum guards standing off to the side no doubt hoping, praying, for *anyone* to touch something, breath on something, or, too much to wish for, attempt a heist, thus alleviating the tedium of what must be the most boring job on earth. I know. I once spent a summer as a lifeguard waiting for someone to drown.

"Aren't you glad you don't have to dust this place?" Kristine said, as we headed to our gallery.

The Met's Greek and Roman galleries are considered a big deal, a multimillion-dollar-renovation big deal with an overhead skylight, a penny-filled fountain, and Greek pillars. Or maybe Roman; I can never tell the difference. And a tile floor designed to look like rugs are spread all over it, except the rugs are made of tiles, too. The main attractions are the white marble figures scattered around the room on gray pedestals. Some of the gray pedestals just have heads, and others have headless bodies. The Met could save a lot of space if they stuck some of those heads onto some of those bodies. There are also a few urns, vases, and a marble coffin or two.

We stood in front of a statue of a fella who looked like, well, a Greek god. I squeezed out a couple of Kegels.

Angela asked, "Why are there never any penises on the

71

men statues? Do you think there's a big drawer in back holding all the broken penises?"

"Yes," Kristine said. "Right next to the drawer with all the women's arms."

"Good one!" Angela said, her thumbs flying into action.

"No penis is a definite deal killer," I said.

So while the other art devotees were conversing about Hellenistic this and BCE that and Greco-Roman whatever, we got into a spirited debate on the biggest deal killers with men, although it's hard to top a missing penis.

"Dirty fingernails," Kristine said.

"Excessive sweating," Angela said.

"Gross Adam's apples," Kristine said.

"Refers to breasts as melons or bazooms!" I blurted out.

"Shhh!" the guard said.

"Nicolas Cage movies," I mumbled, and immediately felt guilty. I thought of Cameron Duncan saying he loved *Sleepless in Seattle*. "Insincere men. A guy who uses romance like a hit-and-run artist."

We checked out a frieze, or a fresco; I get those confused, too.

"How's your Nora piece coming?" Angela asked.

I said, "It's due in a week and hard to squeeze in with my other assignments." The three of us guffawed. The guard shushed us. I contracted my pelvic floor muscle. "I feel like I've questioned half the city. I'll interview a fire hydrant if I can get a good quote out of it. I even talked to the carriage drivers across from the Plaza. One of them told me about some guy making a marriage proposal."

"That's romantic," Angela said.

"Proposing while riding around behind a horse's diaper is romantic?" I said.

"Tell me again why they asked you to write this article," Kristine said.

We walked to the American-furniture wing, which was far less crowded than the wing with the Greek gods. Maybe because it's a room filled with chairs but no place to sit. We stopped to ponder something called a tête-á-tête, which looked like two chairs fused together at one arm in opposite directions. Apparently that was considered a good idea in 1850.

"Designed for soul mates," Angela said, studying the chair-amabob.

"Okay, so how will you know someone's the one?" I asked her.

"Give me three martinis," she said. "Two on an empty stomach."

Kristine sighed. "I should try that."

"How was your date with the pharmacist?" I asked her.

"Dull."

"The stand-up comic?"

"Tortured. But maybe I should give him a second chance. It took Meg Ryan twelve years to realize she loved Billy Crystal," adding for all we non–*It's Academic* members of humanity, "in *When Harry Met Sally.*" Angela and I nodded yes-we-knew-that.

"Didn't Nora write that with her sister?" Angela said.

"Which sister?" I said. "There's more than one sister."

"She wrote *You've Got Mail* with Delia," Kristine said. We were walking through a re-creation of a seventeenth-century living room. "I like the stuff we sell at Bloomingdale's much better than this crap."

"I can't imagine writing with my sister," I said.

"Your sister's an upholsterer. None of us can imagine that," Kristine said.

We paused in front of a Samuel McIntire chair in dire need of some Hallberg reupholstering; the silk fabric on the seat was in shreds.

"You know, Russell reminds me of the boyfriend in *You've Got Mail*," Angela said.

"Greg Kinnear," Kristine said. "But I think he's more like Bill Pullman in *Sleepless in Seattle*. Although they're both interchangeably bland."

"Russell's not bland," I said. "And I like Bill Pullman; I like Greg Kinnear."

"Don't be ridiculous," Kristine said. "We all want Tom Hanks."

After Kristine left for her Internet-musician date, and Angela decided to hang out in the museum store, I walked down Fifth Avenue, squeezing my way though the other pedestrians. I needed a new cord for my laptop.

The Apple store on Fifth is a major tourist attraction in town. Even PC users visit. A three-story glass cube lures you below sidewalk level. A spiral glass stairway wraps around a glass elevator. I found the cord I needed. An apple-cheeked employee swiped my credit card. I was walking up the stairs, feeling pleased with myself, my day, my efficiency, when riding down in the glass elevator, laughing with a curly-haired redhead in a swirly red dress, was the one and only Mr. Cameron Duncan. I didn't turn away fast enough and he spotted me, his smile smug and charming. He waved, kept waving. I could feel my innards tighten. I forced myself to smile back. Wave. Squeeze. Wave. What an ass.

That night I made burgers and salad for Russell and me. He helped clear the dishes. He rinsed while I loaded. He scrubbed the broiler. By now you're probably thinking, *Marry this guy.* I was holding a drinking glass up to the light, looking for spots like a lady in a television commercial, and asked, "How about watching *Sleepless in Seattle*? I'm halfway through my notes."

He looked as if I'd suggested, *Now please scrub my floor.* "Can't you do that some other time?" he said. "I hate the way you pause the DVD to write stuff down. It takes twice as long."

The spotty glass went into the dishwasher.

"And I'm kind of sleepy," he said.

"Did you take your hay-fever pills?"

"Right before I got here." Russell sponged the sink while I sponged the counter. "Do you mind if we go to bed early?" He was bending over, sliding the broiler pan back into the oven.

"Not at all." I smiled, patted him on the butt.

"And read," he said.

"And read?" I stopped patting.

On our sixth date Russell gave me a special foam pillow

that curves at the base to support my neck. By our tenth date he brought over a second foam pillow for himself along with pajama bottoms, an electric toothbrush, two sets of fresh underwear, and the sleep mask he keeps in the nightstand. Russell prefers the side of the bed with the clock radio. I prefer the side closest to the bathroom. We're compatible in so many ways.

In bed, on the clock-radio side, he asked me what I was reading. Stretched out on the bathroom side, I held up *Gone with the Wind.* "Research?"

I nodded yes and asked what he was reading. He held up *Felonies among Friends.*

"Why that?"

"It's good. I like it," Russell said. Five minutes later his eyes were closing, his head lilting forward.

"That must be some swell book," I said.

"It's the hay-fever medicine," he said. Down and out.

On paper, Russell was the perfect boyfriend. Pleasant. Reliable. But in real life, sometimes, not always, he was just Russell. I tucked him in. Didn't bother with his mask. I set his book on my nightstand, Cameron Duncan's smile grinning at me from the back cover. I turned the book faceup and opened my novel to the bookmarked page, Scarlett about to be swept up the red-velvet staircase in Rhett's strong arms. *"Stop—please, I'm faint!" she whispered,* while my boyfriend snored beside me.

6

Tuesday morning I handed in my Kegel story. Tuesday morning Deirdre announced she was off to an important meeting and returned three hours later with a manicure and new highlights. While I was waiting for her feedback, Keith Kretchmer poked his head into my cube. "Hey, don't tell anyone, but Stacy in legal had a nose job." I was trying to remember who Stacy was and what her nose looked like when he said, "Hush-hush, Molly?"

"Hush-hush, Keith."

A moment later I heard him next door, saying, "Hey, Emily, don't tell anyone but—"

I put on my headphones and Lady Gaga and assessed the male employees in the office on their date-ability. The pickings were slim. And the answer to the ever-ongoing burning question: *Why do I know so many great available women and no available men?* At some point all the men who were now paired, attached, snapped up, or spoken for had to be available, right? Wasn't there a layover time when these men were on the market? A transition week, an hour or two between their ex-girlfriend and their new fiancée, their last wife and their current marriage? Then I remembered how the third Mrs. Naboshek was already choosing china patterns before the second Mrs. Naboshek—idiot, chowderhead Mrs. Naboshek—had tuned in to the end of her marriage.

I began with Keith. A knuckle-cracker. Gum-snapper. The first to spread any office scuttlebutt. And married.

Next came Wolfie, the art director. Wolfie's a germaphobe; he keeps a pump-size bottle of Purell on his desk. We went out for pizza once. When the waitress brought our water glasses, he used a napkin to clean off her fingerprints. Wolfie's married to a nursing student.

Brady—the cloud administrator. His title's one of the jokes at the office. Brady's so tall people say he's personal friends with the cloud. Married.

Joel Mooy—restaurant reviewer. On his fourth wife.

Ronald Miller—celeb reporter. Between stories Ron sits in his cubicle eating cannoli and studying Italian on Rosetta. Engaged to a stylist named Gina.

Gavin—Deirdre's assistant. Long-term boyfriend.

Wyatt from editorial hustled by. I didn't know Wyatt's dating status. He was an intern.

I turned off Lady Gaga just as Emily appeared over our adjoining wall. "Do you want to look at new pictures of Rory?" she asked.

"Some other time," I said, meaning *never*.

Rory is Emily's boyfriend. Her long-distance boyfriend. A ski instructor she met in Idaho. Her photos of him are the ones he posts on his Facebook page. Rory is Emily's imaginary boyfriend.

The sound of bracelets and necklaces was heading our way. Emily popped down. She likes to look busy in case Deirdre stops in her cubicle.

Deirdre stopped in my cubicle. "I read the panties piece, it's good," she said.

I did one of my nonchalant smile-shrugs. "Thanks." What I really wanted to do was jump up and down like a cocker spaniel lapping up attention. *Really? Really? Good? You're pleased? Tell me more!* "Nice to hear," I said.

"And the Nora piece?"

"More research tonight!" I said.

So much for sitting on my laurels. And ass.

"What if someone wants to date you?" Angela asked. "What if they think you're their soul mate?"

We were standing in front of the events board in the lobby of the Hotel Pennsylvania, named not because it's in Pennsylvania, but because it's across the street from scenic Penn Station.

"Here it is," I said. I pointed to the listing for SpeedLove. "Second floor." We took the stairs.

"What is it with hotels and carpeting?" Angela said. "Is

there a rule somewhere that no carpeting may be sold to hotels unless it's ugly?" Two sparkly, miniskirted women tot-
tered ahead of us in high heels. They belonged in an elevator,
not on a staircase.

"No one's going to pick me," I said to Angela. "I'm here
to report, not flirt." I'd purposely dressed like a convent student: long sleeves, long skirt, and flats. Angela's outfit wasn't
much sexier, only a notch above her usual sweats and T-shirt,
but she still managed to look cute. "You flirt," I told her.

"I'm not here to meet someone," she said. "If I really
wanted to meet someone, I'd be too embarrassed to be here."

The second-floor landing opened onto a long hallway
filled with single men and women, thirty-four to forty-
five. The reason I so quickly ascertained everyone's age
and marital status was because the event was being held
for single men and women, thirty-four to forty-five. The
website was quite specific about the requirements, saying
that if you didn't fall into the stated age range, you were
going to be *out of place*. The SpeedLove site guaranteed an
even mix of men and women. I had guaranteed Angela that
if she accompanied me on my Nora research, I'd buy her a
month's supply of Twinkies and tuna sandwiches.

Lined up at a registration table, the love candidates
were sticking badge numbers on their well-cut suit jack-
ets and plunging cocktail dresses. Angela and I looked
like the cleaning crew. She frowned at the other participants. "I thought the instructions said dress code *smart
casual*. These people are dressed for *Hollywood opening*."

"The men all look sixty," I said.

"No wonder they call it SpeedLove."

A woman in rhinestones, brandishing a clipboard, told us, "The bar's through those doors."

"Sounds good to me," Angela said.

I pulled her back by the collar. "We have to register first."

We waited in line behind the two miniskirts, one of whom was reapplying mascara and the other removing a piece of gum from her mouth, sticking it in a foil wrapper.

When it was our turn, we were greeted by a woman my grandma Shirley would've described as rode hard and put away wet. Leathery with too much makeup. I can't even begin to tell you how this made me. Was this woman running SpeedLove so she'd have the best shot at meeting the applicants? Had she given up on love so thoroughly that she figured maybe she could at least make a buck off somebody else's attempts? And why was I assuming she didn't have some hot, twenty-five-year-old lover waiting upstairs in a Hotel Pennsylvania suite?

"Welcome," she said, her smile big and welcoming. Her name tag said Fern. I felt immediate remorse for thinking Fern should have taken better care of her skin. "I hope you find what you're looking for!"

"I'm looking for my name tag," Angela said. "Angela Leffel."

"Jeri Jacobs," I said.

Angela gave me a look. I gave Angela a look. Her dimples appeared. "Can my friend Jeri Jacobs and I sit together?" she asked.

"We don't recommend that," Fern said. "It gets competitive." Fern checked her list. "Prepaid. Excellent. Badges twenty-two and twelve. Apply them to the front of your shirts." She eyeballed Angela. "Your T-shirt." She handed us score sheets and pens with the SpeedLove logo. "Mingle in the bar and we'll be giving directions shortly."

I dropped my keepsake pen into my tote and stepped aside for the man in line behind us. He looked thirty-four-to-forty-five-ish, cute, chagrined. Blue-jeaned and T-shirted with a shaved head. And a sunburn. He smiled at Angela. She smiled at him.

"I should be more open to this," she said, as we headed to the doors that would lead me to a vodka tonic. I'd told Angela she was not allowed to tweet during the evening. Otherwise the Twinkies-and-tuna-fish deal was off. It was like telling a four-pack-a-day smoker she can't light up. She elbowed her way to the bar and said, "A double, please! Of anything." She surveyed the crowd. "If you spot cute Mr. Shaved Head, nudge me."

I now know how speed-dating companies make their money. Two words: *cash bar*. Throw fifty nervous people into a room, toss in a bartender, and you're contributing to the GNP. It was like a seventh-grade mixer except the students were all drinking. The setting was also unsettling—one of those windowless business conference rooms, set up like a sad French café with three rows of small tables, a chair on either side of each table. Angela was chatting with the bartender. I was attempting to scribble notes inside my tote bag, hoping I looked like I was shuffling for my wallet. *Atmosphere of hope, fun, nervous tension, loneliness.* Just as I was about to interrupt Angela and her new bartender friend to order my drink, I heard the harsh whine of a microphone being tested, followed by a *tap-tap-tap* and Fern, on the opposite side of the room, saying, "Can you hear me? Can you hear me?" The train conductors in Penn Station could have heard her. Fern kept tapping and testing until the conversations died down. She giggled and said, "I feel love in the air!" I felt fear. Fern was holding a silver cowbell.

Here's what we had to do: Find the table corresponding to our badge number for our first date. After each date, when Fern rang her cowbell, the women would remain seated while the men shifted over one table. She reminded us to be sure to write down the names of our dates and check off the ones we wanted to see again. Dates would last four minutes. About the same time it takes to soft-boil an egg. But Fern assured us four was the magic number and more than enough time to determine if you clicked. Every man would meet every woman, there'd be one twenty-minute bathroom break halfway through, and under no circumstances were we permitted to exchange phone numbers or business cards. When we got home, we should submit our choices on the SpeedLove website, and within a day or two we'd receive e-mails with the names and contact information of our matches. We were at the dating version of sorority rush. "Any questions?" Fern said.

"Why the dim lighting?" someone asked.

"Whose idea was the lame Bono music?" someone else asked.

"Have fun!" Fern said. She rang her bell and off we went.

Hurrying to table twenty-two, I sat across from a nice-looking man whose red tie matched his red pocket kerchief. Under first impressions this guy was *tidy*. Gray hair neatly combed and parted. Perfectly folded kerchief peeking out in a little triangle. Already I knew he used shoe trees and lined up his sock drawer.

"Hello there"—he leaned closer to my face—"brown eyes."

Hello, what? What could I say? *Hello there, bifocals?* I read his name tag. "Hello, Howard Mandel." I pretended to be writing down *Howard Mandel* but wrote *corny line.*

Fern was right. Four minutes lasts a long time. I learned Howard was a retired paper-goods salesman, divorced fifteen years, still looking for that special woman, and was a whiz-bang golfer until he threw out his back.

"You should go to Dr. Russell Edley," I said. "One of the most reliable chiropractors in the city. Upper East Side. I'll write down his number."

"No exchanging numbers!" Howard was also not a rule breaker. Fern rang her cowbell and Howard moved on.

I met Douglas the retired office manager, followed by Eugene the retired advertising guy, and Wayne the retired lab-technician guy, and Myron the retired travel-agent guy. I met James Ward Leonard, a retired man with three names. The men were pleasant. Polite. Nothing exciting. Sixty-year-old Bill Pullmans and Greg Kinnears.

I asked questions. Reporter questions. Why did you choose speed dating? Are you hoping to meet your soul mate? Are you hoping to meet the *one?*

When anyone asked, "So, how about you, Jeri?" I made stuff up, a different story for each man. I'm a physicist. A circus clown. A lighthouse guard. Ballerina. I pose nude for an art studio.

"Really?" Myron the retired travel agent said. "Nude? What do you really do?"

Nobody questioned circus clown or lighthouse guard.

I glanced over at table twelve and saw Angela looking bored senseless. And cute. The bell clanged and cute Mr. Shaved Head moved into the seat across from mine.

"Hello, Jeri," he said, reading my name tag.

"Hello, Charlie Niebank," I said, reading his. I learned he was a high school swim coach, thirty-six years old, amicably divorced, no kids, and wrote a blog for his school's athletic department.

"Do you have a Twitter account?" I asked.

"Pardon me?" he said.

"Wait until you meet Angela. Over at table twelve. She's a social-media expert and loves bloggers."

Charlie looked in the direction of Angela's table, turned back to me, looking confused.

"And swimming," I said. "I'm sure she must love swimming. She's cute. Friendly. Loyal." I had just described a puppy. "I know you'll hit it off."

The bell rang. Time for the twenty-minute bathroom break. Charlie stood, shook my hand. "It was interesting meeting you, friend of Angela," he said.

Other than the sounds of flushing toilets and running faucets, the ladies' room was weirdly quiet. I thought of Fern saying, "It gets competitive."

"I haven't gotten to the cute one yet," Angela whispered to me. She was applying lip gloss and fixing her hair.

"His name's Charlie," I whispered back.

"Charlie! I love the name Charlie."

"A swim coach."

"I adore swim coaches!"

"How many swim coaches have you met?"

"None. Maybe that's why I haven't met the right guy yet."

By the end of the night she was in love. "I hope Charlie picks me back," she said. We were in a taxi heading to our apartment building.

"He will. And he was the only man there who's not a member of AARP."

"Maybe we should have dressed up."

"That wouldn't have made those people any younger. SpeedLove should screen better, vet the participants to make sure they aren't lying."

"If they did that, Jeri Jacobs, they'd have kicked out Jeri Jacobs. Did you get any good lines for your article?"

"Nothing that's not depressing."

"You aren't going to pick anyone, are you?"

"Of course not. Tonight made me appreciate Russell even more."

In our lobby Angela said, "Charlie and I really connected. I could really feel it."

On the elevator she said, "Chemistry's the one thing you can't make up. It's either there or not."

As we stepped out to our hallway, my next-door neighbor Kevin was pounding on his front door. He was clad only in boxer shorts, and his pale complexion looked paler than usual. "C'mon, Lacey!" he was saying. "Don't be like that. I'm sorry!"

7

You might not assume that a chiropractor boyfriend is an entrée into a glamorous world, but you'd be surprised. Russell's patients are grateful to him. He straightens their backs, unkinks their necks, and aligns their spines. They, in return, invite him to parties.

Sarah Greer's debut mystery had already received a starred review from *Publishers Weekly* and been reviewed by the bible of the publishing world, *People* magazine. A bikinied Sarah had shown up on Page Six of the *Post*. John Grisham had blurbed her front cover. Her book party was being hosted in the twelfth-floor Central Park South apartment of Sarah's sister. I didn't know Sarah or her sister, but after Russell introduced me to Sarah, and Sarah to me, and Sarah shepherded Russell off to meet her publicist with the bad L4 vertebra, I helped myself to a vodka tonic. I watched people who knew each other talk to one another. I wasn't in a chatty mood. That afternoon I'd received an e-mail from Fern at SpeedLove asking why I hadn't submitted any picks, but then apologizing because none of the men had selected me. She offered me a 20 percent discount so I could try again along with a PS adding some personal advice. She'd received comments such as "bad attitude" and "felt like the Spanish Inquisition." *Perhaps be more open-minded next time,* she wrote. *And dress a little sexier.*

I was plenty open-minded. I was at a party filled with strangers watching my boyfriend be escorted around by the guest of honor. I sipped my drink, making myself pretend to be deep in thought, as opposed to the way I felt: totally unpopular. About the time I was kicking myself, thinking, *What the hell are you doing here? Why aren't you home finishing your Nora story?*—I spotted Veeva Penney. Live and in person, fabled agent Veeva Penney. I'd seen her interviewed on television enough times to be familiar with her hearty laugh. Her broad gestures. Her louder-than-room-level voice. She was holding court next to the hors d'oeuvres table next to a table stacked with Sarah Greer's books.

Veeva's name first popped up in the trades in the early nineties after her big feud with superagent Swifty Lazar over a power play for Al Pacino. Veeva won the feud, but not exactly fair and square. A week later Swifty died of kidney failure, and Veeva became ten times more powerful than ever. People would say, "That Veeva Penney—she'll negotiate to death!"

She's as top an agent as top agents get. How could I not introduce myself? I was a writer. Writers need agents. I had

my secret collection of essays. Or short stories. I was still figuring that out. We could meet. She could sell my stories. I
could get my column. My sisters could host a book party for
me. All I had to do was waltz over to the pigs in a blanket and
shake Veeva's hand.

I also had to pee. That's the other thing I had to do. I'm
never my best with a full bladder. I was intimidated by
Veeva, and stalling. I'll do loads of things without much
thought—many now qualify as major regrets—but presenting myself to Veeva Penney would require some extra
aplomb and maybe another vodka tonic. I couldn't even
go up and say, "Hi, I'm a friend of Sarah's," and I certainly
wasn't going to say, "Hi, I'm dating Sarah's chiropractor."

I set my empty glass on a passing tray and headed to a
powder room off a hallway between the kitchen and the front
entryway. Bathroom radar is one of my talents. Only my radar
wasn't doing me any favors. Cameron Duncan was standing a
few feet from the closed door.

"Molly!"

"Cameron."

"Hello."

"Are you the bathroom attendant?" I asked, my attempt
at sounding clever. But I probably sounded more like a wedding guest lost in a hotel.

"I'm waiting for a friend," he said. "Good to see you, Molly."
He sounded sincere, which I found sincerely perplexing.

"Great party," I said. "You might want to tweet about it.
I hear great parties are made, not born."

Did he even know I was referring to his post-Hamptons tweet? For a moment there, just an instant, Cameron looked embarrassed. But in a calculated, charming way, like he was trying to look embarrassed. "I didn't realize you follow me," he said.

"I don't. I just tripped over you."

"Well, I apologize for the tweet. Though what makes you think I was referring to you?"

"Because you just apologized to me."

He smiled that amused, crooked smile of his. Not quite a smirk. Not quite a grin. He had an ease about him that made me uneasy. A tiny scab on his cheek said he must have cut himself shaving. His curls could use a trim. But he looked good in a fitted gray suit with no tie. Somewhere between polished and rumpled.

"How do you know Sarah?" he asked.

"How do you?"

"We share the same agent."

"Veeva Penney?"

"You know Veeva?"

"I think I heard a flush. Did you hear a flush?" I said.

"I wasn't listening for flushes."

"Oh. Most people in bathroom lines do." What was wrong with me? Why was I discussing plumbing? We each gazed around looking at nothing, checking out the walls. They were a creamy shade of gold with wainscoting, white trim on the woodwork, and a couple of framed Audubon prints. Rich-people walls. "So why mysteries?" I finally asked. I was making conversation. "Why not politics or historical fiction or haiku?"

He shrugged. "I don't like knowing how things will turn out."

"I do."

"See, that's what I like about you. I never know what you're going to say. I'd have taken you for a loves-surprises woman."

"Really?" I liked that self-image. Maybe someday I'd adopt it.

"What's interesting about knowing an ending?" he asked.

"Well, in *Sleepless in Seattle,* your *supposed* number one favorite movie, we know Meg will end up with Tom. But it's not about who she's going to end up with. We still want to keep watching. We're mesmerized by the journey."

Cameron seemed to be considering my comment, making a mental note. "Maybe the mystery isn't who we're supposed to be with in life," he said, "but what's keeping us from recognizing them."

I waited for him to say touché. Instead we hit another lull. I noticed a scuff mark right above the baseboard. I counted three electrical outlets. I nodded at the door. "You sure your friend's alive in there? Maybe she needs a doctor."

Down the hallway, a woman emerged from another door and walked toward us. She saw Cameron and smiled. She had exquisite brows—clean, sculpted, and delicately arched. I can't tell you anything else about her, that's how transfixed I was by those eyebrows. She paused and kissed Cameron on the cheek, saying, "Poor Mike Bing can't go out on the balcony? The view is divine." She breezed off toward the party area waving good-bye with her fingers.

"Has your detective been banned from balcony privileges?" I asked.

"He has a phobia," Cameron said.

"Like in *Monk*?"

"Yes."

"So you stole the idea of a detective with a phobia?"

"I didn't steal it. It's an homage."

"*Sleepless in Seattle* was an homage to *An Affair to Remember*. Giving your detective a phobia because a TV-show detective has phobias—isn't that stealing?"

"Then I stole it from myself." If a man can blush, Cameron Duncan was blushing. "I have a problem with heights."

"How'd that happen?" I said. "Did your mother drop you as a baby?"

"You want to crack jokes about my phobia?"

"Oh. Sorry. I don't meet a lot of phobias."

"I *have* a phobia. That doesn't make me a phobia."

"Well, what happens if you walk into the living room and look out the window?"

"You don't want to know."

"Actually, I do. I'm curious."

"That's right. You like to know the ending up front."

I frowned at Cameron. He frowned at me.

A man holding a martini glass came around the corner. "Waiting line?" he asked.

"His friend's in there," I said. "Reading *War and Peace.*"

The man left. Cameron told me about his fear of open rooftops and window seats on airplanes and stepping onto balconies. "I'm determined to overcome it," he said. "By Labor Day. That's my deadline."

"How many therapists are involved?"

"No therapists. Just me. I'll go cold turkey. Like a smoker."

"And do what? Ride an elevator to a penthouse? If you've got until Labor Day, leave now and walk up. You'll have more time to adjust."

"Don't bother trying to bait me," he said. "I'm unflappable."

"Really? No one can flap you? Not a soul? Only balconies?"

"Feel free to try."

"Your house is on fire."

"Don't own a house. I live in a ground-floor apartment in Brooklyn."

"A hundred relatives are coming for dinner and the caterer just canceled with the flu."

"Order in Chinese."

"There's no press here to cover your appearance."

"Aren't you the press?"

"No *interested* press."

"Pity."

"I'm fourteen years old and I'm having your baby."

The bathroom door opened. A woman exited. Not the redhead from the Apple-store elevator. A different woman.

Another beautiful woman. With a perfectly made-up face and perfectly coiffed hair. She must have had a beauty-parlor appointment in there.

"Baby?" she said.

I wasn't sure if she was addressing Cameron or referring to my illegitimate spawn, but I was too mortified to care. "My turn," I said, and ducked into the powder room. What was it with this Cameron Duncan? His mere presence unnerved me. He was too smooth, too charming. Totally irritating. I could hear applause coming through the bathroom door, somebody calling out, "Congratulations, Sarah!" It was a lovely powder room. Creamy gold with more Audubon prints. I washed my hands and had a conversation with myself in the mirror. I said to myself: *Why not ask Cameron to introduce you to his agent? What are you afraid of?* My self answered, *You can't trust that tweeter. You don't need his help. Just walk up to Veeva and say hello.* I chucked myself on the chin and patted myself on the back—metaphorically, of course—and returned to the living room.

Veeva Penney was standing near Sarah's book table encouraging a man to purchase a second copy. *Buy one more! You can afford it!* Who wouldn't want an agent like that? I was five feet away from her, ready to extend my hand and introduce myself, Molly Hallberg, *EyeSpy* reporter who happens to have written almost two dozen sparkling essays, when Russell slipped up behind me, wrapped his arm around my shoulder, and said, "Come meet Sarah's mother. She's also a patient."

I met Sarah's mother. A delightful woman. With a bad back. A back that was much improved thanks to my boyfriend. By the time I could extricate myself from discussing Sarah's mother's knee replacement and Sarah's sister's apartment and Sarah's fabulous book and too bad the grandchildren weren't invited, I saw Veeva leaving with Cameron and his powder-room friend.

"Have you ever met a man more bighearted and adorable?" Veeva was saying in her big Veeva voice. She patted Cameron on the ass and the three of them were gone.

8

Father's Day in my family is a two-day holiday. Mother's Day lasts about three weeks and is regarded on the level of a national holiday, which technically it is, but nobody celebrates the celebration of herself like my mother. Fortunately, she's also gracious enough to throw a fuss on my father's behalf, making sure way in advance that her three daughters clear their calendars and get their butts to Long Island on his national holiday.

Before heading out of the city for the weekend, I submitted my big story to Deirdre. I wrote *Nora Ephron romance article* in the subject line. Deleted *Nora Ephron* and left *romance article*. Then changed that to just *article*. I hit the send button and left the office with Emily calling after me, loud and clear, "Leaving early, Molly?"

For me, the pilgrimage back to the town of my youth is a train ride requiring a transfer at the Jamaica Station. For my thirty-seven-year-old sister, Jocelyn the Wharton Grad, it's a five-minute drive in her Prius. And for Lisa, the youngest of the three of us, and the most beloved daughter, the Daughter Who's Produced Grandchildren, it's a major megillah requiring a taxi, a plane, and car service because Lisa now lives in Atlanta. Her husband, Tate Underwood III, and the reason Lisa moved 868 miles away to what my father calls "that Southern speed trap," is usually too busy to attend Hallberg family functions. Tate III manufactures pool-cleaning supplies. Tate III travels to Asia. Not Long Island. Of course the twins, Travis and Tate IV, do accompany their mother back home, and that's what really matters. They're six years old and two of my favorite human beings on earth. They speak with Southern drawls; I'm "Aunt Maaahhlly."

When we gather for our mini-family reunions, each of the Hallberg girls sleeps in her former bedroom, except Jocelyn's room is now a TV room, Lisa's room is my father's at-home office, and my room is my mother's upstairs arts-and-crafts room, versus her basement arts-and-crafts room, and the bedroom most likely to kill off a daughter from the deadly fumes of poisonous glue. The boys sleep on air mattresses in Lisa's room. That way they stand a chance of surviving until adulthood.

The Year Bitsy Gave Up Cooking—that's not a time reference, that's the name my father uses to refer to the year my mother gave up cooking—was notable for another big reason. Within days of her "Enough's enough!" announcement she gave away her chafing dishes, tossed out her cookbooks, said good-bye to her Cuisinart, and started cutting pictures out of her stacks of magazines, relabeling her Tupperware containers and filling them with alphabetized categories—flowers, puppies, butterflies, umbrellas—for her hobby: decoupage. And not just a decorative touch on a tchotchke or two, but decoupage with a vengeance. The bread bin, lampshades, tabletops, picture frames, jewelry boxes, toilet-seat covers, the back of my father's fish tank—any hard surface is at risk. The house went from smelling like brisket and potatoes to library paste and shellac. My father blames this unfortunate turn of events—from cook to kooky—on my mother's getting lost in the wrong aisle at Michaels, suburban America's paean to hobby crafts. If she hadn't turned left instead of right after the pipe-cleaners section, she might be crocheting all of us afghans instead of plastering pictures of fruit on my father's toolbox.

I like to imagine that first night in 1970 when my parents met at Cafe Wha? in the Village, two strangers across a crowded room, one with a business degree, the other the only child of Ziggy and Shirley Grossman, owners of Grossman Upholsterers. Three months later they were married and my father was given the title of president, probably the only upholstery business in the universe to even have a president, but Ziggy and Shirley didn't want their daughter to marry anything less.

My grandparents promptly bought a condominium in Boca Raton, spending winter, then winter and fall, then spring, winter, and fall—every season other than the beastly hot summer—in Florida, until Grandpa Ziggy suffered a massive heart attack while floating on a blowup raft in the condominium building pool, which aside from the tragedy of it all was supposedly quite a sight. A heartbroken Grandma Shirley tried living the widow lifestyle in Florida, but since she didn't play canasta and could enjoy only so many shopping expeditions to the Boca Town Center and had no patience for all the other women fighting over the few available widowers, she sold the condo for a nifty profit, packed up her Hummel figurines, and moved back to Roslyn, where she's spent the past twenty-five years telling my father he doesn't know shit about running an upholstery business. Which even she knows isn't true. Really she's just jealous and regrets that she didn't join the women's movement and run the whole shebang herself when there was still time.

Not only has my dad put three daughters through college and kept his wife living in proper Long Island style, but he's expanded the business beyond Great-Grandfather Grossman's wildest pushcart dreams. In a whirlwind of salesmanship, President Hallberg wined and dined all the big-name interior decorators within a thirty-mile radius to send their sofas and dining chairs and ottomans to him, then worked his way through the New York Design Center on Lexington Avenue, using his interior-decorator clients as references and building the business to include major furniture manufacturers. I once asked my mother how she felt sure enough about my father to marry him after only three months. "Are you kidding?" she said. "The man can sell anything."

I was two and my mother pregnant with Jocelyn when we moved into the Roslyn ranch house. My parents joined a country club even though my mother doesn't play bridge and my father doesn't like golf, but he said country-club membership made good business sense. He'll do anything if it makes good business sense. They attend country-club dances, eat country-club buffets, and swim in the country-club pool. At home, my father bought his fish tank and set up a Ping-Pong table in the basement. He's an excellent player and hustled his way through several semesters' worth of college tuition thanks to his finesse with a paddle. He's spent most of his marriage grumbling, "Goddammit, Bitsy! How's a man supposed to play Ping-Pong when the table's covered with laundry!" It's a running joke. Ever since the Costco opened less than five miles away in Westbury, the Ping-Pong table is also stacked with Kirkland fabric softener, Kirkland paper towels, and Kirkland tissue boxes, along with Costco-size ketchup bottles and boxes of Kellogg's Corn Flakes the size of studio apartments. Overflow items are stored in my parents' garage, next to dried-out gallons of Benjamin Moore paint, rakes, brooms, a snowblower, lawn mower, and a couple of cars. I haven't seen my father play Ping-Pong since I wore a night guard.

For the longest time I wondered what interests my parents had in common aside from raising a family, and what would hold their marriage together once their three daughters were grown and out of the house. I was too young to see the nuances of their connection. My parents are happy. They adore each other's quirks. I envy couples like them, the ones who get it right from the get-go. How'd my mother really know that the young man she met in a Village music bar would build her a lifetime pedestal? What was it about Ziggy Grossman that earned my grandmother's fierce beyond-the-grave devotion? Did it take blind love—or blind luck?

When Evan turned out to be *Evan,* my family circled the wagons and changed the narrative. He was a snake-oil salesman. He was never sincere. He was trouble from the get-go. He went from being Son-in-Law Extraordinaire to (hushed voice) *Molly's mistake.* They're eager for me to find a replacement, but they've never rushed to embrace any of the new boyfriends I've served up.

Russell hates accompanying me to Long Island. He claims his hay fever gets aggravated from all the trees and lawns. He had to work the Saturday before Father's Day and bowed out on taking the train to Roslyn on Sunday. He said he needed to stay home and call his father. Apparently he thinks Roslyn doesn't have phone service to St. Louis.

When I first brought Russell to Long Island, I'd say the reviews were mixed. I'd also say that now that I've reached age thirty-nine, expectations for me have lowered.

"Does he like the Knicks?" my father asked.

"Does he give family discounts?" Jocelyn asked.

Lisa's never met Russell, so her opinion doesn't count.

"Nice looking," my mother said. "He reminds me of someone I've seen in the movies. Although I can't remember the actor's name or what he looks like." But she's quick to point out to anyone who'll listen that "Molly's dating a doctor."

"No, she's not," my grandma Shirley will say. "She's dating a chiropractor."

My grandmother's never had back problems, and even if she did, she believes chiropractors are scam-artist, crooked quacks. And now you know the real reason Russell didn't join my family for Father's Day weekend.

Saturday afternoon the adults sat around on the patio while my father grilled burgers. Saturday night the adults sat around on the patio while my father grilled ribs. Sunday afternoon, in honor of Father's Day, the adults sat around the patio while the day's honoree grilled sirloins. The boys played in the aboveground pool. Every few minutes Lisa would look up from her rum and Coke and holler out, "Don't drown!"

You couldn't drown in our pool if you tried. It can barely hold an inner tube, but even so, it's ruined a sizable section of lawn. My father complains about this throughout the fall and early winter until the first snow. He would have gotten rid of the pool twenty years ago, but my mother insists on keeping it for her grandsons' visits.

"How's everyone want their steak?" my father asked.

"Rare!" my grandmother said, then rolled her eyes.

It doesn't matter what you answer, the steaks will come out burnt.

Jocelyn and I had already set the outdoor table with the Fiesta ware and plastic cups. We'd straightened the seat cushions—the beautifully upholstered seat cushions—and carried out the tubs of Costco coleslaw and Costco potato salad. The containers were larger than the pool. Lisa doesn't help with preparations. She has parlayed her position as the youngest daughter into the lifetime role of princess. She's recently taken up an interest in something called Pinterest, a website that allows her to sit at her computer for hours gathering images of candleholders and red-velvet cakes and press-on fingernail patterns. Jocelyn, on the other hand, is focused on making use of her Wharton degree and is too busy to date or produce children. As my father's executive vice-president she has put herself in charge of franchising the business. So far she's sold one franchise in Teaneck, New Jersey, and is negotiating for a second in Stamford, Connecticut. She's inherited my father's talent for salesmanship. We don't know where she gets her ruthlessness.

I love my sisters dearly; I just can't believe we came out of the same womb.

My father sawed into his steak and tasted his first bite. The boys wrangled over the ketchup bottle. My mother poured lemonade into everyone's plastic cup from a Minute Maid carton. Jocelyn checked her watch. She's always checking her watch, even when she has nowhere to go. "Perfect!" my father said.

"Overcooked," Shirley said. "You've got the palate of a corpse."

"Best steak I've ever made," he said. When it comes to his mother-in-law, he also has the hearing of a corpse.

Six months earlier my grandmother moved into independent living. She's in a building on the water that looks like a Civil War plantation with big white columns. Lisa particularly loves it. The only reason my grandmother even considered such a lifestyle change was because she got into a huge fight with her former building's condominium association over their choice of new lobby wallpaper and taught them all a lesson by selling her place and moving out. She also complains about the food at independent living. "Last night dry salmon, and now this," she said, snatching the ketchup out of Tate IV's hand. The boys wolfed down frankfurters. Travis dropped a spoonful of potato salad on the ground. Tate IV spilled his lemonade. My mind wandered to Deirdre, wondering if she was reading my article over the weekend. And if I'd still have a job after the weekend.

"Can we go swim now?" Travis asked.

"Yeah, I'm done!" Tate IV said, pushing back his plate while my mother mopped the lemonade spill.

"Wanna come swim, Aunt Molly?" Travis said.

"No thanks, sweetie. The pool's a little snug."

"Why don't you work on your Father's Day cards for Grandpa?" Lisa said.

"Let them swim," my mother said.

"Aren't they supposed to wait an hour?" Lisa's hair was done up in a French twist, the hairdo she'd adopted when she moved South. Her tank top was pink, her shorts lime green; she only wears pastels. The life of a Southern belle suits her.

"That's an old wives' tale," my mother said.

"Are you sure?"

"Of course I'm sure! Do you think I'd send my own grandsons to their deaths?"

"Okay," Lisa said. The boys ran off in the direction of the pool with Lisa calling after them, "Don't drown!"

"The boys are lovely," my mother said.

"The cutest," I said.

"Wild Indians," my grandmother said.

"Grandma, have you made friends at your new place?"
Lisa asked. We are all careful not to use the word *home.*

"It's dog-eat-dog in there," she said. "A man with a pulse
isn't halfway unpacked before those women are all over him
batting their cataracts and clucking their dentures."

"Maybe you'll meet a boyfriend," I said.

"Forget it. Any man I'd meet in that place would be a
saggy old geezer. And I don't believe in settling."

"What have you got against companionship?" my mother
asked.

My grandmother made a *harrumph* sound. "If I want a
companion, I'll buy a dog."

I said, "Grandma, what's wrong with a mature relationship between two adults who respect each other and enjoy
each other's company? I think it's smarter to look for long-
term values."

"I'm eighty-four years old. Screw long-term values. Unless
someone delivers on the bells and whistles, who needs it?"

"I agree," Jocelyn said. She was wearing a pantsuit and
pearls, which might be all you need to know about my sister
Jocelyn.

"Well, you shouldn't agree," Shirley said. "You need to
get laid."

"Mother!" my mother said.

"Grandma!" my sister said.

"But once you do get laid," my grandmother told her, "hold out for romance. Everything else you can get from a friend."

"Tate's very romantic," Lisa said. "Just the other night he gave me a neck rub."

"You've got a six-year-old boy giving you neck rubs?" my grandmother said.

"My husband Tate," Lisa said. "Tate the Third."

"Ridiculous Southern names," my grandmother said.

"Anyone want more steak?" my father asked.

"Well, I don't plan to settle," Jocelyn said. She checked her watch. "I want a man who cherishes me."

"Maybe you should go on Match," Lisa said. "You aren't going to meet anyone on Long Island."

"There are plenty of men on Long Island," Jocelyn said.

"Married men," I said.

"I wonder if you and I would have been paired on Match," my mother said to my dad. They were sitting side by side. She elbowed him and smiled like a schoolgirl.

"Absolutely," my father said, "as soon as I wrote 'searching for a woman who can decoupage.'"

"Ziggy Grossman was the most romantic man I ever met," my grandmother said. "Started every morning by making me breakfast. Two fried eggs and buttered toast."

"Oh, that is romantic," Lisa said. "Up until the day he died?"

"Up until my cholesterol went to hell."

"Sid took me to see a romantic movie the other night," my mother said. *"Bridesmaids."* My dad chuckled. My mother did not. Anyone other than my father could tell she was being sarcastic.

"I heard it's amusing," Jocelyn said.

"I want to see it," I said.

"I saw it," Lisa said. "It's not for children."

My mother clasped her heart. It would have been a lovely gesture if a tiny glob of potato salad wasn't on her index finger. "Nobody makes great romantic comedies anymore," she said. "I saw *Desk Set* on TV last week. Did you know it was written by Nora Ephron's parents?"

"Never heard of it," Lisa said. "Travis, don't splash!"

"A darling movie," my mother said. "Katharine Hepburn and Spencer Tracy."

My grandmother flapped her hand like she was swatting a bug. "They were both ancient in that movie. The two of 'em half-dead."

"Katharine wears the most beautiful dresses," my mother said. "How do you suppose somebody working in a research library could afford those dresses? Or a New York apartment with a working fireplace?"

"You realize we're talking about a movie, right?" I said. "Make-believe?"

"Everyone in it's happy. Nothing's raunchy. Nothing's crude. Gig Young was dating Katharine Hepburn for seven years and they never had sex."

"Says who?" my grandmother said.

"It was the fifties, they weren't allowed to have sex," my mother said.

"Were you allowed to be gay in the fifties?" Jocelyn asked.

"Katharine bought Gig Young a bathrobe for Christmas," my grandmother said. "You don't buy someone a robe if you aren't having sex with them."

"Grandma, you buy me robes all the time," Lisa said.

My mother snapped the lid shut on the coleslaw container. "Well, anything Judd Apatow produces is raunchy, not romantic, like in Nora's movies."

"*Julie & Julia* shows older people having sex," my father said.

"She implies it, she doesn't show it," my mother said.

"Stanley Tucci I could enjoy seeing naked," my grandmother said. "Spencer Tracy, no."

We cleared the table and my mother brought out a decorated cake from Stop & Shop; the boys scrambled out of the pool and sang "Happy Father's Day, Dear Grandpa" and gave my dad the cards they hadn't finished drawing. Dad opened the same gifts he opens every year. Aftershave he doesn't wear. Golf sweaters he doesn't need. And two dozen Ping-Pong balls that would end up stored in the basement with the supersize ketchup bottles and corn flakes. My father got all misty-eyed, said a few words about the greatest joy in a man's life was being surrounded by his family. He stood, lifted his lemonade glass, and made a toast. "To the mother of my children," he said, turning to the mother of his children. "The reason we're celebrating today." She looked up at him with such adoration. "Bitsy, you gorgeous broad you," he said. "I've loved you since I first set eyes on you. I don't need

romantic movies. You are the star of the movie of my life."
He leaned over and kissed her as Travis shoved a handful of
cake into his brother's face.

The passengers on the train back to Manhattan were carrying
Tupperware containers, foil packages, and bulging plastic grocery bags. I turned down my mother's offer to wrap some slaw
to take home. I was carrying my purse and *The Great Gatsby*.
After transferring at Jamaica, I jaggedly swayed through the
cars, gripping seatbacks for balance, as the train rumbled beneath my steps. In the rush for seats, I'd flunked out.

"This taken?" I mimed to a guy silently bobbing his head,
wired to his iTunes, sitting next to a gym bag. He pretended
to doze off. I kept walking. Someday I'll write my opinion of
people who hog train seats with backpacks.

Going home had felt good. My family has its share of wacki-
ness, but I consider them my emotional landing place, the one
constant in a constantly changing terrain. I thought about my
parents and my father's toast and how it must feel to star in
the movie of someone's life. To experience that much love. That
much acceptance. I spotted two open seats in the front of the car,
across from one another on opposite sides of the aisle. Over one I
saw a poster advertising Lipitor, how it was good for your heart.
Over the other, Cameron Duncan's latest crime novel, along
with a photo of him, grinning that off-center grin of his. Even
in a photograph I felt as if he were looking right through me in
a way that made me shiver. I chose the seat beneath the drug.

9

EyeSpy is in an office building built over a hundred years ago, back when news reporters sat around playing cards while waiting for the ticker tape, versus now when we sit around playing Angry Birds while waiting for coffee break. The building's tenants are doctors, shrinks, lawyers, and CPAs. If you see someone walk into the lobby wearing blue jeans, you know they're going to our office; we're the only creative occupants. Unless there's some creative accounting going on with those CPAs. The lobby boasts marble walls, a soaring ceiling, gold chandeliers; but it all adds up to dingy because of the gloomy lighting. The small newsstand across from the elevators provides the one bastion of decent light. It's also where I buy my weekly box of Tic Tacs.

"Must be Monday!" Mr. Pupko greeted me. He's my pal. Grumbly, with a beer-barrel chest. When he's not ringing up chewing gum and magazine sales, he sits behind the counter doing the crossword puzzle in the *New York Post* and making inappropriate comments like "What's a four-letter word for *great ass?*"

"How was your Father's Day?" I asked.

"Good."

"How's your wife?"

"Good."

"How's your bad knee?"

"Bad."

I was about to pay for my Tic Tacs when I looked over and noticed Cameron Duncan exiting an elevator, squinting at his phone and hurrying toward the newsstand. I wanted to duck behind a— Well, there was nothing to duck behind unless I wanted to hide under Mr. Pupko, and I sure wasn't about to do that. *Damn,* I thought. Maybe Cameron had a therapist in the building; running into me could be totally embarrassing for him.

"Molly!" he said, looking up from his phone. "I was hoping I'd run into you."

"Really?" Maybe he was with a lawyer. "At a candy stand?"

He picked up a *Daily News,* opened it to the back, and flipped through the sports pages. "Missed the game last night."

"Busy?"

"You can't imagine."

I imagined something blond, brunette, or redhead.

He folded back the paper, skimmed a page, then happily pumped his fist. "*Yes!* Thank you, Miguel Cairo."

"Reds fan?" Mr. Pupko asked, looking up from his puzzle.

"You bet," Cameron said.

Mr. Pupko grunted.

"Is Miguel Cairo your favorite baseball player?" I asked Cameron.

"He is today. He hit a two-run homer."

"But what about the days he doesn't hit a homer?" I glanced down. Cameron was wearing loafers without socks. I like loafers without socks. Loafers without socks are sexy.

"I like him those days, too," he said.

Mr. Pupko was making change for a man buying a *Forbes* and Juicy Fruit. The man took four pennies from the take-a-penny-leave-a-penny dish. Mr. Pupko grunted again.

"I read your restaurant review," Cameron said.

"What did you think?"

"Rather scathing on the brisket."

"Well, don't use my name if you call for a reservation."

Brady the cloud administrator dashed in and bought a pack of Marlboros. "Hey, Molly," he said.

"Hey, Brady," I said. "Those'll stunt your growth, y'know."

Brady is six feet four.

He paid for his cigarettes and dashed out, calling over his shoulder, "See you upstairs."

Cameron checked his watch. "I've gotta go, too," he said. "I guess I should pay for this newspaper now that I've mangled it. What are you buying? My treat."

"That's not necessary."

"No, really. I insist. What were you getting?"

"Tic Tacs." The only thing worse would've been if I were buying a pack of condoms. "I buy them for the flavor," I said.

"Really? I buy them for my breath. Make it two!" he said to Mr. Pupko. He handed me my Tic Tacs. "Now we'll both be kissable."

"Bye, Cameron."

"Bye, Molly."

After he left, Mr. Pupko said, "What's a four-letter word for *horny?*"

Deirdre walked into my cubicle and, despite her perfume, caught me off guard. I was wearing my headphones, waiting for my computer to boot, and leaning over to stuff my purse into my file drawer when I saw her from the feet up in a pair of high-heeled wedgie platforms.

"Deirdre! Hi! Sorry." I sat up straight, tugging off my headphones. She wasn't smiling. She was gripping a handful of paper. Whatever she wanted, it didn't involve a raise, a promotion, or a column. "Nice weekend?"

Okay. That was inane. She didn't come into my cubicle to chat. She'd have sat down if she wanted to chat and she was still standing. I felt uncomfortably aware of her eye level above my eye level. Her breasts at my face level. Deirdre looking down at me like a disappointed parent.

"Molly, what can I say?"

"About what?" But I knew what.

"I believed you could pull this off. That you could handle a bigger opportunity, bring a different dimension to *EyeSpy*."

"But I didn't?" I honestly thought I'd done a good job.

"This lacks sparkle," Deirdre said, holding up the sheets of paper.

"Sparkle?"

"And edge."

"Edge?"

"And any sense of magic or hope."

"Hopeless?"

She read aloud from my article. "'Men who easily say I love you may not love you at all. *Darling* is a euphemism for "I forgot your name." Is there a *one*? Don't ask that question when it's closing time in a bar.' Molly, this is the first piece you've written that I have to reassign." She continued reading. "'Some people never find the one. No, they prefer one option after another.'" Deirdre let out a long, rueful breath.

"I can still work on it, maybe the structure's off," I said. "I can interview more couples."

"Structure's fine. Information's all here," she said. "You just don't have a grasp for romance. You're too detached."

Emily's head rose up like a big ol' smiling man in the moon. "Oh, Deirdre!" she said as if surprised to see her. "Anything you need?"

10

Braless, in a cotton sundress, wearing fishnet stockings and high heels, my hair clipped with barrettes, I was trying to look like Eva Mendes as a prostitute. I'd hauled out the good china, lit a couple of candles, and downloaded the entire sound track from *Bad Lieutenant: Port of Call—New Orleans*. And Russell still hadn't guessed I was creating a romantic dinner the way I figured Eva and Nicolas Cage would've had a romantic dinner if a cop and a whore had bothered to have such a dinner in *Bad Lieutenant*. I didn't know how to make a *National Treasure* dinner, short of decorating the room with cash, but I'd gone to all this trouble to give my boyfriend a romantic fantasy. And to prove to myself that Deirdre was wrong. I wasn't detached. I did have a grasp on romance.

We'd finished the gumbo and were eating the crab cakes and the Cajun chicken I'd brought home from Citarella's. "Do you like the music?" I asked Russell.

"Sure, it's great."

"Like the chicken?"

"Sure," he said.

"It's Cajun. Like they serve in New Orleans."

"Great chicken," he said. He had his tie tucked into his shirt.

I was about to polish off my crab cake but set my fork down and asked, "Russell, do you consider me romantic?"

He paused midchicken. "In what way?"

"In a romantic way."

"Sure. Why not?"

"Well, for starters, I'm dressed like a prostitute and you haven't noticed."

He leaned closer. "I thought your hair was different."

"How do you like eating by candlelight?"

"It's fine if it makes you happy."

"It's supposed to make *us* happy."

"Candles are for women."

"Women?"

"Sure. A woman will light candles in her bedroom. A woman will take a bath and light candles. No guy would do that."

"You've had girlfriends who take baths with candles?"

"No comment."

"Did you take baths with them?"

"We're talking about candles."

"We're talking about romance. I lack sparkle! Magic! I'm trying to fix that."

"Nobody asked you to fix anything. Except maybe you can relax a bit and have a nice, pleasant dinner."

We ate in nice, pleasant silence. For about two minutes.

"Do you like taking baths with candles?" I asked.

Russell took a bite of his crab cake, chewing it slowly before saying, "Every relationship's different. There are women you take baths with and women you don't."

"And with me, you don't?"

"Molly, that's not who you are. If I said, 'Let's take a bath together,' what would you do?"

I didn't answer.

"See? Not you." He looked down at his plate. "This needs tartar sauce."

"So you're saying with other women you might be a man who likes candlelight baths?"

"I'm saying couples bring out different aspects in each other. You might not realize you're romantic until you're with someone who makes you feel romantic."

I blew out the candles. Stood up and turned on the overhead light before sitting again.

"Oh, hello," Russell said. "Nice to see you."

"I worked hard planning this dinner. Lighting these candles. Buying crab cakes and gumbo. I was going to memorize Eva Mendes's cocaine monologue but ran out of time."

"*Bad Lieutenant?*"

"Bad idea."

"It was a lovely effort, Molly."

"It's a terrible movie, Russell."

"Would you feel better if we took a bath together?"

"No," I said. "I don't feel like cleaning the tub."

He pushed aside the chicken and kissed me.

I must pause now to confess that I can't write a sex scene. Some writers are great at describing huffing and puffing and panting and pounding, and if ever there's a sentence that proves I can't write about sex, this is it. How do you come up with new adjectives and surprising adverbs for the same sweaty procedures a couple of pet hamsters can do? If you'd never heard of sex and were reading about it for the first time in a manual, you'd say, "Who? What? *Where?*" The thing is, why are sex scenes necessary? To help the reader visualize the sex? Did we ever want to see Humphrey Bogart and Ingrid Bergman going at it? Would that have made *Casablanca* any hotter? Wasn't *Titanic* still perfect without seeing Kate and Leo jump in the sack? Raise your hand if you'd have voted to view Clint Eastwood's ass on top of a naked Meryl Streep in *The Bridges of Madison County* or to see Tramp humping Lady.

And I guarantee you nobody, absolutely nobody, was watching *You've Got Mail* and thinking, *Gee, how about some hot, sleazy sex?* We didn't want to see Tom crawling over Meg. I'm embarrassed to have even brought the image up. But Russell and I had sex. Nice, satisfying sex. And that's all I plan to say about it.

Thursday morning, when I arrived at work, Keith Kretchmer was leaning on the doorway to my cubicle. "Hey, Molly," he said.

"Hey, Keith."

He was wearing a cardigan; Keith's not at all flashy for a flash developer. "Sorry you bombed out on your story," he said.

"Who told you that?" I stepped around him, walked into my cubicle, and sat down.

Keith cracked his knuckles. "I was just talking with Emily." Her hand flew up and waved from her side of the divider, then disappeared just as quickly. "Do you think you'll get fired? Emily thinks you might."

"Emily's a moron!" I said, raising my voice.

"I think you're a good writer," Keith said. "I hope you don't get axed."

"Thanks, Keith. Thanks for your concern."

He ambled off.

"Good morning, Emily!" I called out again.

"Morning," she said from behind the wall.

I was worried. More than a little worried. I hadn't received a new assignment since *bombing out* on Monday. That happens sometimes. A slow day or two. But I didn't know if the days were slow or I was toast. *No, wait,* I told myself. *Keith's right. I am a good writer.* With a good attitude. Who else would be willing to kayak in the Hudson or walk eight dogs at once or spend an afternoon at a vegan barbecue? Keith? Emily? Okay. A hundred people whose résumés showed up in Deirdre's mailbox every day. But I've been here four years, never missed a deadline except that one time with the sweatproof pantyhose assignment, and everyone agreed those were unavoidable circumstances.

I checked my e-mails. Straightened my desk. Checked my

e-mails again. Called Russell. He was with a patient. Called my mother. Got the machine. I started reading *Rebecca*; Daphne du Maurier seemed like a juicy target for one of my essays, but I stopped after a few pages. I didn't want to be seen reading a book at my desk looking useless. Only Emily had that luxury.

"Hey, Emily," I called over our wall.

"What?"

I walked around to her cubicle. She blinked up at me as if she were stunned I'd walk within a ten-mile radius of her doorway. Stacks of books covered the floor. Three photos of Rory the imaginary ski instructor boyfriend were taped above her file drawers. She shifted in her seat, blocking her computer.

"Emily, you seem to know everything." We gave each other the stink eye. "I was just curious if you happened to hear who's rewriting the romance piece."

She glanced over her shoulder, making sure her computer screen wasn't visible. "Oh, Deirdre probably assigned it to some freelancer."

"You think? Or you know?"

"I think I know."

I looked at her Rory display. "So what does a ski instructor do in June?"

"He's not just an instructor. He's also in management."

"Okay. What does a ski manager manage in June?"

"Hikers. People come to the resort to hike."

"So you're dating a hike instructor?"

"Why don't you take a hike, Molly?"

"Why don't you go call your make-believe boyfriend?"

I turned and walked out of her cubicle. And tripped into Gavin, who told me Deirdre wanted to speak with me pronto.

Deirdre started out by asking if I had free time over the weekend, and for a moment I thought it was a cruel segue into "Well, you'll have plenty of free time next week." Instead, she talked about bike-share programs in Paris and Copenhagen and how the mayor was planning one for New York and maybe we should see how well they work. And yes, there was a split second or two when I thought Deirdre was sending me to Paris, but she was just sending me to a bike shop. "No other forms of transportation for five days," she said. "Do everything you'd do that you'd normally do, only go there on a bike." Good thing I wasn't planning on visiting Long Island that weekend.

I said, "I'll get right on it, Deirdre! I mean—right on that bike!" I sounded like a total fool, blathering because I was so grateful I could switch from being paranoid about my job to paranoid about my life. I didn't mention that the last bicycle I'd ridden had plastic streamers and a Mattel V-rroom.

Friday morning I looked up bike rentals on my computer and found a place only two blocks from my apartment that I must have passed hundreds of times without noticing, having had no interest or desire to notice. I rented an adorable Schwinn with a cute little bell and some gear gizmo on the handle that I never did figure out. It was the biggest, clunkiest bike in the store. The only model that came with a kickstand. I rented a helmet. I rented elbow pads. The nice lady who helped me insisted I couldn't possibly pump fast enough on my Schwinn to warrant kneepads, but I rented them, too.

Despite the hot weather, I wore jeans to protect my skin from scrapes and gouges. I borrowed a backpack from Angela. It was too late to cancel a pressing appointment at Fifty-Ninth Street on the far West Side because I'd waited two months to get the appointment for my first-ever mammogram, so already it was turning out to be a fun day. But at least if I wiped out, I'd be en route to a hospital.

I left early, allowing myself enough time to pedal, my speed clocking in at about one mile per hour. Fresh air. Warm breezes. Potholes. At first I was cautious, stopping for every red light five minutes in advance. Everyone passed me. I mean *everyone*. Babies in strollers. Old men on walkers. It's amazing how fast a gentle incline turns into a mountain when you're riding a bike. By the time I got to my appointment and the receptionist asked, "Which department?" I gasped, "Pulmonary!"

Usually, sitting around a waiting room in a hospital gown makes me grumpy. But this time I didn't mind. I'd've been happy to spend the next five days there. When it was finally my turn, I made jokes about how a man must have invented this contraption and the room being colder than a meat locker. The technician did not laugh. But, hey, squeezing breasts into pancakes all day has to be one of the worst jobs ever, in a serious tie with driving a Hertz bus in circles between the airport terminal and the parking lot. And those museum guards.

Back outside, it took me only three or four hours to figure out the lock I'd used to chain my Schwinn to a NO PARKING sign, and a mere forty minutes to adjust my helmet and elbow pads, but I discovered riding a bike down a hill is far more satisfying than up. As long as you remember not to pass a truck right before the driver opens his door (I won't elaborate) and defer to larger vehicles, say, a bus (I won't elaborate). By the time I hit midtown, heading up Lexington in heavy traffic, empowered by my ability to scoot between cars (illegal) and zip across red lights (also illegal), thinking, *Tour de France here I come!*—life was magical, life sparkled, romance was in the air. I turned on Eighty-sixth riding against traffic (not illegal, but not a good idea) and glanced over to the Hamptons jitney on the opposite site of the street, passengers with luggage lined up along the sidewalk. Cameron was stepping aside to let a woman, a different woman, another woman, an attractive woman, board ahead of him. I swerved to avoid a taxi, the driver yelling out an implausible suggestion to me.

My father always says, once you buy a Subaru, all you see are Subarus. He means this figuratively. It is also true of Hondas and Toyotas. But why was Cameron Duncan Subaru-ing me? Like the universe was trying to tell me, *Watch out.*

Or something.

My parents invited Russell and me to their country club's Fourth of July barbecue. I hate the country-club barbecue, even hated it when I was a kid. The grill's the size of a Buick, and somehow every year the club people set it up so the wind blows the heat into your face, steaming your skin and searing your nostrils while you're cooling your heels waiting for a cheeseburger. Whenever I think of how hot hell must be, I think of the country-club barbecue.

I also turned down Pammie's invitation to spend the holiday in the Hamptons. She sounded miffed, said it was the *primo* weekend for an invitation and the bedroom would get snapped up fast. Maybe she was more of a Pamela than a Pammie than I'd realized.

After five days biking around Manhattan until my butt ached and, I swear, my calves doubled in size, which was not something they ever possibly needed to do, well, after that, hanging out in the city, not subjecting myself to cars, trains, jitneys, or anything on wheels, held a lot more appeal than you might think. Sticking around town was Russell's idea in the first place. He'd been asked to write an article for *American Chiropractor.* That might not mean much to the average soul, but it's a mega-honor big deal if you're an American chiropractor. Russell wanted to get to work on his mega-honor right away, asked if maybe I'd help when he got to the final draft. I was flattered. He'd never asked me to help crack a neck.

So really, staying in the city sounded like a swell idea until July 1 rolled around, a Friday, and everyone else skipped town. Almost immediately the city felt like one of those Japanese B movies after the A-bomb is dropped and the citizens have evacuated. Angela was away for the weekend. Kristine was away for the weekend. Emily let it be known she'd be busy all weekend, and after about the hundredth time she'd materialized over our wall and said, "Don't you want to ask why? Don't you want to ask why?"—I caved and asked why and she told me, "It's a secret."

Friday night Russell worked on his chiropractor article. I read Daphne du Maurier. We fed Joyce and Irwin. We fed ourselves. We ordered a pizza, thrilled to see the delivery guy and know that another human was left in Manhattan. I wanted to invite the guy in to dinner. Russell and I went to bed early. To sleep. By Saturday morning I was wondering if it was too late to call Pammie and see if there'd been a last-minute cancellation for the Daisy Room. By late afternoon, around the time cabin fever was setting in, I insisted to Russell that we go out, take a walk, commune with nature and concrete. We did, and much to my joy we came upon a bevy of humanity.

As soon as summer rolls around, New York street-corner vendors get together with guest vendors who drive in from places like Sarasota, Florida, or Lansing, Michigan, and throw street fairs. Entire blocks are shut down, traffic is rerouted. Policemen guard the barricades set up to guard the fairs. Local bands with bad sound systems wail off the backs of flatbed trucks. The fairs are held for all the people who forgot to go to the Berkshires, Hamptons, or Fire Island. The fairs are also a way for New Yorkers to kid themselves that a city of over 8 million inhabitants is just as quaint and friendly as a small town, only instead of cotton candy and popcorn, you eat chicken kebobs and spicy link sausages.

"Look, honey," I said to Russell. "Here's a booth selling straw hats you can roll up and pack in a suitcase even though none of us are going anywhere."

He was more interested in a table selling tweezers and pliers.

"You can pull some major nose hairs with these babies," I said, holding up a pair of pliers.

Russell was not amused. He bought some toothbrushes, some tube socks. "Can you believe how cheap these socks are?" he said. "This is so exciting."

A fair attendee was sitting backward in a chair with her face pressed through a hole beneath a sign that read ENJOY A RELAXING BACKRUB in the most unrelaxing setting imaginable. Eager young sorts stationed next to the sausage booth handed out pamphlets about cruelty to animals. Russell bought undershirts in bulk. "A third the price of Bloomingdale's," he said. "This is so exciting." He bought an LED aluminum penlight. "This is so exciting."

We walked back to Russell's apartment. He played Words With Friends. I don't know where those friends were, but certainly not in Manhattan. We ordered in Chinese and watched *Windtalkers* with Joyce and Irwin. I've been avoiding even mentioning this, but Joyce and Irwin are Russell's roommates, two turtles whose habitat is on the kitchen counter next to the sink and Russell's vitamin jars. Except when Russell takes them out of their glass tank and lets them crawl around the living-room floor and watch DVDs with us. "Joyce, did you enjoy the movie?" Russell asked afterward, speaking in a deep, serious voice, his Irwin voice.

I was supposed to respond in my Joyce voice. High-pitched and singsongy. "Why, yes, Irwin! I knew Nicolas Cage would save the Navajos!"

"Of course, Joyce. He was a decorated marine!"

This went on longer than I'd like to admit until I finally insisted we go to sleep.

Sunday morning we stayed in bed (imagine sex scene), got out of bed, and Russell cooked omelets. He's an excellent omelet cooker, chops in all these onions and tomatoes and red peppers. We read the *New York Times*. Fifteen minutes later we were done. Reading the *Times* used to be an all-day affair, but now the paper's shrunk to a pathetic sliver, and on a holiday weekend it's barely a flyer. We walked down to Riverside Park and sat on a bench where Russell read old issues of *American Chiropractor* for inspiration and I read *Rebecca*. Mrs. Danvers burned Manderley to the ground.

Monday night we snuck up to the rooftop of Russell's building to watch fireworks. Many New York City apartment buildings have roof decks or roof gardens. Russell's building has a padlock and a chain. But the super was in town and the super has three kids. He also had the key to the padlock. Whatever residents were around made their way upstairs. The sun had set. The kids clapped their hands in anticipation. The Hudson River looked like its own rendition of rush-hour traffic with sailboats and motorboats bobbing together in the dark water, creating a medley of glittery lights. Below us, the waterfront was lined with celebrants, the West Side Highway closed to traffic. But for we lucky ones on that rooftop, it was all about the vista. Our vantage point offered a floating mosaic of ornate cornices and satellite dishes, water towers and air-conditioning units, a broad, twinkling skyline above an urban panorama. The air felt soft and fresh; eerily quiet. A momentary world of calm. I thought of Cameron Duncan and found myself feeling sorry for him. It must be awful to be afraid of heights, to never experience the sweet perspective of being that much closer to the fireworks, that much nearer to the sky. The fireworks looked magical, splashes of color and cascading designs, the handful of neighbors gasping and cheering with each new blossom of light. I saw Russell's face in the illumination. I slipped my arm through his and leaned into his shoulder. He was discussing the building's electrical system with the super. I could see the fireworks. I just couldn't feel them.

11

"How was the Jersey Shore?" I asked Keith Tuesday morning. "How was the Catskills?" I asked Brady. "How was your I've Got a Secret and Who Cares Weekend?" I asked Emily.

Of course, nobody answered. Everyone was sunburned and cranky; the resentment toward the long weekend's being over, tangible. What? Real life? Back so soon?

I wasn't in such a good mood myself. I checked my e-mails. Read *Yahoo! News*. Scanned *Gawker* to see if their features writer was doing any cool articles that our features writer—that'd be me—should have done first. I was listening to Adele and her don't-fuck-with-me songs on my iPod, bouncing to the music, feeling her pain, when I also felt a tap on my shoulder.

I turned my chair to see Deirdre. I said, "Hi! How was the Hamptons?"

"Have you seen Emily?" she said. She was in spit-it-out mode. No time for pleasantries. Not even unpleasantries.

"No," I said. "Isn't she in her cubicle?" *Oh, Molly, Molly, Molly, you blockhead.*

"No!" Deirdre said. "I guess you can do it."

"Do it? Sure! What? I guess so."

"I got a call from Theresa Flynn. She arranges programs at the Ninety-Second Street Y. There's a panel. All writers. Mainly authors."

"And you need someone to attend?"

"No. Theresa needs someone to fill in. Gap Eiffert, the *Post* columnist, is stuck in Mexico with the runs."

I nodded my head to indicate compassion.

"It's an opportunity for us to get in front of an intelligent audience. I think it's a terrible mistake for them not to have *me* on the panel, and I did my best to explain that to Theresa, suggest she speak to my publicist, but they specifically want a writer." Deirdre's expression said just how appalled she was at this Theresa Flynn woman's lack of judgment. "Emily covers authors, covers books, she makes sense, but if you're available, I'll tell them you. You're a writer. So I guess that makes you an author. Sort of." She said *sort of* like she was saying *barely*. "I don't want to say no and have Theresa running off to ask someone at *Gawker.*"

Me? On a panel? At the 92nd Street Y? In New York that counted as the Oscars, Grammys, Emmys, and Nobel Prize of panels, all rolled into one. My inner me was screaming, *Molly, Molly Hallberg, are you out of your gourd? Throw yourself to the wolves, why don't you! Get up in front of an audience of New Yorkers in the arena of arenas for suffering no fools without any idea what the hell you'll contribute?* That was the Molly who turns overly protective when I attempt anything questionable. But the other Molly, Kegel-squeezing, bike-riding, unemployment-avoiding, column-seeking Molly, said, "Sure, Deirdre. When do they need me?"

She shoved a piece of paper at me with where to go, whom to call. "Tonight," she said. "Seven p.m." And dashed away.

Horror. Panic. Terror. Those are the sensations that went roiling through my entire being. Along with excitement. Nerves. And a touch of *What the hell!* Movie stars and heads of state appear at the 92Y. Scientists and CEOs, religious leaders and musical geniuses. Bill Gates. Yo-Yo Ma. Martha Graham. Publicists earn bonuses for booking clients there. People kill to get on panels at the 92Y. They just kill to get on them with at least three months' notice. If I screwed up, said the wrong thing—good Lord, what was the topic?—or worse, said *nothing at all,* sat there like a lox, it wouldn't be a little, sleep-it-off-no-big-deal failure, it would be a call-the-moving-van-leave-town failure. Adios, credibility. Adios, dignity. Adios, life. I asked myself, *Tell me again—why would you want to do this?* And then I knew.

"'The damn ladies' room is always out of toilet paper!" I heard Emily say.

"Sold-out," Theresa Flynn told me when I called to confirm my availability. "Not a ticket available."

"Not a one?" I said. "For moral support?"

She told me the panel members. I gulped. She told me the topic. I gulped. She told me she'd see what she could do about a spare ticket, perhaps there'd be a cancellation. Please arrive early and ask for her.

I spent the afternoon picking and picking apart my wardrobe with Angela, whose renewed interest in fashion coincided with dating Charlie, the high school swim coach she'd met at Speed-Love. She'd say things like "That's workable," "That's questionable," "No way." We voted for a gray skirt, white shirt, and low flats. My image of an author. If I were a man, I'd have worn a houndstooth blazer with elbow patches and carried a pipe.

"They're going to love you," Angela said, shaking her head no to hoop earrings and yes to silver studs. "You'll be asked on a million more panels after this."

"Yes. Death panels."

"My first on-air weather report I couldn't stop shaking. I kept pointing to Hammond instead of Valparaiso." Angela stepped back to appraise the finished product. "Your hair needs fixing." I parted my hair on the left. Reparted it on the right. "Remember to take a deep breath."

"Breathe. Breathing is good. I'll remember that."

"I'll call again to see if any tickets got handed back in. Maybe Russell won't pick up his."

"He better. I had to beg for it."

"I'll tweet about you being a panelist."

"To your grocery-store customers or your Greek-restaurant customers?"

"To everyone! Don't forget anything quotable you say so I can quote you." Angela gave me one last once-over. "Okay," she said. "You are completely presentable."

The 92Y is not an attractive building. Prestigious, yes. Attractive? Not so much. The main lobby is gray. I can't think of anyway else to describe it. It's gray. Maybe solid. I guess I could say it's solid. But basically gray. You enter through either a scanner on the right or past a table with a security guard on the left. I have no way to test this theory, but I feel fairly certain that anyone trying to sneak something untoward into the 92Y would avoid the scanner.

You can judge the fame of a speaker or the popularity of a topic by which of its many rooms the Y uses. The famous-writers-plus-me panel was scheduled for the Kaufmann Concert Hall. The big hall. The important hall. The one that holds over nine hundred people and has a balcony. It's wood-paneled with wood floors and green carpeting and green chairs. It looks like the concert-hall equivalent of a family rec room. In between the lobby and the concert hall, there's a fancy marble lobby. None of the other rooms have fancy marble lobbies, so that's another way to expect a good turnout. You get the marble lobby.

After passing through the scanner in the main lobby, I met Theresa Flynn, who greeted me, thanked me, and said I was the first panelist to arrive. She accompanied me through the marble lobby and through the Kaufmann. I wasn't nervous until she kept telling me not to be nervous. The hall looked a lot bigger than I'd remembered.

"After I welcome the audience I'll introduce Gordon Fenton, and he'll introduce the panelists," she said. "Forty or so minutes of discussion will be followed by twenty minutes of audience questions. That will leave plenty of time for book signings." Then she added, "Well, for the other panelists to sign books."

"Did Gap Eiffert have a book?" I asked.

"Yes," she said. "A new collection of his *Post* columns."

"Maybe I can sign those."

Theresa did not laugh, which made me more nervous than anything.

I sat backstage by myself, waiting for the other panelists to arrive, peeking out like a little kid to watch the seats filling up. Gordon Fenton showed up first, not looking at all the way I'd pictured him from his voice on NPR. Radio announcers never look the way I imagine them. I was expecting John Legend. I got Santa Claus in a brown suit.

"So you're the last-minute fill-in?" Gordon said, holding out his big hand.

"That'd be me."

"Ever do this before?"

"That might not be me."

"You talk? Have opinions?" I nodded yes. "Fine. Just don't interrupt when I'm speaking."

Joseph Gillen walked in next, probably the most famous person on the panel. You usually see him on Sunday-morning talk shows pissed off about serious subjects. He writes about political coups that take place in countries I've never heard of.

"I'm surprised Theresa didn't go with one less person," he said as we were introduced. "I can pick up the slack. What kind of writing do you do? News? Political?"

"Features and entertainment."

He turned away.

Take a breath, Molly, I told myself. But I wasn't sure if I should be breathing or bolting.

Theresa guided Julia Hollingsworth into the waiting area. Julia must be at least ninety years old but she doesn't look a day over eighty. She's birdlike, ultrafeminine, with an excellent face-lift. Her pink dress and ruffled scarf looked like lingerie. Julia writes romance novels under three or four different names, but her most famous name is Julia Hollingsworth. Theresa showed Julia to a folding chair. I walked over and introduced myself. Julia eyed my white top and gray skirt: "Well, you look like a somber young woman," she said.

Theresa kept glancing at a wall clock. "He's always late," she said, like she was talking about an adored son. Three minutes to seven, Cameron Duncan scooted in, all charm and apologies. He kissed Theresa on the cheek, kissed Julia on the cheek. Stopped. Looked at me. Kissed me on the cheek. He saluted Gordon. Chucked Joseph Gillen on the shoulder.

While the men man-talked and Julia examined her face in a tiny, gold pocket mirror, I peeked out. Theresa was at the podium telling the audience members how much the Y appreciated their support. Gordon broke away from his male huddle, waiting to make his entrance. "Let's welcome the host of NPR's *Sorry You Asked*!" Theresa said, to a round of applause, applauding Gordon herself as she exited the stage and he took command of the podium.

Cameron sidled up to me. "You come here often?"

"I'm the token last-minute journalist."

"Nice to see you, token journalist. You're much better looking than Gap. You'll do great."

"Really?" If ever I needed morale boosting, it was now.

"You can hold your own in a conversation. I've seen that side of you."

"Thank you." I paused. "That was a compliment, right?"

He smiled at me. "Yes."

Breathe, Molly, breathe.

Gordon was saying how Cameron Duncan only writes bestsellers, didn't know how to write anything else. The audience laughed. Gordon wished Hollywood luck portraying a character as beloved as Mike Bing, said they'd better not screw it up. The audience laughed, looked around at each other in agreement. Gordon said Julia's novels were printed in thirty-seven languages, that she sold more books worldwide than Danielle Steel and Barbara Cartland. More applause. The audience was almost all women. It looked like an Aleve convention out there.

"Please step back," Theresa whispered to me. Peeking wasn't allowed.

"Sorry!" I said.

"Shh," Joseph Gillen said.

Gordon was talking about Joseph. The coups he's covered, the Pulitzer Prize he'd won. Applause for Joseph. Theresa lined us up. Cameron first, escorting Julia. Joseph Gillen. Then me. The caboose. Gordon Fenton would sit in the moderator's chair, closest to Cameron.

"Gap Eiffert was detained on an important story in Mexico," Gordon was telling the audience, "but we are more than delighted to have—" He looked down at his notes. "Molly Hallberg is stepping in. Molly writes for the online newsmagazine *EyeSpy*. Her most recent story was about bike riding." I waited for the applause. A clap here or there. Probably Russell and a few people who'd clap for anything. We filed out to our seats and the applause started up again. Cameron waved. Julia waved. So I waved. Joseph Gillen nodded. We all sat down. A blue tablecloth covered the table. I was glad I didn't have to worry about keeping my knees together. We each had our own mics. The houselights were off and the stage lights blinding, which was fine by me. It's a lot easier to talk to a thousand people when you can't see the thousand people.

"So let's start with you, Julia," Gordon said, getting right down to business. "We're talking about research. We're talking about inspiration. Do you research your novels?"

Julia dipped her head, smiled up at Gordon through her false lashes like a saucy ingenue. "Well, darling, I can't possibly have had as many love affairs as my heroines do. But I try my best." The female audience laughed, applauded. What was I going to say? I rented a bicycle? Julia sat up straighter. She was still the size of a hummingbird, but her posture was impressive. "I grew up reading the great romances. So in my own way, I was researching even before I knew I'd be a writer."

"I just finished Daphne du Maurier," I said, not stopping to think, *Is it okay if I talk?* "And before that, *The Great Gatsby.*" I sounded like I was giving a high school report.

"I learned so much," Julia said. To the audience. Not to me. "I don't believe character is destiny. I believe love is destiny."

"I don't research my books!" Joseph Gillen said, leaning forward, elbows out, hogging my space, cutting off Julia, and cutting off me. "I live them!" He talked about insurgencies and insurrections and hobnobbing with rebels, hiding with revolutionaries. It didn't seem like a good time to cut in and ask, "Anyone want to hear about Kegel-exercise panties?"

After another coup or two, Gordon finally interrupted, "Cameron, who were your influences? What did you read as a budding future writer?"

The bright lights made Cameron's high forehead shine and his eyes twinkle. His eyes were green. Why hadn't I noticed they were green? He was saying, "My literary heroes then are my same heroes now. Franklin Dixon's *The Hardy Boys.*" The audience awwwed. What could be sweeter? What could be more endearing? A bestselling crime writer who still loved the Hardy Boys. I bet he'd never read a *Hardy Boys* in his life. "I still own my father's original collection," he said. "The only two I'm missing are *The Short-Wave Mystery* and *The Secret of Wildcat Swamp.*"

Okay. So maybe he was familiar with them.

"Do you use the Hardy Boys to inspire plot ideas?" Gordon asked. The audience chuckled.

"Of course!" Cameron said. "But not for my current project. I don't believe Frank or Joe ever signed on to Match.com." Laughter.

Joseph Gillen dropped his big Pulitzer Prize–winning elbow in my space. I nudged back with my elbow. Like the two of us were on an airplane going at it over the armrest.

"Tell us about your new book, Cameron," Gordon said in his NPR voice.

Cameron looked a little shy, a little sheepish. I'd seen that expression on him before. I pictured him practicing the look in his bathroom mirror. "The story's about a murderer who kills women he meets online," he said. "Revenge against the criminal's mother for pushing him to get married." The audience laughed. The plot sounded awful. But Cameron could do no wrong. "Mike Bing goes undercover dating women on Match."

"Did you research the book?" I asked, angling from my end of the table to look directly at Cameron on his end of the table.

"I'm afraid so," he said, looking out toward the black void of the audience, serving up his charming, crooked smile. "And my apologies to all the beautiful women I met online." The audience giggled and cooed. These women should have been throwing cream pies at the man, not rewarding him with cooing.

"You fake-dated?" I asked. "Dated under false pretenses?"

"Who hasn't?" Joseph Gillen said.

"Did any lucky woman rate a second date?" I asked.

"I was the lucky one," Cameron said, so heartfelt, so grateful. "My only regret is that with my writing deadlines, I had no time for follow-up." *Awww.* Another universal aw. "I agree with Julia," he said. "Love is destiny. Someone holds your hand for the first time and you just know." A collective sigh could be heard from all womankind.

"Beautiful," Julia said.

"Know what?" I asked.

"You know your future," Cameron said.

I said, "You must get exhausted in a reception line."

Cameron sounded earnest, fervent, hopeful. "I'm looking for the one woman who understands me, my soul mate. I believe in soul mates." He might as well have been holding up a cue card that said SIGH.

I asked, "Have you ever fallen in love?" The two of us were having a private conversation on the stage of an auditorium.

"A hundred times a day," he said. The audience giggled. The audience laughed. He made those green eyes of his twinkle out in their direction.

"That's not falling in love with a woman," I said, "that's falling in love with love."

"Have *you* tried it?" Joseph Gillen asked me.

"Did you ever marry or live with someone?" I asked Cameron.

"Can we kindly return to our topic?" Gordon said.

"I'd like to recall my time in Niger during the first Tuareg rebellion," Joseph said.

"Not that topic," Gordon said.

"There's a difference between not wanting to settle down and not wanting to settle," Cameron said to me.

You can bet that stirred up applause. It would have been an excellent time for a divorce lawyer to hand out business cards.

Julia Hollingsworth cleared her throat. "Romance is transactional," she said. "It must be reciprocal. A back-and-forth of appreciation." She zoomed in on Joseph. "What's your ideal, big boy?"

"Silent understanding," Joseph Gillen said. "You say it with your eyes. You say it with your heart. You say it with your soul." He laughed. "A woman who doesn't talk."

The audience booed.

"I disagree," Cameron said. "I love a woman who'll go one-on-one with me, who can banter, one-up me, keep me on my toes. That's the heart of the greatest romantic duos. Nick and Nora. Harry and Sally."

"Bogie and Bacall," Julia said.

"Kermit and Miss Piggy," I said. The audience laughed. Finally I'd said something quotable for Angela.

"Fay Wray and King Kong," Joseph said. The audience booed.

"Perhaps it's time we moved on to the Q and A," Gordon said. "Houselights, please?"

Standing mics were set up in the front of each aisle. Anyone with a question could line up and wait his or her turn. I've attended enough writers' panels to know that no matter what the subject, the same two questions are always asked: *What's your writing process?* and *How do you get an agent?* I didn't have a process or an agent so I was pretty much off duty. If anyone asked me—and I sincerely doubted anyone would—I'd just defer to Julia or Cameron. But not to Mr. Elbow Hog. Joseph Gillen scared me.

A woman with gray, frizzy hair, hovering at the first mic, said, "This question's for Julia." Julia nodded, gripped her mic with her long, skinny fingers. "What's your writing process?"

Another woman asked Cameron how to get an agent. A third woman asked Cameron about his writing process. Cameron grinned. "I sit down at my desk, turn on my computer, and hope for the best. And when that doesn't work, I read *The Hardy Boys.*"

Oh, how he charmed that audience! I found myself wondering how a guy who's not attractive could be so attractive to so many women. But I also realized—much to my horror—that he was kind of attractive to me, too.

Cameron turned in his chair to face me. "Molly Hallberg writes my favorite pieces in *EyeSpy*. In between reading Joe and Frank Hardy, I read Molly Hallberg." He smiled at me.

I sat back in my chair out of sight of his gaze.

Another woman asked a question at the mic, this one young with blond curls pulled into a topknot. "Do you need any more volunteers for Mike Bing to date?"

"If only he'd met you sooner," Cameron said, smiling, "but Mike's already solved the crime." Laughter and applause.

Gordon Fenton thanked the panelists, said there'd be books for sale in the lobby and an opportunity to meet the authors for book signings. Theresa Flynn stepped out onstage clapping, calling out thank-you and saying good-night from the podium mic, like a hostess making a not-too-subtle hint that it was time for the guests to vamoose. The panelists rose to leave; Gordon shook hands with the men.

"Come help me, you naughty man," Julia said to Joseph. She wrapped her fingers around his arm and made him aid her down the stairs. Gordon walked offstage with Theresa. Cameron and I followed.

"Thank you for what you said," I told him. "About liking my pieces. Without you, I'd have felt totally invisible up there."

"Feisty Molly Hallberg," he said. Here came the smile again. "We might have to continue our parley."

"Cameron!" Theresa said. "We need you at the signing table."

"Continue it where?" I asked Cameron.

Russell came hurrying up and kissed me congratulations. "Good job," he said. "You got through it!"

Cameron had already walked away with Gordon and Theresa.

12

People who write about their dreams are totally self-indulgent, expecting the reader to (1) give a damn and (2) waste precious time analyzing someone else's dream as if they (#1 again) give a damn. But here goes:

I've just walked out of Saks Fifth Avenue having bought a pair of new socks when Nora Ephron and Nancy Drew drive up in Nancy's blue convertible. Nancy's behind the wheel and Nora's carrying a pot roast and homemade cookies. "Get in!" Nora says. We drive to a bar on Second Avenue, past a mysterious old clock and a crumbling wall, and go inside. I don't know what happened to Nancy's convertible; maybe she valet parked it when I wasn't looking. Anyway, once we're inside the bar I'm eating Nora's cookies and she's giving me the recipe. The bar's really hopping. Backslapping, high-fiving, boisterous energy. Harry

144

Connick Jr. playing in the background. But what's really weird are the two televisions hanging over the bar—that in itself, of course, is normal—but instead of a Yankees game or the Mets, one's playing *When Harry Met Sally* and the other's showing *You've Got Mail*. Nancy Drew orders a gin and tonic and uses her flashlight to point out two men. The bar's smoky so I can never see their faces, but one man's in a shirt and tie sitting by himself, staring at his cell phone. Women, laughing and having fun, surround the second man. Except—even though his face is a blur—he looks straight at me and holds out a rose. Nancy Drew asks, "Which man do you want?" I start to head over to the nice, quiet man with the tie just as Nicolas Cage walks in and sits down with him, and Nora Ephron says, "Don't be an imbecile!" and snatches my cookie away.

I have no idea what this means.

I was meeting Kristine on the seventh floor of Bloomingdale's half an hour before meeting Russell on the fifth floor of Bloomingdale's. Russell needed a new mattress. Kristine and I needed frozen yogurt. And not just any yogurt, but the frozen yogurt at the Bloomingdale's Forty Carrots restaurant. Just thinking about it makes me want to lick this page. Their yogurt's dense, thick, creamy, obscenely smooth, intensely flavored, and—here's the kicker—*fat free*.

I don't actually believe it's fat free. But I also can't believe Bloomingdale's would lie about such a thing.

The Forty Carrots menu has other items on it. Salads. Soups. Chicken sandwiches. But nobody orders those. There's always a thirty-minute wait for a table and standing room only at the take-out counter, and, yes, the clientele is female. Nowhere in all of Manhattan can you get a better sense of sisterhood than sitting at a banquette in Forty Carrots savoring and inhaling frozen yogurt alongside dozens of other savoring, inhaling women. Fortunately Kristine works at Bloomingdale's and she's friendly with the Forty Carrots hostess. With a little surreptitious maneuvering, a secret head nod, and a certain back table, we didn't have to wait the thirty minutes. Which is a good thing. As a Bloomingdale's employee, Kristine only gets thirty minutes for lunch.

She ordered a medium peanut-butter yogurt. I ordered a medium half-chocolate half-coffee. The mediums are huge. Anywhere else they'd be extra larges.

"Exchange tastes?" she said.

We dipped into each other's bowls.

Kristine sat back, closed her eyes, luxuriated in the chocolate, basked in the coffee, sat up, opened her eyes, and adjusted her eyeglasses. "Perfect," she said.

"Perfect," I said.

Kristine and I are purists. We never order toppings for our yogurt.

"Do you think they'll invite you back to the Ninety-Second Street Y?" she asked.

"Yes," I said. "If I buy a ticket and promise to sit in the last row." I said. "I didn't stick to the topic, nobody in the audience asked me questions, and I was warring over elbow room with a Pulitzer Prize–winning dick. We were some panel. Mr. Charm. Mr. Ego. Miss Dirty Old Lady. And Miss Nobody."

"Anyone ask for a refund?"

"I tried but they pointed out that my seat was free."

"I hope they videotaped it."

"Oh, dear God, I hope they didn't."

We paused for new bites, *mmm*ed in unison. All around us women were drooling and moaning.

"How insane you ended up on a panel with one of my dates," Kristine said.

"Say that again?" I set down my yogurt spoon. That's how taken aback I was.

"Your Cameron Duncan. My Frank Hardy. My writer date! I should have known it was a fake name."

"You dated Cameron?" When I said Cameron's name, my voice came out all high-pitched like a cartoon character's.

"No." Kristine smiled. "I dated Frank."

"When'd you find out who he really was?"

"On my way home. When I saw his picture on the subway. How weird was *that*?" Kristine took a bite of her peanut-butter yogurt. I had to wait for her to finish savoring. "The whole date was strange," she said. "More like an interview than a date. He kept asking about my online dating adventures. Like he was researching a book."

A woman at the next table was served a yogurt larger than her face.

"Where'd he take you?" I asked Kristine. *Why do I care?* I asked myself.

"I suggested meeting for drinks at the top of the Times Square Marriott, but we went to Flute, that underground champagne bar on Fifty-Fourth. I think he goes there a lot. They seem to know him. It's like a speakeasy."

"He has a height-phobia thing."

"Oh? Acrophobia? I once dated a guy with coulrophobia."

"And that is?"

"Fear of clowns. Sometimes I'm afraid I have anuptaphobia."

"I'm waiting."

"Fear of staying single."

"Thank you, Miss World Book Encyclopedia."

Kristine looked down at her yogurt. "I'm never going to finish this," she said.

I looked down at my yogurt, said, "I'm never going to finish this."

"But let's try," she said. We scooped up two more bites. Kristine wiped her mouth with a napkin. "I suppose Cameron's cute, if you like that type where none of the features are good-looking, but somehow they add up well together."

"You must have liked his photo online."

"Not particularly."

"So why'd you go out with him?"

"Oh, you know me," she said. "I'll date anyone. We only stayed for one drink. When I left, he gave me a cheek peck. I hate the cheek peck. It's like your grandmother is kissing you." The waitress refilled our water glasses and deposited the check. "That's the biggest flaw with online dating. You can't judge chemistry until you meet the guy, and when you do meet him, you can judge it in three minutes." Kristine removed her eyeglasses and wiped them with her dirty napkin. "Fake Frank Hardy seemed sincere, smart, funny. Just not my type."

"Good thinking. Hold out for the asshole bad boy."

She put her glasses back on. They were still smudged. "Maybe Hunkster500 will be the one. He's next on my list."

"Do you think that's a fake name?"

"I'm holding out for big-time chemistry," she said. "I wish you would."

"I tried chemistry once. I married chemistry. I'm good with comfortable."

Kristine shook two fists the way someone does when they want to shake you, only they don't really want to shake you, they just want to imply it. "Jesus, Molly. Slippers are comfortable! Cocoa is comfortable! Bing Crosby singing Christmas songs—that's comfortable. You shouldn't be sleeping with Bing Crosby!"

"Sex with Russell is fine," I said.

"What about interesting?"

I had to think about that. "Well, sometimes he likes to pretend he's Irwin and I'm Joyce during sex."

"I said interesting sex, not kinky. What do turtles say during sex?"

"Nothing unusual."

"So that's it? You're cool with the occasional turtle talk? You don't want to feel that crazy flutter of invisible connection? That thing that makes your insides buzz?"

"That thing's fleeting."

"It's a foundation. It's your entire everything saying, *Pay attention!* You need to watch *Sleepless in Seattle* again."

"I've watched it more than anyone. I've seen it more than Meg Ryan has. When she gets on that plane to Seattle, I know I'd have never done that."

"And that's why you wouldn't have ended up with Tom Hanks."

"How do we know they ended up happy? We never saw a sequel."

"You got the message, right? What the movie's talking about?"

"Let's not talk about it."

Kristine picked up the check. "My treat," she said. "I can use my discount."

She started unloading her purse onto the table. A wad of used Kleenex. Crumpled receipts. A brush with enough hair in it to weave a wig. Two condom packets. A rolled-up, open potato-chip bag. The bottom half, but not the cover, of a lip gloss.

"That is not an attractive sight," I said.

"Just give me a minute. You know Nora Ephron's essay about hating her purse? In her hating-her-neck book? She was writing about me."

"How about I buy? I'm willing to pay full retail if I can stop you before you whip out an old tampon."

"Oh, here!" Kristine held up her wallet. "My treat!"

The only thing worse than shopping for a mattress is shopping for a bra, which explains the sorry condition of most of my bras. But mattresses are preposterous. What once was a question of soft, firm, or hard is now a voyage into a world of pillow top, tight top, latex, innerspring, cushioned upholstery, motion transfer, antimicrobial, visco-elastic foam. I must be the most oblivious sleeper ever. My criteria for a new mattress is: will it fit through my bedroom door?

Russell was waiting by the escalators in front of the mattress department. Pardon me. Bloomingdale's calls it their mattress *gallery*. They must be getting it confused with the MoMA, six blocks south. Russell was checking his watch, checking his BlackBerry, looking very Russell-esque in gray slacks, a white shirt, and striped tie; his hair neatly combed back. "You're late," he said.

"Five minutes," I said.

"I have patients in an hour."

"Fine. Let's go bounce on mattresses."

He pecked me on the cheek. Grandmother-style.

The mattress gallery at Bloomingdale's is dimly lit in this kind of bluish, kind of grayish light. I guess so the customers can simulate bedtime. Only the mattresses are well lit; spotlights are aimed at each one so the entire room looks like a landing dock for large, white space pods. I'm sure the salespeople are on commission because as soon as you step within spitting distance of a mattress, they all converge, asking to help, asking if you have questions, suggesting you stretch out and see how the mattress feels. A woman who introduced herself as Mina got to us first. We were standing by the first mattress in the gallery. Mina was tall, attractive, her sleeveless, navy dress clean, simple; something about her manner was reminiscent of a college professor. A lot like Russell, only in the guise of a Bloomingdale's saleslady. "Any questions?" she said. The other customers were all couples. Maybe that's why Russell wanted me along; he'd have felt naked without a date. "Stretch out and see how it feels," Mina said.

I turned over the price tag. "Holy shit!" I said.

Mina smiled. She was wise, patient. "That's our top-of-the-line Kluft. Joma wool. Talalay latex. Calico-encased spring unit."

I showed the price tag to Russell. "Holy shit!" he said.

"Seriously. I have to try this," I told Russell. "I need to know what a thirty-six-thousand-dollar mattress feels like."

"Is it for both of you?" Mina asked.

"For him," I said.

"For me," he said.

Russell and I lay down alongside one another, bouncing our shoulders a little, staring at the ceiling.

"Excellent," Russell said.

"Excellent," I said.

"Anything for anything less?" Russell said.

"Hi!" Kristine said as we sat up from the excellent Joma-wool, Talalay-latex Kluft. "Things are slow. I took a break. How's this one?"

"Great," I said. "The price includes a three-bedroom condominium."

Russell stood and whispered something to Kristine.

"Sorry," she said. "Not for mattresses. But maybe a discount on a tie someday."

"What about the kind you can bounce on with a glass of red wine?" I asked Mina. "Can we try that?"

"No," Russell said. "It's impossible to flip a Tempur-Pedic." Russell's a big believer in mattress flipping. Something about dead skin and dust. "Half my patients are people who tried to flip Tempur-Pedics."

I said, "Maybe they were drunk from red wine."

Russell and Mina walked on ahead. Kristine and I followed.

"A chiropractor!" we heard Mina chirp. "So you appreciate the importance of a good mattress."

"Not thirty-six thousand dollars' worth," I said to Kristine.

"Wait. I've got to try that." She headed back to the Kluft. I joined Russell and Mina next to a king-size Shifman Handmade Luxury Plush Pillowtop. You can fall asleep by the time you finish saying the names of these mattresses. "How much is this one?" I asked.

"Hand-tufted," Mina said.

"Seven thousand," Russell said.

"Exciting. You've already saved twenty-nine thousand dollars," I said.

We tried the Shifman.

"Not bad," Russell said.

"Feels just like the other one," I said.

"I liked the first one," Russell said.

"You two talk," Mina said, walking away to give us a moment of privacy in a bed-filled room filled with other couples sharing private moments.

"Please tell me you aren't going to spend thirty-six grand on a mattress," I said.

"If you amortize it out over the course of fifteen years it's only—" He stopped.

"You just did the math, right?"

"Right." He said, "My ex-girlfriend had a Stearns and Foster that felt fine. And the girlfriend before her had a Sealy that couldn't have been expensive, and that felt fine, too."

"Thanks for sharing. How was the sex?"

"You two just had sex?" Kristine said, looming over us. Russell got up, waved down Mina, and walked over to her in the Sealy section. Kristine spread out on the Shifman with me, the two of us side by side, gazing upward like we were lounging on a beach.

"Why do mattress names always begin with an *s*?" I asked.

"Why are mattresses always on sale?" she asked.

"Russell was just telling me about his ex-girlfriends' mattress brands."

"Congratulations on dating Mr. Insensitive."

"He's not insensitive. He's honest."

Kristine and I looked at each other. She looked exasperated. "There's honest. And there's rude. Honestly, Molly, sometimes I wonder about you."

"Stop wondering."

"I once read this thing that said if a person's snoring and keeping you awake, you should clap your hands over their face. That the noise will make them change positions and stop snoring without waking them."

"You won *It's Academic,* right? Your team won?"

"So I'm staying over at this guy's and he's sound asleep going at it full throttle like a beluga whale, and I clap my hands over his head."

"What happened?"

"He opened his eyes and told me I was insensitive." Kristine sat up. I sat up. I saw Russell in animated conversation with Mina. Good Lord. Was he flirting with the mattress lady? Maybe hoping for *her* Bloomingdale's discount? Kristine must have also noticed. She gave Russell a look. "I'm sorry, Molly, but no woman wants to hear about the previous girlfriend's taste in mattresses." She slid off the bed, said she had to go back to her department to sell sofas. "Maybe your boyfriend should buy a Bill *Pullman* sleeper sofa."

Kristine left. I interrupted Russell's exchange with Mina, the two of them going on and on about spines and support and how she loved that he's a chiropractor and really understands.

While lying next to him on the Sealy, I told him he was

rude and insensitive and no woman wants to hear about the previous girlfriend's taste in mattresses.

I went back to my office mad. He went back to his office mad. I'm glad I wasn't the patient whose neck he was cracking next. I can't even recall how things escalated or why I was angry. I just knew that I was right and Russell was wrong so he'd have to be the one to call and apologize. I bet he had no clue what *my* mattress brand was. I sure couldn't. I just knew it began with an *s*.

I conducted a mental inventory of what clothing items I'd left at his apartment and how I'd retrieve them, versus could I live without them? I had a key. I could sneak in while he was at work, toss my belongings into a plastic grocery bag, and haul my ass out of there. Or I could ask Russell to leave my things downstairs with his doorman and I'd pick them up the next time I visited the West Side. Which might be never. Or maybe he could drop *my* things with my doorman at the same time he picked up *his* things from my doorman and . . . I resolved to never again leave personal items at a boyfriend's apartment.

I was surprised when he didn't call that night. Russell's not keen on conflict. It's his nature to smooth things over, clear the air, talk things out, or at the very least deny them.

I went across the hall to hang out with Angela, but she was rushing to get ready for a date with her swim coach. She answered the door holding an open bottle of wine. I'd never seen her dressed so *girlie*. Pink halter dress. Pink sandals. "I think tonight's the night I learn the backstroke," she said.

She sounded all pink and happy. "Don't call the cops if you hear screaming."

I spent the evening watching *Sleepless in Seattle* for the umpteenth time, crying at the ending like I always do, but wondering if I really did understand what Nora was saying.

13

The day before the Bloomingdale's fight, Deirdre summoned me to her office. Even by her standards of low necklines, she'd managed to outdo herself. I sat across her glass-topped desk praying she didn't cough or sneeze, causing her breasts to come flying out at me. Aside from her usual neatly aligned notepads, pens, and laptop, three items were positioned in front of me: what looked like a black metal lipstick tube, a black cigar case, and a short-handled plastic bottle scrubber. "Can you guess what these are?" Deirdre asked. I was about to say a lipstick, a cigar holder, and a bottle scrubber when she said, "Vibrators."

Oh, the twinkle in her eye, the devilish grin! She removed the lipstick cap to reveal a rubber semblance of a red lipstick and pressed the bottom of the tube. We both sat there watching the rubber lipstick vibrate. Deirdre pressed the button again and then a third time, causing the little bugger to speed up each time. If it were a real lipstick, only a clown could apply it.

"Emily discovered these," she said. She removed the top of the cigar case, unveiling a rubber mascara wand, slightly too large for a real mascara wand and with bristles I wouldn't want anywhere near my vagina. Again, Deirdre made it vibrate once, twice, at three speeds. I did not want to ask just where Emily discovered these cosmetically disguised vibrators. The bottle scrubber, it turned out, was supposed to be a blush brush and was the scariest of the three. "Do you know what these are for?" Deirdre asked.

Talk about your awkward questions. "I have a pretty good idea," I said.

"They're designed to fool people so you can toss them in your purse and carry them everywhere. Or leave them on your nightstand without worrying what your cleaning lady might think." Good to know. The day I hire a cleaning lady, I'll run right out to buy vibrating cosmetics. "But best of all"—there was more?—"you can take them on an airplane."

Why? I wanted to ask. *To fly solo in the mile-high club?*

"Emily suggested they'd be a perfect story subject for you." It'd be fair to say that by this point I was pretty much speechless. Not that Emily's contribution to my career opportunities was a total surprise, at least not since the angry note I found deposited on my chair: *You stole my 92Y panel! Thanks for nothing!* Deirdre pushed the three vibrators closer toward me. "Let's see if you can get these through a security scanner," she said. "Then women will know if they can grab a lipstick and hop on a plane." Deirdre loved this assignment. Her smile was amused. Mine was insincere.

"You want me to fly somewhere?" I said. Maybe I could pick the location.

"I want you to get past security," Deirde said. "The courts downtown have similar scanners. See if you can get through. Cheaper than a plane ticket."

"Yes, and if I get arrested, I'll be that much closer to a jail."

Deirdre sat back, pleased with herself. "I appreciate when my staff members come up with ideas for one another. It fosters a supportive work culture."

I picked up the vibrators, stood to leave. "Now I'll have to come up with a book for Emily to review. I hear Proust is snappy."

"Tuesday deadline?" Deirdre said.

"If not sooner," I said.

When I returned to my desk, I didn't bother looking to see if Emily was in her cubicle. I knew she was and I knew she was listening in on her side of our shared wall. "If you used these first, I'll kill you!" I said.

I didn't randomly choose a courthouse. I gave my options considerable thought. Family court? No, too embarrassing if I got stopped. There might be children around. Criminal court? Also unappealing. There might be criminals around. After ruling out the Supreme Court—it just felt *wrong*—

and its appellate division, the one I can never understand, I settled on the civil court building. Landlords suing tenants. Insurance companies suing everyone. Nonthreatening legal activities.

Friday morning I headed down there first thing. I figured a Friday would be less crowded, fewer cases being heard so the judges could head out to their weekend homes early. I didn't want the line to be so short that the scanner guards would have nothing better to do than focus on me and my handbag, nor so long that if they did detain me, hold up my blush brush, and holler out, "Okay! Who's trying to sneak a vibrator into court?" there'd be a large crowd witnessing my humiliation. How would I respond to a "Hey! This isn't a lipstick!" What would I say to a "Will the lady who owns the vibrating mascara please step out of line?" I'd stay right where I was, look around accusingly at the other women in line, and make a face like *How could you! In a public courthouse yet!* And what if my vibrating cosmetics did pass through security? What if they caught on? I'd hate to think what might be taking place in the state bathrooms, let alone the federal ones.

Those were my thoughts while waiting for my turn. A man in a dashiki was dumping his keys and wristwatch into a small plastic bin. A woman who had to be a lawyer—not only was she wearing a suit, but she was wearing pantyhose in the middle of July, for crying out loud—set a leather briefcase on the table. Maybe she had a vibrator tucked inside, a big ol' honking Rabbit. My own big ol' honking Rabbit was hidden in a pouch beneath my bed with its relatives, the dust bunnies. I only used it between boyfriends and preferred a boyfriend to a Rabbit.

Pre-Bloomingdale's, Russell and I had joked about christening his new mattress, how we'd have to spend a great deal of time breaking it in. It was important to him that I help choose the mattress; he wanted me to be comfortable, too. Maybe Russell was content to sit at home when I'd rather go out. Maybe I could barely remember why we were drawn to each other in the first place, or that at times it seemed all he needed was someone, not necessarily *me*. But he was sweet. Thoughtful. Reliable. And I was a few months from turning forty. Good reasons to hang on to Russell and keep my Rabbit under the bed.

The line moved forward. With more than a little trepidation I placed my handbag on the roller belt, then watched it travel merrily on its way right after a backpack and ahead of a long, zippered canvas bag that looked suspiciously like a gun case. One of the guards informed us we could keep our shoes on. Good news. If I ever cross paths with that man with the string coming out of his shoe, it won't be pretty.

I stepped through the security arch. The guard nodded; he looked bored to death. My handbag with its secret stash came riding out. Then stopped. Retreated. The roller stopped. My heart stopped. The roller resumed and my bag reappeared. No detonators went off. No alarms blared. I wasn't carted off to detention and a cell full of prostitutes. I grabbed my bag, waved good-bye to the guards and left.

Stepping into the sunshine, I dug out my phone and called Russell's office. His receptionist said he was with a patient, but ten seconds later he was on the line. I apologized. He apologized. He said he'd bring over a DVD and we could order in Chinese.

A week later, I was sitting in the reception room of Dr. David Lewis, DDS, waiting for my six-month cleaning. On the wall opposite me hung a poster of the Three Stooges dressed like dentists, holding hammers and wrenches, Dr. Lewis's idea of humor. Behind an open sliding-glass window a young woman in a medical smock was cursing at her computer. I sifted through the magazines on the corner end table. *Cycle World. Golf Digest. Field & Stream.* I wanted to curse, too. The one other patient in the waiting area, a woman with close-cropped hair and the bone structure to warrant it, was reading an iPad. "Pathetic choices," she said, wrinkling her nose and acknowledging the magazine selection. "Whenever I come here, I bring my own reading material."

I said, "I'm impressed you remember to do that."

She shrugged. "Bad teeth." She went back to her iPad, chuckling, then sighing, then looking up and asking, "Do you ever read *EyeSpy*?"

"Sure!" I said. Maybe she'd compliment something I wrote.

"Some of their articles are ridiculous," the woman said. "You couldn't pay me to do the crazy things one writer does.

But this piece is adorable. Totally different for them and totally charming."

It didn't sound like it was about vibrators. "What's the topic?" I asked, trying to peek at her screen.

"Love. Romance. Recognizing the *one*." She read aloud: "'Bestselling crime novelist Cameron Duncan writes that finding love is the ultimate mystery.'"

If Dr. Lewis had stepped into the waiting room right that second, it would have been an excellent time to lecture me on grinding my teeth. "May I see that one teensy minute?" I asked the woman.

Her eyes narrowed. She gripped her iPad. Like maybe I'd snatch it out of her hands and hightail it out of there.

"One little second? Please? I'll give it right back. Promise!"

"Only one second," she said, handing it over.

"I swear."

At first I skimmed the article, then I slowed down, absorbed in Cameron's words. *Love is a catalog of emotional needs and you need to prioritize what's important to you. For some it's arousal and erotica, for others it's a playmate or security. Once you choose your priority from the catalog of love, you discover what's critical to you.* I read his interviews with couples who believed the energy and vibrancy of New York fostered romance. These were effusive, rhapsodic, lyrical couples, not the subway cranks I cross-examined. I read his list of New York's most romantic settings. I'd written a list. I'd included a list in my article. I liked my list much more than his list. He wrote how he was waiting for that sense of magic and recognition he knew he'd feel from the first moment he held his soul mate's hand and exchanged that first memorable kiss. I wanted to hate the article. But it was sweet, romantic. *We try. We trust. We make safe choices, foolish choices, wrong choices, wrongheaded choices. We fall off the course and climb back on again.*

He didn't write at all like Nora Ephron. Even the wonder boy couldn't pull that off. But like a Nora Ephron movie, he made love sound fairy-tale idyllic and sparkling with possibility.

The woman started coughing, leaning closer to me. "Excuse me," she said. "Perhaps you can hand me that copy of *Field and Stream*." She was pissed.

If you have good distance vision, it's actually possible to hand an iPad back to its owner while continuing to read the screen. That's what I was doing when I caught one more paragraph. *In* Sleepless in Seattle, *we know Meg Ryan will end up with Tom Hanks. She'll end up with Billy Crystal in* When Harry Met Sally. *But we still keep watching. We're still mesmerized by the journey.*

Cameron had totally ripped off what I'd told him at the book party! Did the guy walk around with a hidden wire? Did he have no shame!

"iPad hog," the woman was saying, stuffing the tablet into her purse.

The receptionist who'd been cussing at her computer was now smiling. She and her computer must have made up. "He's ready for you, Miss Brichta," she said.

Miss Brichta served up one final snarl as she made her way through the door to the treatment rooms.

When I was finally stretched out in a dental chair, a green paper bib clipped around my neck, with Lynn the hygienist gloved and masked and picking away, I thought about how flattering it was, beyond flattering, an homage of sorts, that bestselling author Cameron Duncan had swiped what I'd said. What a compliment! What an accolade! What nerve. I bet he stole half the article, like all that business about magic and memorable kisses. While Lynn scraped, I made a list in my head of my memorable kisses.

Johnny Zwierzko. Fifth grade. Gum in his mouth. Juicy Fruit. I hate Juicy Fruit. Grade: C-.

Pablo Mullen. High school. Sophomore year. Lactose intolerant. Passed gas while kissing me in a Baskin-Robbins. Grade: D+.

Bradley Bernett. High school. Junior year. Making out big-time, kissing me good-night on my front steps. My father suddenly opens the door, pulls me inside, and shoves a corned-beef sandwich in Bradley's hand, saying, "Here! Chew on this!" Bradley: A-. Sidney Hallberg: F.

Nameless Kappa Sigma fraternity pledge. College. Freshman year. Regal Cinemas in Albany. Where nameless pledge somehow managed to poke his penis through the bottom of the cardboard popcorn box in his lap and then offered me popcorn. Grade: Incomplete.

Evan Naboshek. A+. Unfortunately.

Richie Rossier. Five weeks after my divorce was finalized. Washed my tonsils with his tongue. D-.

Russell Edley. Solid B.

"Did that hurt?" Lynn the hygienist asked, stepping back. Before I could answer, she said, "Drink and spit."

That afternoon, I could hear Emily in her office pretending to read Cameron's article and commenting out loud. "Wow, Cameron Duncan did an amazing job on this romance story. Not that it was hard to write, I'm sure. Any fool could have done it, but he sure did a great job!"

I wanted to tell her that the best paragraph in the entire article, the one with the most profound insight, was mine, that he swiped it from me, took an innocent conversation shared outside of a powder room on Central Park South and absconded with it as his own.

But since I'd rather not talk to Emily, at all, ever, period, I didn't mention that.

I slipped my headphones on and researched organic restaurants. That was my next assignment. Writing about food I never ate. My mouth ached. My mind strayed.

Lynn the hygienist had really dug in. There are almost 82 million results when you google *organic restaurants*. That should be a good start. I couldn't get past being called an "iPad hog" even if it was true. Okay, so maybe I held on to it longer than I'd promised, but why resort to childish name-calling? If I had an iPad and someone asked to borrow it, I'd say, *Take your time, no rush at all.* So why was I annoyed with that lady and not upset with Cameron Duncan? I thought I was upset with him. I tried to stay upset with him. I read that the number of organic restaurants was expected to grow 14 percent over the next year. I told myself Cameron didn't remember it was me who said we still keep watching even when we know the ending. He wasn't half as good-looking as Russell. Imagine all the women who must be swooning over his romance piece. Russell's new mattress was too soft. *Oh, Molly, what's wrong with you?*

After work I stopped in the Barnes & Noble on Eighty-Sixth, grateful it hadn't turned into a discount clothing store like the Barnes & Noble on Sixty-Sixth. I paused for my usual five-minute reverie where I imagined my own published book. My acerbic observations on *The Great Gatsby*. My smart-alecky commentary on *Pride and Prejudice*. My snarky appraisal of *Washington Square*. Hallberg, the literary heretic, embraced by critics and fans alike. I tossed in a few book tours and autograph signings.

After I got past that mental malarkey, I found the crime section. Cameron's three novels took up an entire shelf; several copies were available for each title. I didn't know if that was a good sign because the store ordered lots of copies, or a bad sign because nobody was buying any copies. The artwork showed Mike Bing with a different dame on each cover. Probably the girlfriends he kept killing off. I figured I'd buy the first book first and see where Mr. Duncan got his big start. Russell already owned the first book, but I never borrow Russell's books. Russell mangles books, dog-ears them, underlines passages with black marker that bleeds through to the opposite side, drops books in the toilet or leaves them on buses. I don't even want to touch Russell's books.

Maybe I'd go buy an egg-salad sandwich at the Barnes & Noble café. If I read fast enough, I could read Cameron's book while I sat there and not pay for it. I'd just have to be careful with the pages. I have enough of a moral code to draw the line at reshelving books I've smeared with egg salad. But whipping through a couple hundred pages or so while sampling a book for free? I'm cool with that.

I was weaving my way through fiction toward the café when I saw Russell's head. I peeked over from my aisle to see his aisle. Poetry. Russell was in the poetry section. What the hell was Russell doing in poetry? A normal girlfriend would have walked up to her boyfriend, expressed delight at their fortuitous unscripted meeting and casually asked, *What the hell are you doing in poetry?* But I went for option B. I spied on him. Why, I don't know. It seemed like a good idea at the time, more than any deep-down desire to be a sneak. It's fascinating to observe someone who thinks he's walking around unobserved. You never know what you might learn. Like I learned, for instance, that Russell was buying a poetry book. There was only one possible explanation. He was buying the book for me. I'd have to hide and wait until he left. If I showed up now, I'd spoil his gift. I ducked around to the Women's Issues section. He'd never find me there.

14

Later, Russell said it was my idea. I said it was his, even though it really was my idea to invite Kristine and Angela to dinner with their new boyfriends. But Russell's the one who suggested we use his apartment instead of mine because his dining table's bigger.

"Now we have to pay for a cab across town," Angela said when I told her the locale.

"Take a bus."

She was sitting on my floor, her legs straight out, doing stretches. I was sitting on my sofa not doing stretches. The Black Eyed Peas were singing "Rock That Body." "What's wrong with your place? You own good dishes," Angela said.

"One, don't assume this dinner party warrants good dishes. And, two, how am I going to feel if, after dinner, you go across the hall to have screaming sex and I'm stuck here scrubbing pots with Russell? If you leave and get in a cab, I won't have that problem."

Angela extended her arms like a holdup victim. She bent forward toward her toes. "Leave with Charlie and me and only Russell will have that problem." She was joyful, bubbly, giddy, over her swim coach. At first I worried, does she make love with the guy, roll over, and tweet, *It was good for me*. But Angela's relationship with her phone took a serious step backward as soon as she started a relationship with a man. She was counting down the days until school started again, relishing her boyfriend's current availability. "I should have been a teacher and worked for the school system," she said. "It's great having the entire summer off to hang out at home."

"You hang out at home the entire year."

"So what should I wear?" she asked, arms in the air, then back to her toes. She was a new Angela. She still wore her sweats collection, but when Charlie was within a one-mile radius, she whipped out the ruffles and lace.

I smiled at her. "Whatever makes you happy."

"I am happy," she said. She moved onto her back, stretching in all directions, making snow angels on my carpet.

Both Angela and Kristine seemed to feel they'd met the *one*. How did they know so fast? I never know fast. I assess, make lists of pros and cons, and accept another date if the pros outweigh the cons.

After my divorce, when I retreated to Long Island, sleeping in my old bedroom even though it was now an arts-

and-crafts room, my mother came into my room one night bringing me a cup of tea. She sat down on a closed tub of library paste and said, "Molly, if love was easy, it wouldn't feel like magic when you finally got it right."

Magic. I wanted magic. But what's it take to get it right?

I told Angela the dinner wasn't going to be formal, just Russell tossing a couple of chickens under a broiler.

"Can I bring something?"

"Sure. How about a salad, a side dish, some wine, dessert, and two chickens?"

I hoped we all hit it off. Russell was a nice guy. And from whatever foggy, fuzzy memory I retained of our speed date, Charlie was a nice guy. The four of us could go out and have a nice time. But if Russell and Charlie became friends, and then Angela and Charlie broke up or Russell and I broke up, how could Russell still be friends with Charlie while Angela and I were still friends? When Evan and I divorced, we divvied up our friends. You get the casserole dish and Judy Linklater; I'll take the soup tureen and the Seratores. In the end I kept the friends I brought to the marriage, and no matter how friendly I'd grown with Evan's friends, he kept his. I've seen this happen with couples who split after twenty years. The woman gets custody of her college roommate, the man gets custody of his; except for one couple I knew where the husband ran off with his wife's college roommate.

If Charlie and I didn't like each other, how could Angela share her excitement over his dirty talk in bed (already heard about that) or that twisty, flicky thing he does with his tongue (heard about that, too) or the fabulous way he nibbles her ass. I never share sex stories about Russell. He has never nibbled my ass. We never ripped off our clothes and did it on his dining table. Good news, I should think, for our Saturday-night dinner guests.

Saturday afternoon the party host and hostess procured groceries at Fairway. If you've never been there, just imagine the most chaotic, crowded maze of quiches, soups, anchovies, organic this, organic that, whitefish salads, exotic nuts, hand-sorted chilies, cheeses imported from third-world countries, an entire olive oil section (not just a mere shelf), goose fat, dandelion greens; and if you're lucky, you might even pick up a quart of milk and half a dozen eggs.

The Fairway layout makes no sense. The narrow aisles turn every odd way. The cookie aisle requires two sharp turns. It's where New Yorkers play bumper car. But, oh, the quality! People, like Russell, who live on the West Side, bragged for years that they couldn't possibly move to the East Side and give up Fairway. Then Fairway announced they were opening a store on the Upper East Side, and now West Side residents have to say they can never leave Lincoln Center.

"Nirvana," Russell said. "Taste this South African Peppadew."

"You aren't supposed to taste it," I said to him. "They don't want the customers sampling their Peppadews."

"One doesn't hurt. And it's not like I'm not buying

some." He scooped a spoonful of the bright-red little peppers into a plastic container. "Let's taste the grapes and make sure they're sweet."

"Why don't we just ask them to boil up a lobster and see how that tastes?"

We elbowed our way around the coffee-bean section, past the flat-bread section and the dried-apricots section, to the mustards section, where Russell studied labels and I watched two women duke it out over who was first in the ten-items-or-less line. Russell chose a mango curry mustard and we kept going. Our cart was already heaped with Bibb lettuce, feta cheese, walnuts, toilet paper, cauliflower, potatoes, and a giant loaf of sourdough. A pile-up of carts caused a major stall in the aisle with the elevator. One floor of Fairway food heaven is not enough; there's another floor with more soups, more olive oils, more exotic nuts and quiches, along with a health store to stock up on vitamins and Tom's toothpaste, and Fairway's very own restaurant, which displays cupcakes right across from the health store. "Maybe we should order in," I said. "I don't think we'll make it as far as the butcher counter." We angled and banged and snaked through the crush past a fish counter the size of a small submarine and over to the refrigerator case of raw chickens, where I immediately averted my eyes. I hate raw chickens. They look so vulnerable.

"What about dessert?" Russell asked, his eyes widening and my stomach gripping as he said it. The bakery counter was on the far other end of the store and blocked by a sea of humanity.

"Screw it," I said. "We'll serve ice cream." Ice cream was doable. Only an aisle away from the chickens. By the time we got back to Russell's apartment, we were both exhausted.

I set the table. Russell tossed the salad. I washed potatoes. Russell reset the table. He didn't approve of my placemat selection. Russell's the only man I've dated who has three placemat patterns. Gifts from ex-girlfriends. He removed the orange-and-gray basket-weave pattern, replacing it with the sailboats-and-clouds pattern. I wanted to buy him new placemats, but then he'd have four girlfriend patterns. I'd have chosen plastic mats with states and capitals.

"So what do you know about this Hunkster guy?" Russell asked, meaning Kristine's new boyfriend.

"Not much. They've been dating a week."

"And we're entertaining them?"

"An intense week."

"Does anyone know his real name?" Russell was lining a broiler with aluminum foil, sprinkling garlic and salt on a chicken. I was rearranging the freezer to make room for the Rocky Road.

"She only calls him Hunkster. Maybe that is his real name. What would you name yourself if you were dating online?"

Russell paused from his chicken prepping; he seemed to be giving my question careful thought. "Sledge. I've always wanted to be named Sledge."

This was news to me and not necessarily of the positive variety. "That's a pretty scary-sounding moniker," I said, "and probably not wise in your line of business. But if you'd like, I'll call you Sledge."

Sledge went back to his chickens. Covered them in foil and deposited them in the fridge with the salad.

Angela and Kristine had never been to Russell's apartment. You can tell a lot about a person from their decor, although I think most single men's apartments look like they've come off an assembly line, Russell's being no exception. The dark wood. The big leather couch with the rolled arms. The flatscreen TV bigger than the couch. The dining table that also served as his desk was long enough for three chairs on either side—black leather, of course—but it was narrow. If you ate across from someone, the edge of your plate bumped against their plate, ruling out niceties like candlesticks, centerpieces, or serving bowls.

I'd already warned Kristine that under no circumstances was she allowed to show up and suggest rearranging Russell's furniture. Or critique his artwork. The black-and-white photo over the sofa that he had ordered from the *New York Times*. Depression-era construction workers eating lunch on a steel beam of the Empire State Building. In the kitchen, a photo of the *Hindenburg* exploding.

The buzzer rang exactly at seven. By then, the salad was tossed, the chickens were cooking. I'm always impressed with guests who arrive at the precise minute they've been invited. Do they walk around the block for half an hour assuring they can pounce on your bell not at 6:59, not at 7:01, but at the prescribed 7:00 p.m.? I have never been that type of guest but I admire the ones who are.

"Send them up," Russell said into his intercom without bothering to ask send *whom* up.

"How do you know it's not a couple of murderers?" I asked, while we both waited at the open doorway for whatever felons happened to step off the elevator. It occurred to me that Hunkster500 might be a murderer. Kristine hardly knew him; she'd met him online. I was glad the table wasn't set with any steak knives.

Hunkster and Kristine emerged from the elevator. He was tall, like her, and had excellent posture, like her. His build was somewhere between scrawny and skeletal, his Adam's apple as prominent as his nose. He was wearing jeans that looked two sizes too big, cinched in at the belt, and a short-sleeved shirt revealing knobby elbows. Hunkster was holding a bottle of wine. Kristine was holding Hunkster's knobby elbow. She looked happy. Glowing, just-got-laid-type happy.

"This is Hunkster," she said. The men shook hands.

"Is that what you'd like us to call you?" Russell asked.

"Or would you prefer Mr. 500?" I said.

"If Kristine likes Hunkster, that's fine by me," he said, his smile broad, delighted.

"Then that's fine for Sledge and me," I said.

"It's really thoughtful of you to ask us over," Hunkster said. He handed Russell the wine bottle. Russell said he loves rosé. (Russell hates rosé.) We showed the guests in and Kristine surveyed the living room. "Your apartment looks exactly how I expected it," she said to Russell, forcing a smile.

Russell said thank you.

"That sofa sure looks comfortable," Hunkster said, nudging Kristine in the ribs.

"Sure does," she said, nudging Hunkster back. "But I'd move it down half a foot."

"Wine?" I said to her.

"Cheese?" Russell said to Hunkster, holding out a plate.

The buzzer rang again. Russell picked up the intercom. "Send them up," he said again.

While we waited in the doorway for Angela and Charlie, Kristine and Hunkster made out on the sofa. The elevator doors opened and Angela and Charlie broke apart from a giggly embrace. Angela smoothed her hair, smoothed her polka-dot sundress. I felt like Russell and I were the parents of wayward teenagers.

"Nice to see you again," Charlie said to me. He was as sunburned as when I'd met him at SpeedLove, his face and scalp clean-shaven.

"Is this a one-bedroom or two-bedroom?" Angela asked as soon as she walked into the apartment. I hoped she wasn't going to ask if there was a spare bedroom.

Russell turned on a side lamp. I poured wine.

"Kristine, you look beautiful in this light," Hunkster said.

"So do you, Angela," Charlie said.

I turned to Russell, waiting for him to say how striking I looked in the glare of his three-way bulb. "Peppadew, anyone?" he asked.

At dinner I sat next to Kristine and Hunkster, and across from Russell, who sat next to Charlie and Angela. Under-neath the table Hunkster and Kristine were rubbing knees, Charlie and Angela played footsy. More hands were under the table than on the table. It's a good thing we didn't serve corn on the cob.

Where were my girlfriends? These two strangers looked like Kristine and Angela, sounded like Kristine and Angela, but these women were a couple of horny-assed sex kittens. A full-scale traffic tangle was taking place under the narrow table—Charlie massaging Angela's hand, Kristine stroking Hunkster's thigh. I was waiting for Kristine's eyeglasses to steam up. But nobody seemed to notice or care. Our dinner party had turned into a high school make-out party.

"So, dear, how was your day today?" I asked Russell.

Maybe tomorrow morning he'd surprise me with the poetry book, read a poem or two. We'd watch *Meet the Press* and eat omelets.

Russell and I cleared the plates, and passed out bowls of ice cream. Charlie spoon-fed Angela. Hunkster licked a drop from Kristine's mouth. I lost my appetite.

"Gee, nine fifteen already!" Angela said. The guests weren't eager to stick around.

"Crosstown traffic's a nightmare on a Saturday night," Charlie said.

"We have to get up early tomorrow," Kristine said, looking at her watch.

"For church?" I said.

"Well, don't let us keep you," Russell said.

After they'd finally left, Angela whispering, "I knew

you'd connect," and Kristine whispering, "I knew you'd like him," I closed the front door and apologized to Russell. "I had no idea my friends were so immature," I said. "Here I expected an intellectual evening, exchanging views and opinions and getting to know one another better, and what do we get? The back of a bar-mitzvah bus."

I headed into the kitchen to scour the broiler. Russell cleared the ice cream bowls off the dining table and joined me. "We're lucky we have an adult relationship," I said, pounding at the bottom of an Ajax can, drowning the broiler in enough powder to scrub an army barrack. I gave that broiler the cleaning of its life. "All that mindless infatuation. Crazy lust. We should open the windows to clear out the endorphins. It's ridiculous."

But as I said the words, I didn't believe them. And Russell said nothing at all.

15

I stayed over at Russell's Sunday night. Monday morning he did his forty-five push-ups, gargled his salt water, and fed his turtles. Then I fed Russell. I made him toast with jelly. He left for his office and I walked over to Cafe Lalo on Eighty-Third.

If I owned a café, I'd ban all writers. They set up their laptops, shell out two bucks for a small coffee, and hog all the tables while pretending they're Ernest Hemingway at the Café de Flore. I am one of these writers, so I know how annoying we can be. But Lalo's lovely. Italian lights strung through the trees; ivy-filled flower boxes beneath French windows. Inside, the decor is Cheerful Parisian with waitresses as beautiful as the pastries. That must be a requirement for working there: *gorgeous*. Remembering to offer a menu or bring the check? Not necessarily.

Lalo's not only lovely but it's also semi-famous, at least lo-cally, because the scene in *You've Got Mail* where Meg Ryan's waiting to meet her pen pal was filmed there. Every time I see that scene I want to shout, *Meg! What the hell's wrong with you? Don't you realize Tom is NY152 and the guy you're supposed to love!* But that's half the fun, waiting for Meg to figure it out, while she's sitting in Cafe Lalo.

I set up my laptop and ordered a small coffee. I'd only gotten as far as the title for my new assignment, "Or-ganic Restaurants Are Spreading Like Pesticides." Already bored, I clicked on the file for one of my essays. Then my luck, I dropped an index card on the floor and, as I was picking it up, I spotted Cameron Duncan sitting back-to-back to me, wearing his Cincinnati Reds cap. I sat up fast and hunched over my computer, hoping he didn't notice me. Why wasn't he drinking coffee in his own neighbor-hood where he belonged? Even though our chairs weren't touching, once I knew he was behind me, I could *feel* him, like a dog sensing a storm. I wanted him to finish his cof-fee and leave. How was I supposed to concentrate?

About when I was thinking maybe I should say good morning, acknowledge him, get it over with, comment on what a coincidence it was that we were both having coffee in the same place, and then get back to my work, I heard him say, "Good morning!" He turned his chair sideways, leaning around toward me. "What a coincidence that we're both hav-ing coffee in the same place."

"How 'bout that," I said. "This isn't your neighborhood."

"This isn't your neighborhood. We're both crashing."

He moved over to sit at the empty chair across from mine, carrying a coffee cup in one hand and a plate of eggs in the other.

"I'm here to work." I emphasized the word *work* in a way that any normal, sensitive person would take as a hint. "Why are you here?"

"I have a ten o'clock meeting. But I love this place, so I came uptown early." He didn't say what kind of meeting and it seemed rude to ask. What if it was for a prostate exam? Or with his parole officer? "The eggs are great. Want a taste?" he asked. "Maybe you can put down that computer cover of yours. It blocks your lovely smile."

"I'm not smiling. And no eggs, thanks."

"Really? They're excellent." With one finger he pushed my computer lid down, then held out a forkful of eggs toward my lips.

I took a bite, thinking maybe then he'd go away. They were actually really good eggs. "Happy now?" I said. "I tasted your breakfast. Maybe now I can do my work." I raised the computer lid. He closed it again.

"You know you like me, Molly Hallberg."

"Says who? You aren't as charming as you think."

"You're more charming than you think."

"Really?" I must have looked pleased. Too pleased.

He smiled. "See how charming I am?"

"I'm working."

"Would you like to have lunch?"

183

I looked around. "Here? Like get a lunch menu? Or go somewhere else like we're going to lunch? It's nine o'clock."

"Your call."

"I have a boyfriend."

"He's not your type."

"What do you know about my type?"

Cameron patted his chest. "I know it well."

"Do you lie awake at night making up these lines?"

"I mean every word I say, Molly Hallberg."

"Thanks, but I have a lunch meeting with my editor."

"Dear Deirdre."

"Ah, yes. You must be acquainted. From when you took over my article. Did you know your romance piece was originally my assignment?"

For a moment he looked genuinely contrite; he sounded apologetic. "I knew it was *somebody's* assignment."

"I especially liked the paragraph about feeling mesmerized by the journey. Very insightful."

"I didn't know whose assignment," he said.

"Why'd you even want to write the piece? You're a big-time author; we're an online magazine."

"*EyeSpy's* fun. Good-size audience. I used to write for magazines."

"Before you became a big to-do?"

"I liked the topic. Who isn't interested in romance?"

I stared at him. He stared at me.

"More eggs?" he asked.

I shook my head no. He took a bite, wiped his mouth

with a napkin, and sipped his coffee while I watched. I found it extremely disconcerting, the sexy way his lips curled in constant amusement even when eating scrambled eggs, generally not an attractive food for anyone to be seen eating. He looked good in a baseball cap. Better even; it hid his high hairline. And I let myself think, *What if he really is sincere?*

He sat back in his chair; he seemed to be appraising me. "You're like a fizzy beverage, Molly."

I asked, "Is that a good thing or a bad thing?"

He called out to an imaginary waitress, "I'd like to order a Sprite, please!"

The real waitress ignored him, too.

He was acting like a man who liked me, and I didn't want him to like me. No good could come of that scenario. But another part of me *wanted* to believe him. I liked how he saw me. That's what it's really about, right? Liking the you that someone else sees in you.

"I have plenty of flaws," I told him. He didn't respond; he sat there waiting, I supposed, for me to regale him with my many flaws, so I started counting off on my fingers. "I steal Post-its from the office supply cabinet. I pay for one movie ticket, then sneak into a second movie to save money. I argue politics without knowing what the hell I'm talking about. I re-gift. I don't wash the blueberries first. And I didn't fly to West Palm for my cousin Frieda's funeral. I lied and said I had the flu, but I didn't. Don't tell anyone."

"Our secret," he said, easing forward again. "See, already we're sharing secrets. That's a positive sign."

"You tell me a secret."

"I'm afraid of heights."

"That's not a secret. Tell me your flaws."

"I'm attracted to unavailable women."

"Married?"

"I don't know. I'll ask. Are you married to your boy-friend?"

That's how it went. Scrambled eggs and verbal fencing. Lunge. Feint. Advance. Retreat.

Cameron picked up my unused paper napkin, unfolded it, and started fiddling, rolling the edge and twisting it. Half-way down he fashioned a small rhombus shape. "What's your goal in life?" he asked while focusing on his project. "What do you have your heart set on?"

You'd think a question like that would be easy. And you'd hope your answer would be more profound than mine, but I told him about my column. How I wanted it. That it would mean I wasn't a faceless writer. That I'd be Molly with a face.

"You consider a column your big goal?" he said.

"I'm not qualified to balance the national budget." But then I told him about my essays, too. That's the thing about writers; we're often people other people find it easy to talk to. I count on that. But we're the last people anyone should go divulging stuff to. I confessed to Cameron that I'd been working on a *Wuthering Heights* essay on how nobody brushed their teeth in those old romances and that's the real reason Heathcliff and Catherine don't have any sex scenes.

Cameron played with the inner folds of the napkin. "Can

I read some of these literary critiques of yours?" he asked. I said no. He said please. I protested. He insisted. With a final flourish he handed me a paper rose. I pretended to sniff it. How many napkins had given their lives on behalf of Cameron Duncan's roses? He spun my laptop around. Typed something and swiveled it back with the screen facing me. "That's an e-mail addressed to yours truly. Attach five essays. Or else."

"Or else what?" No one had ever asked to read my essays. Not my parents. Not Russell.

"Or else something really bad. I'll let you know as soon as I think of it."

"I'm shaking in my boots." I attached the ones on *Washington Square, Gone with the Wind, Pride and Prejudice.* Seven of them. Then stopped as I was about to hit the send key. What if he hated them? What if he loved them and stole them? What if he never said anything? He pulled his chair around closer and pressed his finger over mine, the two of us clicking the send button.

I know people are always saying things like my heart raced or my pulse sped up or there was this current of electricity, all of which I usually think is bullshit or bad writing, but that's how I felt. The physical sensation of his finger on my finger pressing a simple computer key startled me. I had no idea I'd ever feel that way about e-mailing my essays.

"The media portrays you as a player," I said.

"Good," he said. "My publicist says the real me's too boring."

"Why haven't you ever married?"

He moved his egg plate from my table and placed it back on his table, turned back toward me. Now he was counting on his fingers. "High expectations. I'm an idealist. I didn't want to marry until I was thirty, and since then, a couple of women I might have married didn't want to marry me. My writing. Book deadlines get in the way of dating. And, oh!" He leaned closer. "I have a shameful flaw. One most women don't tolerate." He sat back, grinned with the confidence of a man who knows he's got a killer grin. "I don't wash the blueberries first."

I closed down my computer, tucked my paper rose in my purse. "I can't be late for my lunch meeting."

"That's in three hours."

I said, "I have a boyfriend."

16

Emily was out on vacation, which felt like my idea of a vacation. By the end of July the entire office slows down and remains that way through August. Readership dips, ad revenues shrink. Beach-bound employees disappear in droves. The ones who are still around leave early on Friday and return late Monday. Basically, we're down to a three-day workweek.

I'd requested the meeting with Deirdre. I wanted to plead my case with as few distractions around as possible, sit down mano a mano, womano a womano, and finally convince her why giving me a column was for her own good and the good of *EyeSpy,* a way to increase loyalty, build a daily following, add brand value and create a unique property that only *EyeSpy* could offer.

Those last two points were courtesy of my sister Jocelyn and her four years at Wharton.

Gavin the assistant was also on vacation, so at 12:30 I stood in Deirdre's doorway and tapped lightly, asked if I was interrupting, which clearly I was. Her desk was covered with wrapping paper and tissue and bows, and she was scolding her scissors. It wasn't clear what the scissors had done wrong, but Deirdre was in a tizzy. She's one of the bosses who need an assistant. I don't know why she doesn't get a substitute assistant when her regular assistant is out. She must figure training one's more trouble than living without one. Or it may be her way of saying, *See! I can live without you!*—so that way the assistants never ask for raises. Which is pointless. Her assistants never last long enough to ask for raises.

"Do you need help?" I asked.

She looked up at me and frowned. "We have a meeting, right?"

"Right." I stepped into her office, but only two steps, in case Deirdre was in half a mind to throw that naughty scissors at my head.

"I don't know what's wrong with these Hallmark people," she said, "but this paper's impossible to cut, and it's totally the wrong gift. Why am I even bothering to wrap this awful gift?" The gift was misbehaving, too. She held up a small box that had been hiding in her wrapping supplies, explained it was a gold money clip she'd gotten talked into by some evil salesman at Bergdorf's. "Stephen won't use a money clip! What was that salesman thinking?" She told me that Stephen and she, Stephen meaning Mr. Dolson, whose photograph graced the frame on Deirdre's desk, were celebrating their twentieth anniversary that night and she'd be screwed if she didn't have a decent gift for him. "So what is it you want to talk about?" she snapped.

That was not a good opening for making my request, so I said, "Why don't we chat on our way to, say, Tiffany's?" Hopefully, no security guards would remember escorting me out. "A nice twentieth-anniversary watch or a jeweled tie clip? A leather desk set?"

"They sell leather desk sets at Tiffany's?" she said.

"I don't know."

"Who uses desk sets? Nobody uses desk sets."

"Desk set. Bad idea."

She grabbed her handbag. "We'll buy a watch."

In the taxi, Deirdre called her publicist. A taxi, I must note, is an exceptionally small environment to share with a woman who wears heavy perfume. I envied our driver on his side of the divider. While I cracked a window, Deirdre asked the publicist if her anniversary was good for any PR angles. I found that touching. After she hung up, I asked why she didn't make the Bergdorf's salesman wrap her gift. She was back to normal Deirdre again; she laughed a throaty, low-decibel laugh. "I wasn't putting money in that money clip."

I did not care to know what kind of IOUs for sexual favors or vouchers for carnal services Deirdre was wrapping for her husband. But they sure sounded more exciting than a watch. "Tiffany's will do everything," I told her. "Who doesn't love that blue box?" Our cab stalled in a mess of traffic, a truck on one side, a bus on the other, two more cabs and a red light ahead of us. Deirdre banged on the divider for the driver to keep moving. She must have confused him with one of her assistants. "Twenty years," I said. "That's an impressive long time for a marriage. What's your secret?" I was trying to engage Deirdre in conversation, keep her in a good mood before I went in for the kill. A more patient, rational person might have told herself, *Gee, Molly, maybe you should table this discussion, come back another day, a more propitious, less-likely-to-get-your-ass-kicked day.* But patience and I, we're not such a good team.

"Our secret?" Deirdre said. "Patience. One of the reasons I was *hoping* you could pull off Nora Ephron's style on the romance piece was those couples in *When Harry Met Sally*. Not Harry or Sally or Carrie Fisher, but the other couples, the old ones. The movie came out the year I met Stephen. And when I saw it, I wanted to be one of those couples, build a life together and still find joy in each other years later." This was a new side to Deirdre, a sentimental side. "One of the women said she and her husband met when they were counselors at camp; she said she knew right away, the way you know a good melon." Deirdre sounded wistful, caught up in her memory. I had never heard her speak with such affection in her voice. Of course, I'd only heard her speaking to employees. She smiled. A tender-for-her smile. She said, "Stephen's my melon."

I tried to dovetail the photograph on Deirdre's desk with a rounder, more melonlike face. "That's a lovely story," I said. "A watch will be timeless."

Deirdre checked her own watch, slid open the little parti-
tion window, and barked at the driver. "Can't you find a better
goddamn street!" He shut the window and ignored her. Traffic
began moving again. "Stephen's a good egg," she said, "a real
peach; he's my sugar." Deirdre had just given me a recipe for
cobbler. "I'd been dating someone else, but when I met Stephen, I could imagine myself as one of those couples."

In the men's-watch section on the third floor of Tiffany's, Deirdre reverted to executive decision-making Deirdre,
scrolling across the glass display case, pointing and commenting, "Not the chronograph, nothing stainless steel, the gold
one with the Roman numerals. . . . No, not that one. The one
next to it. . . . Yes, that one!" She didn't ask my opinions.
I waited and observed, pretending I was Audrey Hepburn
having lunch at Tiffany's. The salesman in his well-cut suit
with his well-cut manner presented Deirdre's selection on a
velvet tray. She picked it up, held the watch against her own
wrist, handed the salesman an American Express card. The
same woman who put a halt to lining the office garbage cans
with plastic bags in the interest of saving money, who, when
you asked her for a salary increase, responded as if the entire
journalism industry would fold if the coffers were depleted of
that extra $2,000 a year you sincerely felt you deserved, and
who cut out free coffee in the office kitchen after the price of
sugar packets went up, *that* woman was dropping $8,000 on
a watch in under ten minutes. In my next life, I wanted stock
options and a Christmas bonus.

We were waiting for the salesman to return with a receipt and the blue box. Deirdre was busy straightening her wallet, arranging twenties with twenties, tens with tens. There no longer seemed to be an opportune time or clever segue to bring up my column. I'd blown my chance. Should have gone for it in the taxi when she was a captive audience. "Didn't you want to see me about something?" she asked, zipping her wallet shut. So there I was at Tiffany's talking about brand values and unique properties, tossing out whatever buzz words my sister had prepared me with, doing my best to convince Deirdre that a column called MyEye was an edgy, yes, daring concept, an advertisable proposition unlike anything *Gawker* offered; maybe I could even start it with my Thursday assignment; what a perfect example that would be! Of course, I'd need a headshot taken because columnists need headshots, but that could be arranged.

"I know it's a great idea," I said. "I know it like a good melon."

Thursday I jumped out of an airplane. It was an assignment, of course. I'm not someone who does that sort of thing casually. *Gee, there aren't any good movies this weekend; I think I'll leap from a large airborne vehicle.* But what better way to demonstrate my column-worthy daringness; and if things didn't go well, I could always write an obituary column.

The previous week Deirdre had left a note on my desk: *This has potential!*

For whom? I wondered. *A funeral director?*

Along with her note was a Groupon and an article torn from the *Post* about the booming interest in skydiving—3 million US jumps a year. No mention of how many US fatalities. A photograph showed two people wearing helmets and goggles and the kind of jumpsuits you usually see on gas-station attendants and prisoners. The people were strapped to one another with a harness that looked no sturdier than the straps on a backpack, their arms stretched out, their legs stretched out, like they were in the midst of doing jumping jacks when they happened to fall out of a plane one on top of the other, pancake-style. The image of a pancake is the main reason it had never occurred to me to go skydiving, the image of *me* as a pancake.

The Groupon was for a company called Manhattan Skydive, so already I knew I couldn't trust these clowns. If there's one place in this world you won't find a soft landing, it's New York City, unless the sunbathers in Central Park don't mind your landing on their towels. I checked out Manhattan Skydive's website. I read about jumping from ten thousand feet and free-falling for four thousand feet. I read about not being allowed to wear sandals or high heels; they recommended running shoes. Made sense. Good for running away at the last minute. Drinking alcohol beforehand was also not advised. For me, it was going to be mandatory. When I made my reservation over the phone, I asked just how a company seventy miles outside Manhattan got off naming themselves Manhattan anything. The chirpy young woman—who was more interested in recording my charge-card number than answering questions—informed me that Manhattan Skydive did not refer to the location, but was meant to evoke the thrill and excitement of Manhattan. "Then maybe I should just stay in Manhattan," I said.

I rented a Zipcar for my seventy-mile drive. While driving through small towns and villages, past farmlands and cows, I imagined my funeral and my unusually flat, custom-made coffin with the one-of-a-kind lining supplied by Hallberg upholstery. My sister Lisa would fly in from Atlanta with the twins, making excuses for her husband, who had an emergency pool-equipment meeting in Asia. Jocelyn would keep checking her watch, complaining that the service was running long. My grandmother Shirley would carp about the folding chairs hurting her ass. Pammie would be busy rearranging her Memorial Day guest list, wondering who should get the Daisy Room next year.

Maybe Russell would deliver a woe-filled eulogy on how he tried to put my bones back together but they were in too much disarray. As an apology, he'd hand out business cards offering one free neck crack per mourner. Deirdre, dressed in black with inappropriate cleavage, would be unable to speak through her tears of regret, having come up with the assignment in the first place. "I was about to offer her a column!" she'd blubber through her sobs.

The entire *EyeSpy* staff would attend—publication suspended in my memory—the employees all thrilled to have a free day off; Emily Lawler in the front row snickering, and Kristine and Angela in the back row making out with their boyfriends. And afterward my father would grill burgers for all the guests, and my mother would distribute memorial plaques with my decoupaged face. The thing is, throughout my entire imaginary circus, I could picture Cameron Duncan standing off in a corner, sad, alone, making a rose out of a paper napkin and crying genuine tears.

When I arrived at what looked like the middle of a mowed-down cornfield, I walked into the aluminum-sided Manhattan Skydive office that looked a whole lot bigger in the website photo than in real life. Damn fish-eye lenses. The first thing I did was fill out paperwork, most of which boiled down to "I won't sue you, I won't sue you, I won't sue you." On the last page was the line *Skydiving can kill you. But on the bright side, that's rare.*

Way to go, optimists!

My class was small, only six of us, so already I was nervous. Why weren't there more people here? Where did the smart skydivers go? We sat on a bench in the back of a hangar, one plane in the hangar, two others parked out on the runway. We watched a video for all first-time jumpers. It was like a Disney cartoon, except instead of singing chipmunks and birds we got happy people flying through the air. Our instructor, an upbeat young man named Haywood with reassuring broad shoulders and a jutting jaw, informed us that he'd personally logged over four thousand jumps. He asked us to go around and introduce ourselves, say what brought us to Manhattan Skydive. The woman next to me was celebrating her thirty-fifth birthday along with her fidgety friend, who was celebrating her thirty-eighth birthday. Dickie and Patty were celebrating their engagement, and a gung ho sort who introduced himself as Denby was celebrating his divorce. I felt bad not having anything to celebrate, so I said I was celebrating my rich aunt's dying and leaving me money in her will with the one condition that I try her lifelong passion, skydiving.

Haywood ran us through twenty minutes of ground training before suiting us up and assigning us to our planes and our jump buddies. Denby's jump buddy was a statuesque young woman with a sexy mole above the corner of her top lip. He was pleased, but not as thrilled as I was to be paired with Haywood and his four thousand jumps. The birthday girls were assigned to the first plane on the runway, the engaged couple to the second plane on the runway. I was happy. It could take hours to pull my plane out of the hangar. Then Haywood and I were assigned to a new contender, a plane that appeared out of nowhere—well, out of the sky—and swept in on the short runway, landing amid a flurry of noise. I worried it was low on gas.

I boarded last, stepping up onto the strut and ducking into the low doorway. "What? No stewardess?" I said. The pilot directed me to strap in. He wasn't wearing a parachute, a good sign. He turned a key to start the plane. *A key?* Even the engine sounded picayune. I gripped the sides of my seat until we were airborne. By then I had to holler to be heard over the noise. "Has anyone ever chickened out!" The plane was so cramped my knees were bumping against all the other knees, Denby's knees and mine shaking in unison. Haywood shouted for us to remember to hold the straps, bend our feet back, keep our eyes open, and look at the canopy.

All I cared about was remembering to pull the rip cord. Haywood and I were jumping first. He opened the door to a blast of thundering noise and cold air in my face, checked my harness, and hooked his front to my back. Having to choose between the fear of jumping and the indignity of riding back down in that tiny plane, stepping off onto the runway with my parachute and Haywood still attached to me, was reason enough to plummet forward.

I jumped. We plunged. I don't remember much between that point and the ground. I was floating in a wind tunnel, almost unaware that Haywood was lashed behind me. It was beautiful. Then scary. I pulled the cord. Felt the lurch and jolt of the chute's opening and tugging us upward, until we glided earthbound and free. I loved it. I fell in love with it. If only falling in real life love were this easy. Take a big breath and open your eyes.

17

Russell showed up after a day of Saturday appointments, sniffling and blowing his nose, unable to get through half a sentence without a *ker-chew!* "Why's the TV so loud?" he asked.

"Kevin and Lacey." I pointed to the wall. I listened. "I think they're done." I turned off the television.

Russell sneezed. "Damn ragweed," he said.

"Ragweed season's not until August."

"That's in two days." He sat on the sofa, loosened his tie, and complained about his watery nose, his scratchy eyes, and his enlarged tonsils.

"You still have tonsils?" I sat next to him, held his hand, then remembered he'd sneezed into it. "What did your patients say while you were sneezing all over them?"

"They have allergies, too."

"All of them?"

"One out of five Americans do."

"And four out of five of us don't. Did you take an antihistamine?"

He nodded yes. "You know, mosquitoes breed dengue fever."

"And you should worry about that why?" My solid, dependable, more-or-less-member-of-the-medical-community boyfriend was not demonstrating impressive behavior. Evan was the same way. Toss him into court with a jury for an audience, a demanding client, and a hanging judge to boot, and he'd manage to rip the opposition's net worth and self-worth to shreds. But at the first hint of a head cold, the man crumbled. I suppose I should muster up more sympathy for the ailing man-babies in my life, at least offer to fulfill a sexy nurse fantasy or two, but my mother never fussed when any of her daughters claimed poor health. She'd hold palm to forehead and say, "Yep, a little warm. Now throw some clothes on and don't be late for school." She seemed to honestly believe that looking illness straight in the red, itchy eye built character. Even if you did stay home, there was no upside. We'd have to help vacuum and dust, iron our sheets. My sisters and I developed strong immune systems early in life. There was no point not to.

Russell sneezed.

I handed him a fresh Kleenex. "We better not go to the movies," I said.

"But I want to see *Cowboys and Aliens*."

"How do you think the other patrons will feel after they've

forked over thirteen bucks for a ticket and you're sitting next to them spewing mold spores?" I maintained that common courtesy required sneezing people to sacrifice their own pleasure for the good of the majority. Russell pointed out the extenuating circumstances; it was opening weekend.

"What if you take a nap, a short one?" I said. "Not one of those naps where you wake up two days later and say, 'I can't believe I slept so long,' but just long enough to make sure you feel okay and then we'll go. The nine o'clock show instead of the seven? You can wait that long, can't you? While you rest, I'll go online and order tickets in advance." That was a lie. It galls me to pay an extra $1.75 handling fee on ticket prices that are already offensive. We'd buy them at the theater at the regular offensive price, instead of the really offensive price. "A power nap," I said. "You'll take a power nap."

Russell agreed to my plan as soon as I said the word *power*. I followed him into my bedroom. He removed his loafers, lining them neatly at the foot of my bed, unbuttoned his shirt, and draped it on the back of the upholstered chair. He took off his watch and set it on the nightstand next to the clock radio, a copy of *The House of Mirth,* and the paper-napkin rose that Cameron had made. "Are you sure we don't have to set the alarm?" Russell asked.

"I'm your human alarm. Do you need your sleep mask?"

"Not for a power nap," he said.

I pulled back the covers and he climbed in, sneezing twice before drifting off. I curled up on my chair and watched him sleep. Some men look sweet and innocent when they rest; sleeping brings out a tender boyishness in them. I once dated a man for months longer than I should have because I confused his sleep face with his awake personality. But Russell's jaw hangs loose, his face goes slack, and his tongue hangs out; it's not what you'd call his most attractive time of day. He wheezed, grunted, and rolled over. *You have many fine qualities, Dr. Russell Edley,* I thought. *You really do. And you deserve to be loved for them, not just appreciated; adored, not just accepted.* In the back of my closet a pair of brown leather boots had been taking up residence for years. They were never quite right. Not from day one. While shopping, I tried them half a size larger, half a size smaller; something about the cut was off. But they're lovely to look at with many attributes—water-resistant, midheel, rubber-soled bottoms—so I ignored the way they pinched and bought them anyway, hoping that one day I'd slip them on and discover they magically fit.

I woke Russell at 8:15, asked if he felt well enough for the movie. He insisted he was fine. He coughed. Then sneezed. He picked up the paper flower on my nightstand and used it to blow his nose.

The movie theater was at Eighty-Sixth and Third, an easy walk if you don't count the time navigating sidewalk vendors, garbage cans, bus-stop lines, newsstands, baby strollers, dogs, chaos, tree guards, and pedestrians. Russell was upset with me because I forgot to buy the tickets. "I'm sure it won't be a problem," I said. "The reviews were terrible. There'll be plenty of seats."

As we came around the corner, we could see a line formed outside the theater.

Russell walked up to a woman wearing one of those wide headbands like Hillary Clinton wore in the nineties. "Is this the line for buying tickets or the line for people who already have tickets?" he asked.

"The buying line," the woman said.

We took our places at the end of the line. It was still light out. A man was selling sunhats and sunglasses on a table a few feet away. Ahead of us, two people up, another woman was shouting into her cell phone, "You're never on time! You're late on purpose so I get stuck buying the tickets!" The decibel level of her voice was an assault on the city's usual noise assault. I couldn't imagine being so angry that I'd scream in public. I'd be too embarrassed to scream in public.

Russell seemed to relax a bit when other people lined up behind us and we were no longer *last,* but he kept leaving to peek inside at the movie-times board. He was waiting for the words *sold out* to appear so he could march back to me and say I told you so.

"Still good," he said after returning from his second reconnaissance.

"Good," I said. "But what's your alternate choice?"

"There's nothing else I want to see."

He was silent.

I was silent.

He sneezed.

I said gesundheit and went back to being silent.

A guy behind us was saying, "I hear that alien/cowboy movie really sucks."

We inched forward through the theater doors. Inside, in line, Russell kept his eyes peeled to the digital board above the cashiers. "There's an eleven-thirty show. We can go to that if the nine's sold-out, but it'll be your fault we have to wait."

It seemed like a good time to talk about something else, *anything* else. I asked, "Russell, what did you do with that poetry book you bought?"

He raised his brow the way baffled English detectives do on PBS. "How do you know I bought a poetry book?"

"Is it for me?"

"You?"

"Yes, me."

"No, it's for me."

"*You?*" I must have sounded incredulous. I could see I'd hurt his feelings. The line moved forward.

"You really don't know me, do you?" he said, keeping his voice low as if he didn't want anyone to know him. "I like poetry. Walt Whitman. Billy Collins. Robert Frost."

"You read Robert Frost? Why would you not mention that to me? Where along the lines of communication when you were telling me you hate Cobb salads and you were two badges short of Eagle Scout, and you once almost choked to death on a fish bone at your grandmother's seventy-fifth birthday, did you fail to bring up poetry?"

"I thought you'd laugh at me," he said.

The woman up ahead barked into her phone, "Asshole!" and stomped out of line.

"Why would you think I'd laugh at you?"

"C'mon, Molly, you're not what I'd call a poetry kind of woman." I had no idea what a poetry kind of woman was like, but I was pretty certain she was someone Russell saw as softer, more sensitive, more Elizabeth Barrett Browning, than me. He said, "You read literature to make fun of it."

"You watch the same crappy DVDs over and over again."

"So?"

"So nothing."

Russell sneezed. He searched in his pockets. I searched in my handbag and handed him a tissue.

When Evan and I uncoupled, it was a dramatic, name-calling, accusation-hurling parting of ways. For Russell and me it was a fizzle, a lazy animal that stopped plodding down the road and died. I prefer nasty split-ups. They're more clear-cut; you aren't left with any internal wavering.

"The simplest normal conversations with you turn into verbal banter," Russell said.

"Is that bad?"

He exhaled a long, rueful sigh. "I feel like a trained bear running to keep up. *Can you top this?* Snappy dialogue's for characters in movies. You want someone who doesn't exist." It was our turn at the ticket counter. "Maybe some people enjoy sparring," he said to me. "I don't." He asked the cashier for two tickets for *Cowboys & Aliens.*

"Only one," I said. Then I bought a ticket for *Crazy, Stupid, Love.*

It was a mature breakup. We agreed I'd keep the coffee-bean grinder he gave me for Valentine's Day; he'd keep the Waterpik I gave him for his birthday. In the popcorn line, Russell asked if he should stop over after his movie to pick up his belongings—his movie would run longer than mine. I had his shaving cream, sleep mask, some boxer briefs, socks, a razor, a shirt, and his Morton salt. No, I said, because we both knew we'd end up sleeping together, and farewell sex muddies the waters. He sneezed, I said God bless you; he said good luck with my writing; we'd drop off personal belongings with each other's doormen. After our purchases at the snack counter, I asked him to say good-bye to Joyce and Irwin; we wished each other a happy life. Popcorn in hand, he headed off to his movie, followed by two women.

I woke up the next morning thinking, *What if I've made a huge mistake? What if Russell is the best I can do? Isn't somebody better than nobody?* What if no matter how hard I tried, how many times I pulled a Sisyphus and pushed the boulder back up the mountain, I'd never get it right—this romance thing, this choosing-the-right-mate thing, this thing where you're supposed to connect on a soul level, an emotional level, instead of what I'd been doing, connecting on a levelheaded, this-ain't-bad level. I pictured myself living alone with a houseful of cats. Then told myself to buck up. I could probably have a short-term affair with Cameron Duncan. That might be good for a night or two. Before he moved on. I could sign up for Match.com and fill my evenings with go-nowhere coffee dates. I might not end up with a boyfriend, but I could always end up with a caffeine addiction. Or I could stop trying altogether. I could just lean over and pull out my Rabbit.

"You decided you weren't compatible over a cowboy/space-monster movie?" Angela said. Angela and Kristine and I were getting pedicures at Sheila's Nails on Lexington. I'm no expert on other cities, but New York's a town where you can get your toes done on a Sunday afternoon. I was in the middle chair soaking my feet, while on my right Kristine was getting her calluses buffed, and on my left Angela's toenails were being subjected to an emery board. Our pedicurists, three pint-size, diligent women in pink smocks, were chatting in Korean while we pedicurees discussed my less-than-twenty-four-hours breakup. You know your girlfriends really love you when they're willing to crawl out of their own boyfriends' beds to offer moral support for your now no-boyfriend bed.

"We sort of split up at the cashier's window, but officially broke up while waiting in line for popcorn," I said.

"Who paid for the popcorn?" Angela asked.

I was turning my head like I was watching a tennis match. "He did. But I got Jujubes."

"Nobody eats Jujubes," Kristine said.

"Who paid for the Jujubes?" Angela asked.

"He did."

"Classy," she said.

"I really decided to break up before we got to the theater, while we were still at home and I was watching him nap."

"He naps?" Kristine said.

"Not classy," Angela said. "Good thing you dumped him. My policy is, if there's no buzz with a man, tell him to buzz off."

"I never realized you had an official policy," I said.

"I made it up just now."

"It takes courage to end a long relationship," Kristine said. "It's like the MTA. You wait for the bus and you wait for the bus and you can't give up on waiting for the bus, by hailing a taxi or something, because by then, you've already invested so much time waiting for the bus."

"Clip short or long?" my lady asked in her musical voice, the pitch rising and falling.

"Short," I said. She focused on clipping while I continued my story. "These two women were standing behind us, and as soon as Russell and I agreed it was over, one of them hit on him. She went all sexy-voiced on him and asked what movie *he* was seeing."

"It's so easy for men," Kristine said, switching feet.

"Way too easy," Angela said. "Did that woman make you want him back?"

"He hadn't gone anywhere yet."

"Dumping a guy's like putting an item back on the sale table at Saks," Angela said. "As soon as somebody else picks it up, you want it." Angela's pedicure lady said something to my pedicure lady and the three women laughed. "You should find some guy and have wild sex tonight."

"Who? Her?" Kristine said.

"Who? Me?" I said.

"You need a new affair to forget your old affair," Angela said.

"Russell wasn't an affair. He was Russell."

"When's the last time you hooked up just for fun?" Kristine asked.

I reflected, then said, "I once had this crazy thing with a customer I met while working at Hertz. He'd leave dirty messages on my voice mail."

"What kind of car did he rent?" Angela asked.

"A convertible. His messages said things like 'I want you top down' and 'turbocharge my pop-off valve.'"

"And that turned you *on?*" Kristine said.

"No. But the convertible did. I was young and he was Hertz Gold."

This led to Angela's and Kristine's offering up examples of their own wild affairs. To inspire me.

"A docent at the Guggenheim," Kristine said.

"A divinity student!" Angela said.

"The floor manager in glassware and fine china."

"This supercute meteorologist from Terre Haute. We met at a convention." Angela's cheeks pinked.

"Married?" I said.

She shrugged. "Oh, well."

"Uncle Freddy." Kristine smiled. "Only he wasn't really my uncle."

I didn't want wild affairs. I didn't want tawdry affairs. I didn't want slapdash, superficial, rash, foolish, any affairs. I wanted to feel cherished. I wanted to feel adored. I wanted someone to look at me as if the sun and moon set on me or rose on me or whatever it is you want planets to do when someone thanks their lucky stars for you. I wanted someone to *get* me and then love what he got. Most of all, I wanted to believe, re-believe, that was possible.

"You'll meet someone," Angela said. "Love is in the air."

"And ragweed," I said. "Spores. Pollen. There's all sorts of grief out there."

18

Emily Lawler was standing in my cubicle. She was tanned, and dressed in a flouncy, lavender skirt with a lavender floral top. "Want to see my vacation photos?" she asked.

Emily was not a flouncy, lavender kind of girl. I was immediately suspicious. Of what, I didn't know, but something was strange. "I'm holding out for the slide show," I said.

"A lot happened."

"A lot happened here. Nobody disturbed me."

"You'd miss me, you know, if I weren't here." She sat down in my *guest* chair.

"I've already tested that theory. I survived."

"I did a fabulous interview for my column last night." If it's possible to convey smugness in the pronunciation of one word, that's what Emily did when she said *column*. "Emily Literati," she added, in case I didn't know just which column she meant. She stretched out her legs, crossed her ankles, and sat back with her head resting in her hands, elbows up.

"Anyone ever tell you that it's rude to drop by uninvited?"

"One of my best columns ever," she said.

"Thanks for sharing. And thanks for bragging."

"Cameron Duncan? I believe you were once on a panel together." She sat up straight, folded her arms across her chest. "Of course, you weren't *supposed* to be on a panel together. He was pretty amused when I told him what happened. Y'know, that thing about you stealing my appearance."

"Cameron's easily amused."

"His new book sounds amazing. Mike Bing's girlfriend won't be killed off. Mike's ready for commitment. Like in Spenser novels, Spenser's psychiatrist girlfriend."

"So now Cameron's copying Robert Parker?"

"It's an homage."

"And Cameron's cool with you telling the ending of his book, that the girlfriend lives; it's okay if you blab that news?"

"Oh, no. That's completely confidential. I'm not revealing a thing."

"You're off to a good start."

"We shared many secrets."

"You and Cameron? Secrets?"

Emily smiled, looking heavenward like that was where she hid her secrets. Miss Innocent, Miss Smug. "He's not conventionally handsome, but I think he's really handsome, don't you? And what self-effacing charm." I'd never noticed him being self-effacing. I thought of him as cocky and presumptuous. "We talked for what seemed like hours," Emily said. "About his growing up in the Midwest, how it affected his values; what it's like for a guy to have all those sisters; my column and how much he liked writing his column when he wrote for *Ellery Queen*. We share a bond you couldn't understand."

"A columnists' bond?"

"He's so sensitive. You should have heard him—not that you would have been there—he was talking about love and romance, and old expectations that get in the way of love. How many men think about these things? He said cynicism's self-protection, a defense mechanism used by cowards who give up on love because they're afraid love's given up on them. Mike Bing's new girlfriend will fall so in love with him that she'll stop being a cynic."

"And because of that, she deserves to live?"

"Because of that she gets to be an ongoing character."

"Well, thanks for the update." I looked at my watch. "Gee! Check out the time! And I have so much to do! I wish we could gab longer about your great night last night, but I'm swamped."

"Have it your way," flouncy, lavender Emily said, standing up. "Cameron is so sweet. He made me an origami flower out of a napkin. Do you want to see it?"

I said, "Let me just imagine it."

A week later, Deidre had me enlisting to be a Rockette. Her ideas were becoming diabolical. I couldn't wait for her to assign "I Was a Crack Addict" or "I Was Buried Alive." This latest one involved something called the Rockettes Experience—two hours of my learning to high-kick in a chorus line. It's how the Rockettes keep themselves employed until Christmas.

Dancing is not my sport. Some people are naturals. My sister Lisa, for instance. Any type of music you pop on a stereo and her body can't help but react; she starts tapping her toes, swinging her hips, snapping her fingers. Within minutes, she knows all the steps to a rumba, the latest moves for hip-hop. If we were passing a fire station with a radio playing some frolicky music, I'm sure she'd do a pole dance. Whatever family DNA existed in the dance-talent gene pool, Lisa snatched up all the goodies. Jocelyn and I, we're sideliners.

In seventh-grade dance class, boys wanted to dance with me because I'd developed early and ballroom dancing was a good excuse for a twelve-year-old boy to accidently smash against the budding breasts of a twelve-year-old girl; perhaps the first and only time I was truly popular. But after I trampled Artie Brodsky's feet box-stepping and severely damaged Allan Greagsbey's instep during a jitterbug (don't ask me why they were still teaching the jitterbug in 1984; George Orwell couldn't predict the Roslyn public school system would still be teaching the jitterbug in 1984), having established myself as a bona fide klutz, even the prepubescent boys decided my boobs weren't worth it. My relationship with dancing became one of avoidance. School party? That was me in the parking lot, making out with my date to avoid dancing with my date. Live-band bar mitzvah? Meet me at the sweets table; I'll be hanging out there.

I even tried ducking out of my own wedding dance. But as luck would have it, Evan considered himself a regular Arthur Murray. If Evan had married Lisa, the two of them could have spawned a superstrain of miniature Michael Jacksons and Twyla Tharps. I should have tossed my wedding veil over my sister's face and made her go onto that dance floor, because no way was Evan going to miss his shot at showing off his footwork to all his litigator buddies. Unfortunately he was dragging along a white-laced lummox. Talk about getting off on the wrong foot! Some days I think the marriage headed downhill right after the band started "Wind Beneath My Wings." I made the mistake of telling Deirdre that story one day, how my own flesh and blood booed me off the dance floor, tossing cocktail shrimp and lamb chops at me until I got out of Evan's way and let him finish with his big one-knee slide into the cello player. Maybe I'm not remembering the details exactly right, but Deirdre thought there might be some humor opportunities in my learning to be a Rockette, and now I was sitting in my cubicle trying to register online.

Turns out Rockette experiences were in big demand, sold-out a month in advance with only one date still available, probably because it was a totally undesirable date, the Saturday of Labor Day weekend. I'd be dancing with out-of-towners. And hopefully the website didn't really mean that part about the class's only being offered to *advanced* dancers trained in tap, jazz, and ballet. I signed up anyway. By the time I got there, they'd already have my money; it would be too late to send me to the principal's office or wherever Rockette students are sent when caught lying.

About then's when I stopped and felt a wave of Russell Withdrawal. If I threw out my back or kicked myself in the face, I couldn't call Russell. *Hi! Remember me! We used to date up until two weeks ago when I decided I could do better than you, which I probably can't, but I was wondering if you'd unfurl my spine?* I was more likely to die of humiliation than *die* die in a dance class, but I missed the comfort of having my own personal medical-type person at my disposal.

I also missed walls. Emily's head appeared. "Everyone loves my Cameron Duncan interview," she said. "Have you read it?" She was wearing snowman earrings.

"Who's everyone?"

"Just everyone."

"What's with the Frosty the Snowman baubles?"

"A gift from Rory."

"Summer sale?"

I asked if she'd read my skydiving piece.

"I'd love to, but I'm so busy with everyone calling to compliment my piece." On cue, I heard her office phone ring. She must have been dialing herself on her cell phone. "See what I mean!" She slipped out of view.

I hadn't spoken to Cameron since he showed up behind my back at Café Lalo. If you've ever given yourself a secret writing project, essays you haven't shown to any other human on earth, the writing you consider your *real* writing, reflective of the *real* you, and then you finally, in a moment of insane weakness, let a smooth-talking author talk you into sending those essays to his personal e-mail and you don't hear anything back, you're going to be pissed. At him for starters. But even more at yourself.

I pulled up Emily's interview on my computer and read the opening sentence: *Last week I hung out with my friend author Cameron Duncan.* Already I wanted to barf. I heard Emily squealing, "Really? You love it!" I skimmed through the interview. I wanted to finish reading it before she finished her phone call so she wouldn't catch me reading it. Emily was laughing. "Honest? The best interview ever!" Unless her caller had some serious hearing problems, she was raising her voice for my benefit.

The interview had nothing to do with Cameron the writer. Emily's questions focused on sensitive, understanding Cameron, beloved by women readers who wanted to mother him or ravage him. Lay it on thick, why don't you, Emily.

Men with limited experience with women—perhaps they married their high school sweetheart or originally studied for the priesthood—they are the men who later have affairs; they feel like they've never lived. But if you've been privileged to know many women, you'll gain self-knowledge about what you want and who that special someone needs to be. After that, recognition comes swiftly. Almost instantaneously. There's only one thing left to do.

I asked him, "What's that, Cameron?"

He said, "You need to kiss her."

"Oh my God, I could kiss you!" I heard Emily saying. "Thank you, Cameron! You've changed my life!"

I clicked off the article. Interesting, maybe. Life changing? I think not, Emily Lawler.

My phone rang. *Outside call,* the ID window said, about as useless a piece of information as you can get. *Inside call* in our office means someone standing up and calling across the cubicles. I picked up the receiver, said hello. My first few months at *EyeSpy* I'd answer the phone with *Molly Hallberg! Reporter!* or, when I was in the mood and had extra time, *Molly Hallberg! Entertainment reporter for online newsmagazine EyeSpy!* But after my mother complained and Kristine guffawed a few times, I just went with *Hello, Molly Hallberg.*

"Hello, Molly Hallberg," the caller said. "Exemplary skydiving piece. Made me want to walk up to a third floor."

What was this guy doing? Working his way through our cubicle jungle? Wait until he found out a guy named Keith came next. "Hello, Cameron," I said. "Thank you for reading my article." I wished I felt as cool and professional as I tried to sound. I wanted to ask him about my essays while at the same time I wanted to tell him he was a jerk.

"I was thinking about our coffee date," he said.

"Coffee *date*? That wasn't a coffee date, that was a coffee run-in."

"What time can you run into me again? You owe me a lunch."

"I don't remember it quite that way. Aren't you too busy getting interviewed?"

"Oh, did you read Emily's piece?"

"Is there a pop quiz?"

"Let's get back to us."

"Us?"

"Your essays."

"Oh. My essays."

If anyone ever tells you they want feedback on their writing, substitute the word *feedback* with *praise*. No writer wants feedback. Asking for feedback is an invitation for constructive criticism or, worse, plain old criticism. My essays were still in my computer; they couldn't seem to get any further than that, but I had nightmares of the *New York Times* reviewing my book, nightmares that usually ended with my flying to Brazil for plastic surgery to change my identity.

Mind-boggling mindlessness!

Insomniacs rejoice!

Trees died to print this shit?

Not meant for human consumption.

If Mr. Simon and Mr. Schuster were alive today—they'd wish they were dead.

The Rockettes were high-kicking on my computer screen. What did they care? Their reviews were always great.

"Can't we talk now?" I said. "What's wrong with over the phone?"

"Lunch is better."

"Okay. A business lunch," I said. "Just for feedback." I meant praise.

"Our place?"

"We have a place?"

"Cafe Lalo."

"That's not our place and I'm no longer hanging out in that neighborhood."

"Boyfriend trouble?"

"A short business lunch. That's it."

"I promised to stop in the Barnes and Noble on Eighty-Second Street Saturday afternoon," he said. "To sign books."

"Your books? Or just anyone's?"

"Meet me there at noon?"

I agreed. In a loud voice. Loud enough to be heard over the wall. "Yes! Looking forward to seeing you, Cameron!"

19

Saturday, Angela was sitting on my bedroom chair, tweeting for her grocery-store client and eating a Twinkie for breakfast. She was wearing pajama bottoms and a tank top, her hair uncombed. Charlie hadn't slept over the night before or she'd be in lingerie. "How's this sound?" she asked, reading off her telephone screen. "'Flo sez slice onions under cold water to avoid tears. Vidalias now 2.29 per lb.'"

"Compelling." I was debating between flats or sandals for my lunch with Cameron. Flats said *business*. Sandals said *I don't want you thinking I thought about this too much.*

Angela began tapping again. "Flo's also got a good one for burgers, how you shouldn't put the grilled ones on the same plate you use for the raw meat, but I haven't cut that one down to one hundred and forty characters yet."

"I have faith in you. Does this work?" I held up a straw handbag. "Or this one?" Held up a canvas handbag.

"You're thinking about this too much," Angela said. She pointed to the canvas one. "Looks more bookstore-ish."

"Fine. With the flats."

"Why'd you never show me your essays?" she asked.

"You'd tweet them."

"Not unless they're short."

I sat down on the bed. "He made me show them to him."

"You like this man." Angela sounded both accusatory and pleased.

"He's trouble," I said.

"Perfect! Sleep with him."

"Sex doesn't help me get over a man. Sex makes me think I love men I don't. He's a congenital dater."

"Mike Bing's not."

"Angela, Mike Bing is not real."

"Let's see what he's up to," she said, tapping. "Ten thousand followers are standing by." She made a face. "Oh."

"Oh?" I hated her *oh*-face.

His tweet said, *Off to lunchtime obligation. Hoping somebody's ego can handle it. Mike Bing says brace yourself. Could be uncomfortable.*

He was late. Not technically late, but I arrived early. I waited for him at the crime table, reading the cover copy on Sarah Greer's book. When he came hurrying up to me, he apologized, explained he'd stopped in to say hello to the manager. "She's a friend," he said.

"I'm sure she is."

"She's young. Enthused. Very supportive."

My idea of a bookstore manager is someone who walks around in a three-piece suit with a boutonniere, lovingly straightening books and making recommendations to little old ladies. "Did you ask your supportive, young friend why your books aren't on the crime table?"

"They're upstairs on their own table."

"You have your own table? How about a sofa and chairs?"

"Follow me," he said.

He was wearing his baseball cap and sunglasses. I didn't ask, *What's with the indoor shades, buddy?* Maybe he was afraid somebody would recognize him. What better place than a bookstore? Then again, maybe he was worried nobody would recognize him, and this way he could blame his sunglasses. *Can somebody's ego handle it?*

"Do escalators make you nervous?" I asked, half over my shoulder, as we rode to the second floor. I was two steps ahead of him.

"I look straight forward," he said. That meant he was looking at my butt.

Cameron did have his own table, a big display of his three bestsellers stacked up, fanned out and faced forward on metal stands. "This will just take a moment," he said.

I didn't tell him I had never read his books. I'd decided to put off reading the one I'd bought until after he commented on my essays. That way, if I didn't like his feedback, I could read his book and decide he was a terrible writer, so what difference did his opinion matter anyway?

He checked his jeans pockets and asked to borrow a pen. I dug one out of my handbag and watched while he scribbled his name on the title pages of *Larceny among Lovers*. I kept waiting for a salesperson to come running over to scold the ball-capped man in sunglasses bent over a table defacing Barnes & Noble property, but nobody seemed to care; I wondered if I could go around signing a few books. *All my best, Willa Cather. Best wishes, Charlotte Brontë.*

"Aren't your other two books going to be jealous if you don't sign them, too?" I asked, picking up a copy of *Felonies among Friends* and pointing to the pile of *Murder among Mistresses*.

"Shh," Cameron said, midsignature, smiling. "Didn't your mother teach you to keep your voice down in a bookstore?"

"What's your next book going to be called? *Arson among Acquaintances*?"

"It's about online dating. Not fires."

While he signed, I suggested titles. *"Jury Tampering among JDaters? Misdemeanors among Match.comers?"*

He removed his sunglasses, looked up at me, and shook his head. "Would you like to wait for me in the children's section?" He smiled that goofy, appealing smile of his that I refused to find appealing.

"Why'd we meet here anyway?" Was I supposed to stand there admiring him signing his three bestsellers before he trashed my essays and ego? "Are you trying to impress me?"

"Yes," he said. "Is it working?" Then, more softly, whether for me or out of respect for those customers whose mothers did teach them not to disturb the other patrons in a bookstore: "Your being here makes me feel less self-conscious. I consider this an obligation, but it makes me uncomfortable."

My brain detweeted. "An uncomfortable obligation?"

"Yes."

"Oh. I hate those, too." He hadn't meant me; he'd meant *him.* Only later would I think, *Jesus, Cameron, then why didn't you sign the books in your friend the manager's office?*

Cameron finished his obligation and suggested we go for a walk. "Unless you're hungry?" he said.

"I'm good." My stomach wasn't looking forward to hearing feedback.

So we walked. If we were in a movie, we'd have been in the middle of the montage, those quick scenes directors use to let you know a couple's hitting it off, without dragging out the movie an extra twenty minutes. There's rarely any drama in the scenes, no big mystery over whether the happy couple will giggle when they splash each other in the swimming pool; will they collapse into laughter when they pretend-wrestle on the picnic blanket? I suppose somebody could drown in a swimming pool; that would be dramatic, but I've never seen it happen. Not even in foreign films.

Cameron and I wandered past the Starbucks on Eighty-First, down Broadway and through a farmers' market. Picture corn, tomatoes, zucchini, homemade breads, and goat's-milk soaps. We strolled over to Riverside Park along the Hudson River. Envision dogs, grass, water, boats, and dog shit. We looped our way up to the flower gardens at Ninety-First. Sometimes a montage has conversation snippets, hints of how the relationship is developing.

In front of Starbucks:

CAMERON: Why do I threaten you?

ME: Don't flatter yourself.

CAMERON: What if you believed I'm sincere?

ME: I pride myself on not believing you. Or any lothario.

CAMERON: Nobody's been a lothario since the eighteenth century.

ME: You look good for your age.

On Broadway at Seventy-Sixth:

CAMERON: You're a romantic, Molly. You just won't admit it.

ME: Me?

CAMERON: Anyone who reads Thomas Hardy for fun is a romantic.

ME: Is it time to discuss my essays? I'm afraid to ask.

CAMERON: Were you scared to jump out of a plane?

ME: No. I just closed my eyes and jumped.

CAMERON: You should try that more often.

Farmer's Market:

ME: Tell me about a woman who broke your heart.

CAMERON: Easy. Amanda Carson.

ME: Easy Amanda Carson?

CAMERON: We were sitting at an outdoor café. She sees a guy at another table, by himself, with a fuzzy little dog.

ME: Doesn't sound like a guy kind of dog.

CAMERON: She goes over to pet the dog, starts talking with the guy. I'm still at our table. I see them laughing; the guy hands her a business card. She later married him.

ME: Too many dogs in this town. How long had Amanda and you gone out?

CAMERON: Only once.

ME: Heartbreaking.

Along the Hudson:

CAMERON: You're the Nora to my Nick.

ME: Nora Ephron?

CAMERON: Nick and Nora. *The Thin Man?* You and me, Molly. I'm using Nick and Nora's banter as a prototype for Mike Bing and his new girlfriend.

ME: You're stealing it?

CAMERON: An homage.

Riverside Park flower gardens:

ME: Do Emily Lawler and you really have secrets?

CAMERON: That's a secret.

*　　*　　*

He pointed at one of the overhead banners hanging on the lampposts. The banners promote park events: free kayaking; yoga classes; free movies shown on the Seventieth Street pier. "Spontaneous movie date?" he asked.

I looked up and read that night's selection: *Bad Lieutenant: Port of Call—New Orleans.*

"Nicolas Cage," he said.

"I've got plans," I said.

We walked up and out of the park without speaking. We didn't even exchange snippets. At West End Avenue, I waved for a taxi. I needed to leave. I wasn't sure why; I just knew I needed to.

"Next time?" he said.

"Are you sure we'll have a next time?"

He pulled off his baseball cap and with two hands gently placed it on my head, giving the brim an extra little tug. "Absolutely," he said. "You have to return my hat."

He never mentioned my essays. Few montages include essays.

20

I wasn't lying when I said I had plans that night. I could have broken the plans. My mother would have been thrilled if I'd broken the plans. It depressed her when her thirty-nine-year-old daughter asked to come home for a Saturday-night sleepover. But I'd ruled out staying home with my television cranked up to drown out Kevin and Lacey's sex moans. I'd ruled out the Hamptons and the thought of Pammie's introducing me to her other guests as "This is Molly. She's between boyfriends. *Again.*" And I'd ruled out an evening with Cameron Duncan when my insides began to panic. I was clicking with a man I knew for a fact was on automatic click-pilot with every woman he met. As soon as my taxi drove off, he probably whipped out his cell phone and called the next number in his date-o-dex. Maybe even *Emily.* They might be sharing popcorn and secrets right now. But why didn't he already have a Saturday-night date? Why was he even in town for the weekend? And why was I sitting on the LIRR heading to Roslyn wearing his baseball cap? How many other women were riding around town in his baseball caps?

I wanted him to be sincere yet I didn't believe he was sincere yet I wanted him to be sincere. Why couldn't I trust a man who'd never married, ran around with a hundred different girlfriends, and had perfected the art of always saying exactly the right thing in exactly the right way, making even the most levelheaded, intelligent women require smelling salts? Gee, you'd think I'd be fine with that.

I changed trains at Jamaica, sat across from a woman sucking on one of those fake, I'm-trying-to-quit cigarettes. She tapped her foot, drummed her fingers on the armrest, chewed on her plastic cigarette, and chewed on her lip. She was skittish the entire ride. By the time we got to my station, she had me biting my nails and craving a cigarette.

My father grilled corn and salmon for dinner. My mother made a salad out of something called Grand Parisian Mix from Costco, although nothing about it seemed particularly French. Or grand. I set out three plates, three glasses filled with ice, the silverware, a bottle of Pepsi and a bottle of Coke. My mother insists Coke tastes too syrupy, and my father insists Pepsi tastes too bubbly, and everyone else in the family insists you can't tell any damn difference, but to end the debate and keep peace in the household, my mother's been buying both brands for years. I was drinking vodka. I sat in my Molly seat. Even though my sisters and I were grown and out of the house for years, when we returned home, we still sat in our assigned seats. Mine was across from my mother and next to Lisa's empty chair. My mom sat next to my dad, who sat next to Jocelyn's empty chair.

"So, seeing anyone new?" my mother asked when we were settled in our places.

"If she was, would she be here?" my father said, peppering his fish. The salmon was blackened. It wasn't supposed to be blackened, but that's what we called my father's overcooked salmon.

My mother had conflicted emotions about my liking Russell, and now she had conflicted emotions about my breaking up with Russell. On the other hand, she'd found him dull. On the other, at least I had a boyfriend. "I might know someone for you," she said.

"Really? Who?"

"I don't know. But I might."

One time only in my life, my mother had procured a potential boyfriend for me. Elliot somebody or other. I was home on Easter break my sophomore year at SUNY Albany. Elliot was home on Easter break from his junior year at Cornell. In the hierarchy of schooldom, for people who keep track of that sort of thing, Cornell ranks about ten trillion universities higher than SUNY Albany; so for me, dating a Cornell student would be considered an upgrade. Two months earlier my mother had met Elliot's mother, Frances, in a steps aerobics class, the one step class my mother ever attended before deciding it was all a bunch of crap; but she was there long enough to buddy up with Frances, become girlfriends, and have the two of them decide they'd be excellent mother-in-laws together. (They no longer speak. Something to do with a dispute in 1998 involving matinee tickets for *Ragtime*.) Over break, my mother invited me to lunch with her new friend—tossed out a carrot by saying we'd go to Trattoria Diane, with their to-die-for arancini rice balls. Diane's is also famous for its Sunday prix fixe, not that that matters if you're there on a Tuesday. My mother didn't mention her friend was bringing a son, and I'm sure Frances sprung me on an unsuspecting Elliot. My mother had never set eyes on this young man other than a wallet photo Frances showed her in the locker room. I should also point out that my mother hasn't replaced her wallet photos since I was in fifth grade, so I don't know what Frances was agreeing to unless she was impressed with my Girl Scout uniform. But the two plotting mothers, the Ivy League son, and state-university Molly met for lunch.

I'm pretty certain I was the only one at that lunch who knew Elliot was stoned out of his mind. Even Elliot was too stoned to know he was stoned out of his mind. "How do you like Cornell?" I asked. That was the extent of our conversation. He sat there staring at the saltshaker and finishing his ravioli, knocking off the remainder of his mother's linguine and whatever was left in the bread basket. At the end of the meal the mothers suggested, "You two kids should get together again!" I later suggested to my mother that she resign from the matchmaking business, that I'd manage on my own, thank you very much. Ever since my divorce I've lived in fear that she'd try again; that she'd bring home nephews of women she met in grocery stores.

Sitting at my parents' kitchen table, I decided it would be far better for my mother to think I was involved than for her to get involved. I told her that, yes, I was drawn to a particular man.

"Drawn to?" she said.

I picked at my salmon. "I can't tell if he likes me, or if he hates when a woman doesn't like him, making me some sort of challenge. He's what your generation would call a ladies' man."

"What would your generation call him?" my father asked.

"A man-whore."

"Do you like him?" my mother asked, spearing her Parisian Mix.

"I don't want to like him."

"Do you like him?" my father asked.

"I suppose."

"If you already like him, then you're no longer a challenge," he said. "He'd have moved on. Your man-whore's sincere." My father the problem-solver.

I said, "He's forty-two years old and never married."

"Good," my mother said. "The last thing you need is a married man."

"I believe we can all agree on that, but I'd feel better if he were divorced."

"Why? What's the difference between someone who's never married and someone who married someone they shouldn't have married?"

"One of us is capable of commitment."

"Yes," my mother said. "And one of you is capable of bad judgment."

She was defending Cameron without even knowing it. That's the kind of power he had on women.

"I was quite a ladies' man myself," my father said.

"Oh, Dad, you were twenty-two years old when you met mom. How much of a ladies' man could you be?"

"I had quite a lot of girlfriends in college."

"And I had a lot of boyfriends!" my mother said.

"So how'd you two players know you were ready to commit?"

"Look at your mother!" my father said, waving at her with an ear of corn. "She's a beauty!"

My mother giggled. "It's impossible to resist a man who always says the right thing."

Sunday afternoon my sister Jocelyn showed up with her new boyfriend. Sunday afternoon my grandmother showed up with her new boyfriend.

"Dave Rooney, Molly Hallberg," my sister said, making her introductions. "Molly, Dave Rooney." She seemed to be confusing a business meeting with a family brunch.

"Arnold," my grandmother announced, indicating her gentleman friend with her thumb, hitchhiker-style. "Introduce yourself, Molly."

Everyone else had already met. Long Island bonding and all that.

While I was busy reassessing my relationship with Russell, my sister had gone out and found herself a fella. And more shocking, so had my grandmother.

Jocelyn was scoring higher on the shock-o-meter. She was wearing capris, a lacy pullover, and flip-flops; her toes were polished a frosty peach. Somewhere from the soul of a Wharton grad, a new sister had emerged. I was happy for her. Dave Rooney was clean-cut and ruddy cheeked with short-cropped hair that gave him the look of a handsome choir leader. Dave's family was also in the upholstery business, except Dave was only second generation, not fourth like Jocelyn, and Dave's family sold supplies. Twines, foam, muslin, Dacron wraps. I knew all this from my mother, who'd been reporting on what was now called Jocelyn's Romance with Dave the Supply Guy.

Happy couples create romantic narratives; they tell meet-cute stories worthy of a romantic comedy. Dave and Jocelyn's was *Isn't it amazing? We were negotiating over shirring tape and fell in love!* I imagined their conversations in bed: "Darling, the earth moved." "I noticed that, too, sweetheart. Do you think this is memory foam or down feathers?"

My grandmother met Arnold while waiting for a free blood-pressure reading at her independent-living residence. He tried to cut in line and she gave him hell. One thing led to another, and now they were inseparable. Arnold spoke in idioms. "Shirley and I are two peas in a pod!" "Since meeting Shirley, life is just a bowl of cherries!" "She's a horse of a different color." According to my mother's reports from her girl-to-girl conversations with my grandmother, Arnold was a hot commodity at the residence, other women making goddamn fools over themselves trying to snag him. He was two years older than my grandmother. Slim. Courtly. With a vein protruding in his forehead that looked ready to pop any second. I just hoped he wasn't here today and gone tomorrow.

We were sitting outside on the patio, our chairs arranged in a circle, drinking Bloody Marys my mother had made from a mix. Jocelyn's chair was pushed against Dave's, and the two of them were holding hands. My mother's chair was next to my father's, and every now and then he'd squeeze her knee. My grandmother and Arnold were also within squeezing distance of one another. I was the heigh-ho-the-derry-o cheese who sat alone. The outdoor table was set for brunch, but so far, nobody seemed all that interested in corn flakes.

"More Bloody Mary?" my mother asked Arnold.

"I'll drink to that!" he said, chuckling, holding out his empty glass.

"Me, too," Jocelyn said. My sister seemed relaxed with her Dave. She didn't slip into her habit of checking her watch every five minutes; she was content right where she was. I'd felt comfortable with Russell. But never content.

Arnold saluted my grandmother with his cocktail. "I knew what I wanted since I first started dating at age fifteen," he said, "and when the girl of your dreams finally shows up, you strike while the iron's hot."

"Were you widowed, Arnold?" my mother asked.

"No."

"Divorced?"

"No, single!" Arnold said the word *single* with utter glee.

"You've been dating for over seventy years?" I said.

"Didn't want to settle," he said.

"That's admirable," Jocelyn said.

"That's romantic," my mother said.

"That's insane," my father said.

"*We're* happy," my grandmother said, frowning at her son-in-law.

"These are our what-the-fuck years!" Arnold said, tossing out a more colorful idiom. My grandmother laughed her ass off while the rest of us looked uncomfortable.

"Jocelyn tells me you do pranks for an online newspaper," Dave said to me.

I shot my sister a look. Told her boyfriend, "That's not quite how I'd characterize it."

"What kind of pranks?" he asked. He was stroking Jocelyn's arm with one hand while swirling his drink in the other. Multidexterous Dave.

"I sneak vibrators through security stations. Walk around in kinky underpants."

"What do you really do?" Dave asked.

"Dave has a finance degree from Duke," Jocelyn said.

"So your Wharton degree talks to his Duke degree?" I said. Dave grinned.

"You speak the same language," Arnold said.

"That's important," Jocelyn said. Not that anyone was arguing. "People have conversational patterns. Dave and I, our patterns are in sync."

"Two peas in a pod!" Arnold declared.

My grandmother elbowed Arnold.

I was surrounded by pea pods. My girlfriends. My family. Soul mates were falling out of trees.

"We should discuss doing more business together," my father said to Dave.

My grandmother cut him off. My father's talking business pisses her off. "They played *Vertigo* for movie night last night," she said. "Jimmy Stewart?"

"Alfred Hitchcock?" Arnold said.

"Heard of it," we all said.

"Best scene is Jimmy Stewart's dream with the swirling hallucinations," Arnold said.

"Half the residents got sick to their stomachs," my grandmother said. Arnold and my grandmother shared a big laugh over that one. Jocelyn and Dave rubbed their calves together while looking around in opposite directions pretending we weren't noticing.

"Jimmy Stewart overcoming his fears, climbing that tower for the woman he loves," Arnold said. "Now that's romantic."

"Romantic?" my father said. "He killed Kim Novak!"

My grandmother shook her head and hooted. "She fell off that bell tower like a limp dick!"

"Top off your drink?" my mother said to nobody in particular.

"Tonight's *The Thin Man,*" Arnold said. Every night's movie night in independent living. "Nick and Nora?"

"Heard of it," we all said.

"Even with the Hays Code, you could tell from their snappy dialogue, they were screwing all the time," my grandmother said.

My mother topped off her own drink, polishing off the pitcher. "All gone! We'll need more."

"I'll go!" Jocelyn said, grabbing the empty pitcher.

"I'll help!" Dave said. The two of them dashed off into the house.

"We won't be seeing them for a few hours," my grandmother said.

"Play some Ping-Pong later?" my father said to me.

"Can you wait until I fold the laundry?" my mother asked.

"Jesus, Bitsy, I'll be in my casket before that happens."

"Gotta see a man about a dog," Arnold said, standing up, excusing himself and heading into the house. He kissed my grandmother on the cheek before he left.

"He's got prostate issues," she announced as soon as the screen door slammed behind him. "Pees incessantly."

"I'm glad you're happy, Grandma," I said.

"He's a good man. He doesn't want to change me."

"He's a little late for that," my father said.

"I had plenty of time to change you, Sidney, and I didn't," my mother said. "I love you as is."

My grandmother and I watched my parents kiss. We kept watching until it got embarrassing. "I'm glad you dumped the quack," she said to me.

"Grandma, chiropractors are respected medical—oh, never mind."

"I wasn't looking for Arnold, but I had the good sense to open my eyes when he showed up. It doesn't take a rocket scientist to know your quack of a boyfriend was a reaction to your pig of a husband. Get that Evan out of your head. Send him packing already! He's clouding your judgment and turning you into a coward."

"Me? A coward?" My grandmother had just insulted me in the guise of giving advice.

"Are you telling me that in a town of eight million people there isn't one man who gives you heart palpitations? And I don't mean the kind that require digitalis."

"Grandma, I'm bad at love."

"Baloney. Maybe you're just bad at spotting it."

"What I miss?" Arnold asked, returning from his mission.

"Brunch!" my mother said, pulling away from my father and standing up. "Sidney will make omelets."

"Swell," my grandmother said. "How do you like your eggs burnt?"

21

Monday morning Emily gave notice. Keith Kretchmer told me first, when he leaned into my cubicle and said, "Did you hear?"

There's only one appropriate response to that. "Hear what?" I said.

"Your buddy." Keith indicated Emily's office with a nod of his head. "She's moving to Idaho." I about flew out of my chair; looked over into Emily's cube. She wasn't there. "She's going to live with some guy out there," Keith said.

"Rory the ski instructor?"

"Yeah. A ski guy in Idaho." Keith wandered off. I'd have been less surprised if he'd said she was moving there to be a potato farmer.

I rarely visited Emily's office; I avoided stepping foot in it. Even if I'd wanted to, it was impossible to find a place to put your feet; the floor was covered with books from publicists and books from publishers and bound manuscripts from self-published writers angling for a review by the ever-literati Emily. Her office was a zoo. She never cleaned it. Half the books were probably already out of print. But I couldn't help myself. I marched around from my office to hers, removed two stacks from her guest chair, piled them on top of another tottering stack on the floor, and sat down. New photos of Rory and Emily were tacked to her wall: Rory and Emily at the Central Park Boathouse; Rory and Emily against a backdrop of the Queensboro Bridge; Rory and Emily in Little Italy. A framed photo next to her computer of Rory and Emily with fireworks exploding overhead. And next to that, a Cameron Duncan rose.

A minute later a smiling Emily appeared, stopped, looked at me. "A visit from Molly Hallberg!" She sat down in her chair.

"What gives?" I said.

"You heard my good news?" she said.

"Keith, the town crier, told me. You and Rory? This guy's for real?" Emily smiled. I'd like to say that for once it was a sweet smile. But it was a smug smile. "You're giving up your job—your *column*—for a guy?"

"He said he'd move mountains for me."

"So you're moving to mountains for him?"

"Molly, it's what people in love, do." Her smile changed. It amped up from happy into radiant. Emily in love. Rory the ski instructor in love with *her.* I wrangled with the concept.

"Congratulations!" Brady the cloud administer said, poking his head in the doorway and running off.

"When did you decide this?" I asked Emily. "What did Deirdre say?"

"She's devastated, of course. I wanted to tell her in person before she left for vacation. In two weeks I'm blowing this pop stand. Deirdre's in her office shooting herself right now." Emily smiled her Emily smile. "She said I can write my column from Idaho."

"She agreed to that?"

"I told her *Gawker* has writers in Idaho." Emily stood, picked up her paper rose, and held it aloft like the Statue of Liberty. "Yes, I can have it all!"

"You can have it all in Idaho. Do you really see yourself living there?"

"Now I can." Emily sat down. "Cameron Duncan's the one who convinced me to take the risk. About Rory. And me." Emily held her rose in her lap with both hands like an earnest debutante. "He said the two driving forces in the world are love and fear. My rose is supposed to be like Dumbo's feather. He made it to give me the courage to fly." She spoke with fervor. "He said, when you realize you love somebody, you want the rest of your life with that somebody to start right away."

"Cameron didn't say that. Billy Crystal says that in *When Harry Met Sally.*"

Emily frowned at me. "Well, they're both right!" she said.

Tuesday afternoon, Cameron called me at work. *Outside call.* "You owe me a movie," he said. "And a hat."

"I've incorporated your Reds cap into my wardrobe," I said. "I can no longer part with it."

"Then Mike Bing will have to hunt you down and steal it back."

"Forget it. He kills off any woman he comes near."

Cameron sounded like Cameron again. A serious Cameron. "I'm trying to change that," he said. "Movie on the pier Friday night? Seventieth Street in Riverside Park?"

"The office is going out for good-bye drinks for Wyatt."

"Wyatt who?"

"Our summer intern. He's going back to college."

"The movie's not until eight thirty. You can do both."

"And just where would I meet you for this movie on the pier?"

"Front row," he said. "I only sit in the front. I like to feel like I'm right inside the movie."

"And how do you suggest I get a few hundred people to let me cut through to that front row?"

"Jump out of a plane?"

"I can do that."

"I know," he said. "You inspire me."

"Bullshit."

It was a moment or two before I heard him say, "Molly, when are you going to stop needing so much convincing?" I didn't respond. "First one there, save two seats," he said, before hanging up.

*　　*　　*

It's a good thing I forgot to ask what movie we'd be seeing; I might have said no. Romantic movies on a first date make me nervous. I end up feeling all pressured and awkward about unspoken expectations. It's like being seated at the singles table at a wedding.

Friday morning I dressed for Friday night instead of for Friday at work: cotton, cropped pants and a gauzy top, platform sandals more stylish than comfortable. I skipped Wyatt the intern's farewell party and took the subway uptown, wearing Cameron's Reds cap, and carrying the beach towel Angela insisted I take. She didn't want me getting dirt on my butt. *Not sexy,* she said.

When I got to the pier, it was still early; the movie didn't start until dark. I love the Seventieth Street pier. It's one of the few quiet spots in the city, a long deck flowing out into the sparkling Hudson. Only a scatter of people were milling about, except down by the far end, where a large screen was set up and a small group of moviegoers had already congregated. I sped up as I walked in their direction, my competitive side urging me forward to grab two places. It sure beat waiting till later and crawling through a mosh pit of New Yorkers. I saw one woman positioning a low stadium chair; two guys were sitting cross-legged and playing cards. There was no sight of Cameron. I was hoping he'd arrive first to hold our spots. I hate saving seats; it's like asking for a fight.

I sat as close to the screen as I could without landing in the opening credits. A woman wearing a denim jumper and sensible shoes sat down and busied herself spreading out sandwich bags and soda cans, a jacket and a backpack. She reminded me of a land surveyor staking out a property. "Do you *mind?*" she said when a molecule of my towel brushed against a molecule of her blanket. "Do *you* mind?" I said. We dagger-eyed each other. I pulled Cameron's cap lower on my forehead, stretched out my arms, and protected my turf.

The pier began filling up quickly and soon looked like a giant happy picnic ground with people weaving their way around blankets and coolers, calling out to each other, settling in to watch the sunset over the Hudson and wait for the movie. More women than men. Lilith Fair at the movies.

By the time Cameron showed up, I had defended his spot half a dozen times. He looked appealing in loose-fitting jeans and a button-down shirt. He was holding a brown paper bag in the crook of his arm. "You're here," he said. He sounded delighted. I felt like a woman who might delight a man.

"Oh, my God!" my pal the space hog said to him. "I saw you at the Ninety-Second Street Y!"

You saw me, too, I wanted to say.

Cameron and the woman chatted. She loved his books. She adored him. She was more than happy to make room for him. She'd have shoved me off the pier if necessary. She scooted over. Cameron sat down and turned to me, shrugged like *What can I say?*

"Thanks for the sunset," I said to him. "Nice touch."

He asked if I'd seen *Sleepless in Seattle.*

I asked, "Is that a trick question?"

He unpacked the paper bag, unveiling two plastic cups, a bottle of white wine, a popcorn bag and a box of Jujubes.

"You eat Jujubes?" I said.

"They're my favorite food group," he said.

During the movie we drank chardonnay. We passed Jujubes back and forth. I chided myself for not bringing floss. We watched Tom and Meg playing Sam and Annie. I could have recited half the lines. Sam on the telephone telling the radio psychologist about the first time he touched his wife's hand and how he *knew*. Like magic. Annie sitting in her car on Christmas Eve listening to the radio and crying. Writing a letter but afraid to send it; Rosie O'Donnell mailed the letter. For the slightest moment, as I reached into the popcorn, still focused on Annie, my fingers grazed Cameron's. A soft, scratchy warmth. Was I dreaming it? Did I imagine it? *Magic.* We looked at each other and smiled. The unspoken message: *This is nice.* Sam's son, Jonah, picked Annie's letter out of hundreds, choosing her as his future mother because she liked Brooks Robinson. I cringed when Sam dated the woman with the hyena laugh. Bill Pullman did remind me of Russell. I held Cameron's baseball cap against my heart when Annie flew to Seattle and Sam sees her at the airport. She sees Sam across a street but gets scared and returns to New York and her Russell. But it's Valentine's Day and the world's conspiring for her to fall in love. She says farewell to Bill Pullman and hurries to the Empire State Building and her destiny. She takes the risk. In the reflected light I could see Cameron's profile as he concentrated on the screen, captivated and transfixed, watching Sam finally meet Annie.

Okay. I cried. I always cry. I know what's going to happen, but every time I cry. Jimmy Durante sings "Make Someone Happy." The Empire State Building windows light up with a big red heart. Fireworks explode over an outline of the city. As the screen went dark, the audience applauded. It's that kind of movie, the kind that makes you want to applaud. Couples hugged. Girlfriends exchanged wistful looks. The crowd behind us began to disperse, gathering their empty soda cans and popcorn bags, folding up blankets. The air felt fresher, clearer, and romantic.

Cameron handed me a napkin. Not a rose one. A regular one. I dabbed my eyes. Put his Reds cap on my head.

He stuffed our wrappers and cups into the brown bag. "Walk out to the railing?" he said.

"You can do that? Mike Bing won't panic?"

"It's dark. I can manage." He smiled. "I need the practice. Before this summer's up I will overcome my fear of heights."

"Aren't you cutting it a little close on the end-of-summer timeline?"

"I keep visualizing myself on the city's tallest building."

"That'd mean the Empire State Building. Sounds a bit ambitious."

"Well, that's what I imagine." Cameron deposited the bag into a trash container; we walked to the end of the pier. We looked out toward the silent river, Cameron keeping his gaze steady on the horizon, the streetlights and window lights of New Jersey.

"If you're uncomfortable, stare at those blinding fluorescents off to the right." I pointed across the river. "That's a hospital."

"Good to know." His smile made me smile.

Other couples gravitated toward the rail, embracing and kissing, amid a rumble of soft voices and laughter.

I said, "You really do like *Sleepless*. When you said so, I thought you were just saying so."

He nodded. "I like how there's always a grand gesture in her films. Arranging to meet on Valentine's Day. Tom bringing Meg daisies when she's sick in *You've Got Mail*. Billy Crystal declaring love at the New Year's dance. Grand gestures tell someone how you feel about them."

"I like when Annie's staring at the sky in Baltimore at the same time Sam's staring at the stars in Seattle." I looked up.

Cameron looked up. "No Manhattan stars," he said.

"Nope. Just the usual weird vaporous glow, an occasional planet or flying saucer. Wouldn't it have been great if Tom Hanks and Meg Ryan each saw the same flying saucer?"

"Molly?"

"Yes?" We stood facing each other.

"Take a deep breath, Molly."

"A deep breath why?"

"If you're done with flying saucers, this would be a perfect time to kiss."

He placed his hands on my shoulders and I felt a kind of

chill, but it might have been from the wind off the river. I took a deep breath. We leaned closer, our lips centimeters apart. I stopped, leaned back. "Your expectations for a first kiss are pretty extreme. What if the kiss isn't good?"

"We should find out," he said. "It could be a real time-saver. And if it's no good, we'll be friends. Or colleagues."

"Colleagues?"

"Yes." He laughed. "We could have an office affair. Deirdre offered me a column." He tilted his head toward mine again. I stepped back, out of his grasp, bumped into a couple behind me, excused myself, and turned back to Cameron.

"Column? You've got a column?"

He smiled his dopey, crooked smile, shook his head like *Isn't life funny?* "We discussed it a couple of weeks ago," he said. "She wants to announce it when she's back from her vacation and start after Labor Day. Something edgy, daring; she sees it as an advertisable proposition. Wants to name it GuyEye."

"GuyEye? What guy? You're the guy? Are you stealing my column?" Cameron looked hurt and confused, but not as hurt and confused as I felt. "You don't need a column! You have your novels. That's *my* column!"

"You're kidding, right?"

"This is not me joking. You stole my column! This—this—" I flailed my arm in the direction of the pier, the movie screen, the Hudson River, and all of New Jersey. "This is you being you making an idiot out of me! How could I buy into all this you-me-beneath-the-stars crap? You're a sales-

251

man. And a thief! Half the things you say or write about you've stolen, so why should I be surprised you'd steal my idea? *My* column. Or do you consider this a goddamn homage? 'Don't get upset, Molly. Isn't it flattering when I rip off your concept, Molly! Nobody else complains to the beloved Cameron Duncan. Why should you, Molly?'"

By now, other people were watching.

I snatched Cameron's baseball cap off my head and flung it out into the Hudson. Well, I thought I flung it. It landed three feet from the pilings and floated back toward the pier.

Cameron was gripping the railing with both hands, gaping down at the water. I don't know if he looked unnerved from the height or unnerved by his hat's sinking to its death.

"Thanks for the movie," I said. "Enjoy your grand gesture!"

I stormed off, leaving him standing there alone, looking like *What the hell did I say?*

22

Deirdre wasn't halfway out the building and off to vacation before the headphones were off and the music cranked up. By the time her elevator hit the lobby floor, the photo editor and the traffic coordinator were conducting chair races in the aisles, spinning around the cubicles doing wheelies, while the interactive designers placed bets. Water guns appeared from nowhere, squirting over the walls in surprise attacks. All inner-office correspondence was conducted via paper airplanes. The *EyeSpy* employees were busting out like third graders throwing erasers at the substitute schoolteacher. Only there was no substitute teacher. Deirdre was so hands-on she'd never leave her responsibilities in anyone else's hands. Instead, she *trusted* us.

I was the first to whip out the paper cups, contributing cheap vodka to the cheap wine, gin, and tequila that made up the office makeshift bar. I was so crazy-mad upset about Deirdre giving Cameron my column idea that I couldn't see straight. I was so drunk, I couldn't see straight.

However, there was one happy sight in my blurred vision: Emily was packing up her cubicle. By day three of Deirdre's vacation, around the time my headache cleared, Emily had made real progress with mowing through her hoard. "Free books, everyone!" she called out.

"It's my mother's birthday next week," Santiago the videoconference engineer said. "What have you got?"

I could hear Emily and Santiago sorting through possibilities. "Does she bake? Does she have low-self-esteem issues? Is she interested in Henry Kissinger?"

"About time you cleared off that floor," I called over the wall. "Your space has been an ongoing fire hazard!"

"Well, I'm off to be with my hunka-hunka burning love," she called back. "If this joint burns down, don't bother sending a postcard!"

Emily's jubilant disposition was an affront to my miserable one. How was she able to have such faith in her Rory that she could toss her entire life into the air?

Somebody tossed a paper airplane into my office. It landed on the floor behind me so I didn't see the pilot. I picked up the plane and read the note scribbled on the wing: *You okay?* I looked up to see Keith standing in my doorway. "May I?" He pointed to my chair.

"Sure."

He sat. Cracked a few knuckles. Leaned forward with his

elbows on his knees and his hands clasped. If he were gray-haired and thirty years older, he'd look like a grandfather about to tell a bedtime story. "You're not you the past week," he said.

I looked over both of my shoulders to see what other me might be standing there and turned back to Keith. "Who am I usually?"

"Somebody with zest," he said. "You've got no zest."

"I'm zestless?" I didn't realize I had zest, so how could I lose it? "I'm fine. I'm really fine, Keith. Thanks for your concern."

"You have friends here. Other friends besides Emily. Try not to be so distraught about her leaving." I didn't say a word. There were no words. "And if you've got man problems, you can talk with me anytime. My wife has a nice cousin in Westchester if that's what you're looking for."

"A cousin in Westchester. I'll keep that in mind."

"Not that he'd want to meet a woman without zest, but I'm sure you'll snap back."

"Thanks, Keith, I'm glad we had this talk."

He stood up, reached over, and patted me on the head, then asked, "Did you bring any vodka today? We're running low."

"I'll pick some up at lunchtime."

Keith walked out as I heard Emily saying, "Woo-hoo! Y'know, I *am* gonna miss this place!"

When Emily wasn't handing out books, she was planning her good-bye party, making suggestions for where it should be held, hinting what she'd like as a good-bye gift, and bemoaning that Deirdre was on vacation and nobody had thought to ask for a contribution to the gift fund before she left.

"Why do we have to go to all this fuss if you'll still be reviewing books and writing your column?" I asked, raising my voice. I was at my computer researching a piece on New York pretzel carts.

"Who needs a stapler?" Emily called out. "You can't have it until Friday, but first come first serve!" She popped up over my wall.

"I do not need your stapler," I told her. "You are dismissed."

"I have some books for you."

"Thank you, Emily Literati, but I've got enough to read."

She used two hands to hold up a book, making it dance along our ledge. "How's this?" I read the title: *He's Just Not That Into You.* Emily replaced it with a dancing *Anger Management for Dummies.* She laughed. "Just kidding!" she said. "Except about the dummy part. You're not as smart as you think."

"What's that supposed to mean?"

She disappeared. The photo editor, pushed by an art director, whipped past my cubicle on an office chair. Cocktail hour was about to start.

A pink-covered paperback came tumbling over the wall. *Heartburn.* By Nora Ephron. Followed by Emily's paper rose.

Despite my numerous invitations (zero), I chose to spend the weekend holed up in my apartment feeling sorry for myself. So far, this was one hell of a summer. I'd broken up with my boyfriend. Liked a guy I shouldn't have liked. Lost a column I never had in the first place. And my nemesis Emily had squeezed fifty bucks out of me—along with everyone else at the office—for her farewell drinks and a new silk blouse. Who even wears silk blouses at a ski resort? Why didn't she ask for a down vest?

Her party wasn't half-bad, though a bit redundant after a week of debauchery in Deirdre's absence. I hugged Emily good-bye. She hugged me good-bye. Like one of those scenes in the movies where mortal enemies find common ground just as it's too late.

"We can skype," I said to Emily.

"Why?" she asked.

"You're right," I said. "Why?"

Her parting words to me were "You're a blind fool, Molly Hallberg."

I didn't ask her to elucidate, and it was too late to get my $50 back.

On Monday I'd tell Deirdre how mad—no, I'd say *disappointed*—I was about the column. Saying *mad* could get me fired, a scenario I hoped to avoid until I found a new job. Maybe I'd be a Rockette. My class was only two weeks away. Right in time to audition for the Christmas show. Who didn't love Rockettes? And as a Rockette, I might even meet a new boyfriend. I heard Santa Claus is nice.

I was thumbing through the TV guide, planning my weekend activities, when Angela dropped by before leaving for the Catskills with her swim coach. She suggested maybe

I should go back to SpeedLove, only for real this time, as me, instead of undercover as Jeri Jacobs, and meet someone good. "I'd meet the same guys Jeri Jacobs met," I said. "You got the one good one."

Kristine called Saturday afternoon while on break at Bloomingdale's. She groaned into the telephone. "The mattress salesgirl is dating a chiropractor."

I was in my bathroom balancing the phone between my ear and shoulder and polishing my toenails, one foot up against the ledge of the tub. An accident victim waiting to happen. "How did you come upon this news flash?" I asked.

"She's telling everyone. I think she's having it printed in Sunday's flyers."

"And why'd you feel compelled to tell me this?"

"Closure," she said. "I thought you'd like closure."

"I already had closure. Now I have to think about it some more."

After we hung up, I thought about Russell long enough to realize I no longer thought about Russell. That made me feel guilty. Didn't he deserve a mourning period? Apparently I didn't either. I hoped he and his mattress saleslady would be happy together. She could hand out his business cards. He could tell clients their backs needed a firmer mattress and hand out her business cards. Russell could borrow her Bloomingdale's discount. It sounded like a good match. I moved on from there to feeling sorry for myself.

Self-pity's actually an excellent way to pass the time. You

don't have to dress for the occasion. Makeup's not required. Ice cream's often involved. Nobody demands you hold up your end of a conversation. The only conversations you have are with yourself.

You realize you're turning forty in two months, don't you?

Oh, God, I'm turning forty.

You don't like to think about it but it's hanging there like a big casaba melon about to drop on your head. Single in your thirties? People cut you some slack, maybe you're concentrating on your career. Traveling the world. Getting a grad degree. Single after forty? They start to wonder.

I'm not single. I'm divorced.

Semantics. Either way, you're alone. You've turned into a cynic. You stopped believing in love. You've been using your divorce as an excuse for five years to choose men you don't care about so you don't care if they leave. What's with that?

Unfair! Russell and I had some nice moments together.

We're aiming higher than nice moments. How about someone who gets you? Makes you sparkle? Feel challenged, alive, adored? Brings some romance into your life! How about some magic?

I know who you're talking about and I can't trust him.

You admit you felt magic?

Yes. Maybe. Okay. Maybe magic.

We don't decide to trust. We decide not to be afraid. Those movies you love—and while we're at it, you can't love Nora Ephron's movies and be a good cynic—in every one, Meg Ryan trusts something within herself. How else does she get on that plane to Seattle or get past Tom Hanks ruining her bookstore? How else does she marry

Billy Crystal? She gets her happy ending because she tries something different and ends up with someone she didn't imagine.

Well, Tom Hanks wasn't a liar. He never stole Meg's idea for a column.

Fine. Good luck curling up with your column. Hopefully your indignation will keep you warm at night.

I spent Saturday doing all the things you tell yourself you'll do if only you had time to do them. I dropped off a pair of heels needing new heels. That was it. For weeks I'd been complaining I had way too many errands to catch up on, and they boiled down to ten minutes at the shoe repair. I organized my sock drawer by color. Then reorganized it alphabetically. Checked expiration dates in my medicine cabinet. Checked expiration dates in my fridge. Half my life had expired. *Forty, forty,* I kept thinking. *I'm turning forty.* My mother wanted to throw me a party. My father said he'd barbecue. They'd suggested a party while I was still dating Russell and could guarantee I'd have a date. I'd said, sure, okay, I wouldn't mind a party. But a party when you bring a boyfriend is one thing. A fortieth birthday party with only relatives is pitiful. Just imagining that party made me sad. Which led to laundry.

There's nothing like spending a Saturday night in a laundry room to underline you've screwed up your love life. I suppose some people have actually fallen in love in laundry rooms. Their eyes meet across a crowded folding table and there it is. Recognition. Simpatico. *You're a mess? I'm a mess!*

We're in love. I was embarrassed for Dennis the doorman to see me in the laundry room on a Saturday night. We have a security camera our doormen can watch from the lobby. So far it's led to the discovery that the man in 5B steals women's panties and the woman in 7A snatched another neighbor's Tide. But otherwise it just makes you self-conscious that your doorman's watching you do laundry.

I hunted down quarters, picked a book, stuffed my soap and dryer sheets into my laundry bag, and dragged it down the hall into the elevator and to the basement. I normally don't drag, I carry, but I was in a draggy mood. To my surprise, Lacey and Kevin Gallo were downstairs, the two of them holding hands while watching the spin cycle on their dryer, like new parents gazing into a nursery ward. We greeted each other.

"Hello, Lacey."

"Hello, Molly."

"Hello, Kevin."

"Hello, Molly."

"Kevin and I are moving out," Lacey said.

"You just moved in."

"The walls in this building are too thin. We can hear your television at night."

I didn't point out that they were *two-way walls*. Not only could I not keep a boyfriend, I was driving away neighbors. Their dryer buzzer went off. Lacey opened the door and removed some of the most pornographic underwear I've ever seen. I wanted to swallow detergent.

At this point a judgmental outsider might note that I had no business pitying myself, that I was the one who broke up with Russell; I was the one who threw Cameron's baseball cap in the Hudson; I was the one who married that no-goodnik Evan Naboshek in the first place. But it wasn't my past decisions that were depressing me; it was the fear that I'd continue to make lousy choices in the future. What sign from on high did I have that I'd ever figure love out? What would it take to feel hopeful and optimistic, bullish instead of foolish? Hopeful people get on a standing-room-only bus and look around for an open seat. Hopeful people step on a bathroom scale and say it's water weight. Hopeful people don't carry umbrellas just in case or buy life insurance. Was I willing to go through the rest of my life not feeling anything, even if all I ever felt was hopeless hope?

Lacey and Kevin left with the x-rated undies. I started two washers—thankful that I didn't have to compete for their availability. I settled into one of two orange plastic chairs, waved hello to the security camera, and picked up *Heartburn*. That same judgmental outsider might question why I'd want to sit in a laundry room rather than return to the comfort of my own apartment. Normally, I do that. But I'm hideous at timing laundry. I'm always zipping back downstairs and discovering there's still fifteen minutes left on the washer, and I end up standing there twiddling my thumbs. Or I arrive late and somebody else has pulled my wet clothes out of the washer, not because that somebody else is a thoughtful and considerate neighbor, but because the somebody pounced on the washer as soon as the buzzer went off. Leaving my clothes in a big soggy heap.

As long as nobody was around to force me into being sociable when I preferred being miserable, I'd sit and read and wait for my laundry and spare myself the stress of running up and down. I have long been an advocate of staying home with a good book over going out with a bad date. Not that any men, good or bad, had asked me for a date that night, but if one had, he would have found it impossible to compete with Nora Ephron. The washer tubs filled with water while a seven-months-pregnant Nora took off for her father's apartment in New York after learning her husband in Washington, DC, was having an affair. She called herself Rachel in her novel and called her husband Mark, but everyone knew the story was true and whom she meant. Suds foamed, the washing machines did that agitator thing that makes them shake and ruin brassieres, and Rachel went to group therapy, used a kreplach joke as a metaphor, and wove in recipes for key lime pie and bacon hash. A robber followed her off the subway and robbed her therapy group at gunpoint. I held up the book toward the security camera and pointed at it for Dennis's sake. The way my chair was angled, I was afraid he wouldn't see I was reading, that he'd think I was some madwoman sitting alone in the laundry room throwing my head back in laughter while watching towels spin.

I'd read the novel before, of course, but that was years earlier, before I had my own husband cheat on me, my own heartburn. Evan liked to think he was a public figure, but unless you were suing someone for divorce, you probably never heard of him. A famous husband cheating on you, your second husband in a row to cheat on you, while you were pregnant yet; this was a woman who earned her right to distrust men, to not trust herself or her instincts. But she kept believing, hoping, doing her best. During the bleach cycle Mark showed up and brought Rachel and their two-year-old son back to Washington. I was so engrossed in the book that I forgot to add the softener sheets. I stopped the dryers, added the sheets, and went back to reading about Nora—I mean Rachel—discovering Mark and his lover were looking to buy a house, and Rachel smashing a pie in Mark's face at a dinner party.

Back upstairs in my apartment, I hung my T-shirts on the bathroom shower rod. I folded my towels and bed linens and left the rest so I could continue reading. Rachel went into labor, knowing her marriage was ending, asking Mark to talk about the birth of their first son, when Mark and she were both happy in the marriage; not just her. A vinaigrette recipe later, healing from her second cesarean, she left DC with her children and headed back to New York to start again. And she did. Of course she did. She had faith in love; she believed in romance; and she found the Nick to her Nora. A real-live Nick. A crime writer. Whose real name was Nick. You could sense her joy in *When Harry Met Sally*. You could see it in *Sleepless in Seattle*. You could feel it in *You've Got Mail*. Her dogged determination to create happy endings. We *can* get it right; we can surprise ourselves with our courage and heart. And when we do, hearts will light up on the sides of buildings, Jimmy Durante will burst into song, kisses will be shared in flower gardens, and we'll dance to "Auld Lang Syne." And with time, we'll find ourselves sitting beside our beloved on a red velvet love seat, sharing memories of how we first fell in love.

Except for those of us who are total idiots.

23

Monday morning I walked down to Gavin's desk and asked to get on Deirdre's schedule.

"You and everyone else," he said. "Her day's a nightmare." He lowered his voice. "She's a nightmare." Deirdre never returned from her vacations relaxed.

"It's important," I said.

"To you or to her?" Gavin said he'd see what he could do. Juggling Deirdre's schedule was Gavin's only opportunity to exert power. Other than that, he was at her mercy all day.

I returned to my cube and my pretzel-cart article. I stared at my computer screen. It stared back. This would have been about the time Emily and I would be going at it. She'd have been tossing pretzels over the wall. Somehow, without her, the office was less entertaining. I actually kind of missed her.

Since her grand exit, her cubicle had been ravaged. As soon as anyone leaves or dies around our office, the vultures sweep in, swapping chairs, upgrading garbage cans, stealing notepads, Post-its, pens; prying filing cabinets and bulletin boards out with crowbars and sledgehammers. Keith and Brady were already fighting over Emily's cube. Brady wanted it because it was larger than his cube, and Keith liked that it was closer to the men's room. Nobody wanted to ask Keith why that mattered to him.

My office phone rang. I screened the caller's name on the ID. Oh! Outside caller! I picked up the receiver and in my best journalistic voice said, "Molly Hallberg."

"Good," a woman said. She was either on a bad cell connection or talking into her hand.

"Good why?" I asked.

"This is Veeva Penney."

"*Veeva Penney* Veeva Penney?"

"No. JCPenney." She chuckled. "Old joke." The phone broke up, crackling. I didn't say anything. What if it was a crank call, Emily phoning from Idaho pretending to be a famous agent? "I hear you're the new columnist for *EyeSpy*," she said.

"Very funny!" I hung up.

The phone rang a minute later. An outside caller. I snapped up the receiver. "What do you want! You can't live without me? I hope you're enjoying your blouse!"

"I enjoy many of my blouses."

The reception was excellent. I was not speaking with

Emily. Chances were quite likely at that point that I was speaking with Veeva Penney. "Oh, hello." I was mortified. "We had bad reception before. Were you able to hear me?" *God, please say no.*

"Perfectly," she said. "I read your essays. They're quite good."

I'd had this conversation a million times. Except all the other times it was in my head. "My essays?"

"Cameron Duncan sent them. Ever consider putting them together as a collection?"

I said, "Every day of my life."

"You'll need at least twenty of them."

"I have at least a hundred of them. Are you saying you want to be my agent?"

If hearts can stop, mine had just gone into a holding pattern.

"Cameron said you're a terrific writer. With a terrible temper. You won't be one of those pain-in-the-ass clients, will you?"

"Not at all! I had cramps one day. Made me testy."

"I hear you, sister. We'll talk. And congratulations. Nowadays everyone needs a platform." Veeva rattled off her phone number, her e-mail address, her address address, and the name of her favorite flowers for some reason and hung up.

I had an agent? And a platform?

Hank Brandt, the ad sales manager, was passing my cubicle. "Hey, Hank," I said. "Have you heard anything about our running a new column?"

"No," he said, "but if we are, I am totally applying for the job." He hurried off.

I walked down to Gavin's desk again. He was studying his computer screen: Craigslist. Job openings. He hit his keyboard, made the screen go black. "Don't tell Deirdre," he said.

"I hear you, brother."

"I was about to call you. She wants to see you when you're available."

"When *I'm* available? Am I being fired?"

"I don't think so."

"Then I'm available."

He buzzed Deirdre's intercom, whispered to me, "She's been a witch all morning."

"I heard that, Gavin!" Deirdre barked into his intercom.

"He meant me, Deirdre," I said into the speaker. "It's Molly. Good time to talk?"

"Come in," she said.

Gavin and I exchanged thumbs-ups. "Good luck," he said.

I pressed his shift bar. Craigslist popped up again. "You, too," I said.

As soon as I walked into Deirdre's office, I knew why she'd been hiding out. She had a hideous sunburn. The kind that's bright red and peeling in splotches and announces to the world that your SPF was way too low. She was wearing sunglasses indoors. Then I realized that wasn't a sunburn. Deirdre had had a chemical peel. I waited for her to say something, share some girl talk, maybe exchange beauty tips. Like the name of her plastic surgeon. Or malpractice lawyer. "Have a seat," she said barely moving her mouth. It must have hurt to talk.

I never know the protocol for these things. Was I supposed to say, *Appears to be a great job! That complexion of yours is on its way to looking like a baby's bottom!* But Deirdre didn't say anything, so I didn't say anything. I sat across from her in her dark-lensed, egg-shaped frames, neither of us acknowledging that she looked like a Moon Martian. "Enjoyable vacation?" I asked. She ignored my question. Got right down to business before I got down to my business of asking how Cameron Duncan ended up with my column idea! What was really maddening, though, was that I could no longer be mad at him after he'd hooked me up with Veeva. His agent. *My* agent! I'd have to apologize, thank him somehow; at the very least be willing to maintain a pleasant working relationship as colleagues.

"A MyEye column is a good idea," Deirdre was saying. "You'll do your same type of articles, but with a column head, a photograph. We'll make it a brandable property."

"Excuse me?" I said.

This was turning out to be a very strange morning. A when-will-the-other-shoe-drop morning. My father had a Great-Aunt Ruta whom I never met but is legendary in the family for her cynicism. Any happy occasion she'd manage to point out the dark side and make a sour comment. Her motto was "Behind every silver cloud there's a pogrom."

Weddings lead to divorces. Adorable babies grow into surly teens. Houses burn down. Men who steal your heart turn out to be thieves. That's how strange a morning it was. I was waiting for my great-aunt's ghost to appear and say, *Here come the Cossacks!*

"I want to launch with your Rockettes assignment," Deirdre said. "We can promote it as a kickoff to *EyeSpy*'s exciting new column. Kickoff. Get it? *Kickoff?*"

"Got it. Kickoff."

She sat back, smiled. The smile seemed to hurt her face.

I said, "Isn't Cameron Duncan writing the column?"

For a moment I thought I saw Deirdre's face redden, but it was difficult to tell with her face already so red. "I may have considered other candidates," she said, her words slow and measured. "Perhaps I offered it to him. But he, frankly, talked me into you."

Cameron didn't want the column? He wasn't a thief? That was a good thing. Deirdre's having to be talked into me? Not so good. But I wasn't about to be fussy; I'd deal with my ego later. I thanked Deirdre, told her I wouldn't let her down, thanked her again, and headed back to my cube. I wanted to cheer and shout, *Hey! Guess what! I'm getting a column!* Good news doesn't feel half as good without someone to chuck you on the shoulder or give you an *attaboy.* But telling anyone at the office was off the list. That'd be like expecting a coworker to be happy I got a raise. I could call my parents, but I already knew what they'd say. *That's nice, honey. Does this mean you can stop jumping out of airplanes?* Kristine would be pleased. Angela would tweet the news to her grocery-store followers. The truth is, there were only two people I really wanted to talk to. One was now living in Idaho. And the other had no interest in talking to me.

24

That night I tried sleeping on my back, sleeping on my side, sleeping on my stomach. I tried sleeping with a pillow over my head, but only for a few minutes; I worried I'd suffocate. No matter what position I tried, I couldn't shut off my head. Oh, my thoughts were mad at me! I wanted to call Cameron. I was embarrassed to call Cameron. I wanted to call Cameron. I was scared to call Cameron. I wanted to call Cameron but didn't know his phone number. Our relationship hadn't reached the texting stage. And male authors with thousands of female fans don't have listed numbers.

At 4 a.m. I wrote e-mails in my mind:

—*Dear Mr. Bing, I need to hire a detective. Can you please help a big-time fool track down a big-time author?*

—*Trying to find the right words to apologize, but it's difficult to type while hitting my head against a wall.*

—*What if the guy who seems too good to be true isn't make-believe?*

I didn't send them. They seemed wrong. Too pat. And if he didn't respond, I'd spend the rest of my life wondering if he hated me or if I'd landed in his spam folder.

At 7 a.m. I turned on *Good Morning America* to drown out Kevin and Lacey saying good morning next door. Sylvester Stallone was being interviewed by George Stephanopoulos, talking about playing Detective Mike Bing. "The character's hard-boiled," Sly said. "Like Rambo. But also sensitive. Like Rocky. He's a romantic waiting for that one kiss that will change his life."

I did want to hit my head against a wall.

This was the perfect time for a feminist intervention, Gloria Steinem showing up saying, "Molly, repeat after me: *I Am Columnist, Hear Me Roar!* You do not need to go running after a man. Send a polite note thanking him for his recommendations on your behalf, then get on with your life, focus on your career."

"But, Gloria, even you eventually got married."

"I was sixty-six. I didn't go rushing into anything. And what's with bringing up marriage? You haven't kissed this guy yet."

I felt sad when Gloria said that. I realized I wanted to kiss him. I wanted to kiss Cameron Duncan more than any man I've ever wanted to kiss. And that included River Phoenix, whom I spent all of 1986 wanting to kiss.

"Okay," Gloria said, seeing the woebegone expression on my

face. "Some women aren't cut out for eschewing men. And I know you gave it your best shot dating the chiropractor with the turtles. But don't tell anyone I made these suggestions. Ask your boss Deirdre for his number. Ask your new agent Veeva Penney for his number—and congratulations on that. Your buddy Emily interviewed him. She must have his phone number. But personally, I'd never speak to her again. No man's worth it. Although, Cameron Duncan is an extremely appealing man."

"You know each other?"

"Of course. Famous people hang out together."

"Then why can't you give me his phone number?"

"Because I'm in your imagination, Molly. How the hell am I supposed to know his number!"

At work, I started with Gavin. He had Deirdre's contact list. Deirdre's door was closed so I could ask Gavin for Cameron's number without the embarrassment of Deirdre knowing I was asking for Cameron's number. Embarrassment was Plan B.

"I'm not allowed to give out numbers. I could get fired," he said.

"You hate your job, Gavin. You'd get severance. I'd be doing you a favor."

"Whose number is it you want?"

"Cameron Duncan."

"No can do. Deirdre keeps a few secret numbers on her private cell."

"Cameron has a secret number?"

Gavin shrugged. "Crime-writer mentality."

I looked at Deirdre's closed door. Took a deep breath. Asked Gavin if he'd mind buzzing to see if I could worm a secret phone number out of her.

"She's not in there," he said. "She left early for Labor Day weekend."

"She just got back from vacation."

Gavin rolled his eyes. "I guess her *sunburn* is uncomfortable. You can call her at home, but I don't recommend it. She's in a pisser mood. Furious at her dermatologist for lying about the recovery time for the world's worst chemical peel."

"Good advice, Gavin. I'll move on to Plan C."

Back in my cubicle I could hear Keith banging around next door, arranging his files and computer, having won the Battle for the Cube. I dialed Veeva Penney's office. Got a recorded message saying her office was closed until after Labor Day. I was down to Plan D. "Hey, Keith," I called out. "You don't happen to have a phone number for the dearly departed Miss Lawler, do you?"

His head appeared over the wall. "Sure," he said. "I like to ski." His head bobbed down. A minute later his head bobbed up. He handed me a torn piece of notepaper with Emily's cell number.

"Thanks, Keith."

"You're welcome, Molly. The cousin in Westchester's still available."

"Thanks, Keith."

I dialed Emily's number hoping I'd get her voice mail, that I could leave a message and she could leave a message back, sparing myself the embarrassment of asking for Cameron's number. I'd just casually mention she wasn't the *only* person with an *EyeSpy* column, and, oh, yes, could she please pass along some phone info?

How grateful I felt when her recorded greeting came on. The beep beeped and I started to relay my question.

"I knew you'd miss me," Emily said when she cut in. "I heard about your column."

"How?"

"Please, Molly. I'm me."

"How are you? Enjoying mountain life?"

"It's so romantic," she said. "Every night Rory gives me a foot rub."

"I didn't call to discuss your feet."

"First thing every morning he brings me a fresh cup of coffee."

"Gavin does the same thing for Deirdre."

"I heard her chemical peel's a disaster."

"Heard how?"

"Please, Molly."

"I don't want to take up your time, but—"

"That's what people say when they don't want you taking up *their* time. What do you want? I'm very busy."

"Doing what?"

"Editing an interview. Reviewing romance novels. I'm thinking of changing my column's name to Emily Loverati."

"Can't wait to read it. Do you happen to have Cameron Duncan's phone number?"

"Congratulations. You finally ran out of excuses to run away?"

"What do you mean by that? What did you hear?"

"Please, Molly. In my opinion he can do a lot better, but he seems unwilling to believe me. Seems to think you're the Nora to his Nick Charles. Not Nora Ephron. God knows from that assignment you blew nobody means Nora Ephron."

"Have you talked with him?"

"Jeez, my cell phone seems to be dying."

"Can I have the number please, Emily?" She didn't say anything. "Emily, please."

"Okay, fine!" She put me on hold, came back, and gave me Cameron's secret number. "How do you plan to apologize? Calling's rather lame, don't you think?"

"What do you suggest?"

"You need a grand gesture."

"Like what?"

"How should I know!"

If I were watching myself starring in a Nora Ephron movie, right about now I'd be yelling at Molly to quit dawdling and win back the affections of the man every other person in the audience knew from the get-go was the man for her. What would Nora have Molly do next? Like a true Nora heroine Molly had dated the wrong person. Supportive friends rallied round. References were made to other movies. *An Affair to Remember* in *Sleepless in Seattle*. *Casablanca* in *When Harry Met Sally*. Molly keeps referring to Nora's movies.

Of course the movies all have misunderstandings, but our beloved characters choose fighting for love over fighting. Billy Crystal did as Harry. Tom Hanks as Joe Fox. Meg did as Sally and Kathleen. In *Sleepless in Seattle* nobody had to, but still, there were complications. And running. Lots of running. Billy running to the New Year's Eve dance to declare his love. Tom running to the Empire State Building to find his son and find his heart. Now it was Molly's turn to run for her life; the life and the man she really wanted.

Okay. Enough with talking about myself in the third person; it makes me feel psychotic. And the only running I've done so far is run out of ideas. But along with saying, *Don't settle, love is worth risk,* Nora taught me something else: I'd have to write my own happy ending.

Phone message #1 (Tuesday, 4:00 p.m.):

"Help! I was standing on the Seventieth Street pier and jumped to conclusions."

E-mail #1 (Tuesday, 11:00 p.m.):

I'm sorry. I'm sorry. I'm sorry. Cyber-apologies suck. But I'm sorry. I'm sorry. I'm sorry.

E-mail #2 (Wednesday, 3:00 a.m.):

Please regard previous e-mail. I'm sorry. I'm sorry. I'm sorry.

Phone message #2 (Wednesday, 11:00 a.m.):

"Hello? I'm calling from the New York Scuba Society. We found your hat. Call for details!"

Phone message #3 (Wednesday, 6:00 p.m.):

"Cameron? It's Molly. Author of the new book *Mea Culpas among Morons*. I mean, I'm the moron. Not you. You're the one who sent my essays to Veeva and turned down the column. Although maybe you never even wanted it. But you knew I did and you talked Deirdre into me and we both like Jujubes and we both like sitting in the front row at the movies and maybe that's not important but maybe it is. I don't know anyone else who likes sitting in the front row eating Jujubes, so please call."

I phoned Angela. "Coast clear?"

"No men on premise," she said.

"I'll be right over."

I opened my front door and she was already standing in her doorway wearing some semi-sheer, baby-doll, lacy, short jumpsuit thing. It was truly uncategorizable. But I knew Charlie was on his way. "Where did you buy that?" I asked, eyeing her outfit.

"Online," she said, closing the door behind me.

"I won't ask the name of the site." Angela's apartment is decorated in Early IKEA crossed with *Peanuts* posters.

A small suitcase was open on her floor with half her ward-robe scattered around in tangled piles. I followed her to the kitchen as she sashayed in feathered mules, one hand on her hip, swinging the shoulder with her Snoopy tattoo. I said, "I doubt Charles Schulz would approve of this getup."

"Then good thing he's dead." Angela opened her fridge and stared inside, frowning at the contents. "Want something? Wine, vodka, hemlock? Cameron's still not returning your calls?" She closed the fridge.

"No."

"Call again and pretend you're not you. Maybe then he'll want to talk to you."

"And be who?"

"How about Jeri Jacobs calls to invite him to a SpeedLove event?"

"Apologize by introducing him to other women?"

"You can be there and surprise him. You'll have four minutes to apologize face-to-face."

"Thank you. I'll take that plan under consideration. The hemlock plan, not the SpeedLove one."

I resumed my campaign.

Text #1 (Thursday, 10:45 a.m.):

Just in case your phone machine's broken . . . somebody named Molly is trying to reach you.

Text #2 (Thursday, 10:46 p.m.):

P.S. She's not a stalker. She's an apologizer.

Phone message #4 (Friday 8:00 a.m.):

"Hello? This is Nora. Charles. Not Ephron. I'm looking for Nick. I hope I'm not calling too early. I don't even know if you're an early riser or write until all hours of the night and then like to sleep late because we never—"

The machine cut off; I heard the phone pick up. "I do sleep late." Cameron's voice sounded warm and husky. And half-asleep.

"Oh! Hi! It's you. Real you! Thank you for picking up." I was so used to talking to his machine that I wasn't prepared for the actual him.

"How'd you find my number?" he asked.

"I hired Mike Bing when you weren't looking."

"You're saying he takes assignments behind my back?"

"Please don't tell him I'm the one who squealed."

"What am I supposed to do about you, Molly Hallberg?"

"Can we fix it?"

"We? It?"

"Yes. You. Me. A possible us? Maybe give me a redo?"

"Redo you going ballistic on me? By the way, that flaws list of yours? You forgot to mention temper."

"That wasn't me. That was crazy, insane, aliens-have-taken-over-my-body me."

"You upset me, Molly. I care for you and you didn't let me explain. The energy and passion you have that lets you jump on a bike or jump out a plane or go on a Ninety-Second Street Y panel totally clueless—that part of you can be beautiful and fun, but it can be hurtful. And it hurts you, too." The sadness I heard in him matched the sadness in me. "When I come home at night, I want excitement," he said. "What I don't want is a gun pointed at my head. I don't know if I can be friends with a woman who doesn't trust." My mind was racing for the words that would make it okay again. But I never got the chance. I heard Cameron sigh. "I don't know what else to say, Molly. I'm sorry." He hung up.

That was supposed to be my line: *I'm sorry*.

I called Angela. I knew I'd wake her. But I knew she'd understand.

I could hear her fumbling with the phone. "Sweetheart?" she said.

"Other sweetheart," I said. "Not Charlie. Molly."

"Oh."

"Sorry." At least I got to say sorry to someone. "I just spoke with Cameron."

"He called?"

"I called. He picked up. He said no."

"To what?"

"To me."

"Final no? No way no?"

"He said no."

"Oh, no, I'm sorry. Will you be okay this weekend? Are you going out to your parents'? Kristine's gone, too."

"I'll be fine. I suppose. I guess." I hoped. "I have the Rockettes class tomorrow."

"Charlie and I'll be back early Monday," she said. "Forget Cameron. You'll find someone tons better."

"Angela?"

"Yeah?"

"Do you really believe I'll meet someone better? That people are replaceable?"

"No," she said. "But I'm your friend. That's what I'm supposed to say."

25

The citizens of New York peeled out of the city, grasping for that one last weekend of summer. I spent Friday afternoon walking down Third, walking up Lex, down Park, up Madison; I walked through Central Park trying my best to tune out humanity, only I felt assaulted by humanity. *Look at all these couples. Everyone's a couple. Hand-holding, starry-eyed, in-my-face couples.*

Saturday I slept in late. Not luxuriating-in-bed-catching-up-on-your-sleep late, but more like suicidal-can't-face-the-day late. It was so unfair! I'd been fine with Russell. Fine enough. Then Cameron wormed his way into my shut-down heart and I messed up everything. I glanced at the nightstand and the clock. My Rockettes Experience started at 1:15. If I wanted to kick myself, I was about to learn how. I bolted out of bed; I only had thirty-five minutes to get to Radio

City Music Hall! I couldn't be late and blow my first official column. Hey, art department! Don't bother photoshopping Molly's headshot!

I showered, threw on clean underwear in case I ended up in a hospital, slapped on some blush, and tugged on my leotard. I actually owned black tights and a leotard, souvenirs of a 2005 Halloween party where I dressed as a cat and Evan dressed as a dog the year before we divorced because he really was a dog. I added a skirt and sneakers to complete the look, pulled my hair back with an elastic. It was important to dress like a dancer to make up for not being a dancer.

By the time I got downstairs, hurrying through the lobby, I had less than ten minutes to get to my experience. I was running past Dennis the doorman when he stopped me, holding up his hand like a traffic cop. He said, "Molly, you've got mail." I heard the elevator door go *ding!* He handed me a small, white envelope. "Angela left it yesterday before leaving for the weekend."

"Yesterday?" I said.

"I forgot," Dennis said.

I stuffed the envelope in my purse and ran out and down the block to the corner, where I grabbed a cab. I'd have body-blocked and tackled one if necessary. I told the driver, "Radio City Music Hall. Fiftieth Street backstage door! And hurry!" His driving was worthy of a movie car-chase scene as he zipped to midtown, asking questions. Was I a dancer? A musician? An usher? Did I have access to discount tickets for the Christmas show?

I was the last to arrive in the mirror-lined dance studio. Purses, shoes, and sweaters were stashed and strewn among a long, wall-length row of thick chairs attached at the arms; the chairs looked like Rockettes. I dumped my stuff and joined the other students, who were seated on the floor around a beautiful, long-legged, bun-topped woman who introduced herself as Miss Melodie. She introduced ponytailed Mr. Seth, sitting at an upright piano off to one corner.

"And you are?" she asked, checking a note card.

"Molly."

"Molly?"

"Jeri Jacobs. Sorry! I'm nervous."

Beautiful Miss Melodie smiled. "No reason for anyone to be nervous." She told us there had been over three thousand Rockettes in the past seventy-five years, and the average performance required four hundred kicks. Before I could whip out the multiplication tables, she had us up and on our sneakers spread out behind her like a yoga class, except we were channeling Bob Fosse instead of Rodney Yee.

Mr. Seth banged away and Miss Melodie called out dance steps that everyone in class, other than one black-leotarded klutz, seemed capable of following. I told myself, *I don't need to be good at this; I just need to write about this.* "One-two-three-five-seven!" Miss Melodie called out. I was wondering what happened to four and six when she also started calling out corrections. "Reach, Ginny! Shoulders, Tina! Left, not right, Jeri!" I was having fun. I never got in step with anyone else, but I did get into it.

About the time I was thinking maybe I'd been harboring a hidden talent for jazz all these years—interpretive jazz—Miss Melodie switched us to tap. I'd be lying if I didn't say it's thrilling to put on those beige, T-strapped Rockette shoes, even though they're technically only a notch better than community bowling shoes. But I loved the way my toes tapped and my heels tapped, and I just wanted to tap-tap-tap-tap-tap until Beautiful Miss Melodie instructed us to line up for synchronized kicking—tallest women in the middle fanning out to the shorter ones. "Quickly, ladies, quickly!" We were on a strict schedule. Jazz choreography. Tap choreography. After our kick line we'd go through mock auditions, have a photo op with Miss Melodie, and a backstage tour of Radio City Music Hall.

Despite being tall enough to belong in the center of the line, I landed at the far end next to a hyper little creature who, had we taken a vote, I'm sure would have been the second-most-unpopular girl in class. It didn't take much to know who was the most unpopular. A derisive look here. A scowl aimed in my direction there. Nobody wanting to stand on either side of me in the kick line. But I didn't care! *Hit it, Mr. Seth!* Kick! Kick! Kick! I was dancing and kicking and writing about the Rockettes for my first column! I was so excited I wanted to pass out from shortness of breath. Kick! Kick! Kick! "Synchronize, ladies! Synchronize!" Miss Melodie called out. "Jeri, kick when the others kick!" Mr. Seth switched into playing "Rockin' Around the Christmas Tree," and Beautiful Miss Melodie, tapping and kicking to lead our tapping and kicking, directed us to salute with our right hands while maintaining our line formation with our left hands. "Salute! Salute!"

I got my salute mixed up with Miss Hyper's salute, kicking in the wrong direction, treading on her foot and tripping forward. I decided it might be an excellent time to tap-tap-tap my way over to one of those nice cushy upholstered chairs and take a short break, maybe review my undercover questions for the Q&A. Like how do the Rockettes in their skimpy, sequiny uniforms keep from freezing their asses off in the Macy's Thanksgiving Parade? Probing, incisive questions like those.

The other ladies were now dancing in circle-kick formation, arm to shoulder, arm to shoulder. Kick. Kick. It was ten to three; I'd been tapping and jazzing for over an hour and a half. My arms and shoulders needed a time-out. My legs wanted to kick *me*. I dug into my purse for my memo pad and remembered Angela's note. I pulled it out of its envelope—written on Snoopy stationery—and read: *Hey, Molly! FYI. Cameron tweeted something strange. "Sleepless from wondering were you the one? Mike Bing misses you and needs new perspective. Time to face up up up to problem. Saturday @3." He sounds crazy. Good thing you didn't get involved. xoxA.*

I read the note again. *Up up up. Sleepless.*

"I'm sorry! I've gotta go!" I said to nobody in particular. Mr. Seth was pounding out "Santa Claus Is Coming to Town"; the ladies were kicking and saluting; and Miss Melodie was calling out, "Chin up! You can do it!"

I scuttled out of the studio with seventeen blocks between Cameron and me, flying down a staircase past a tour group, and kept running out onto Sixth Avenue. About then I became conscious of my leotard and stolen tap shoes, but unless a Radio City Hall security guard came chasing after me with a gun, I had to keep going, down Fiftieth past the Radio City posters, dodging pedestrians and cutting across the street and zipping around the corner at the Cole Haan store onto Fifth Avenue, almost bumping into a man playing a saxophone, all the time praying for a taxi. An SUV with a raised hood had traffic at a standstill. I kept running. Past Rockefeller Center. Past T.G.I. Friday's. Past Forty-Seventh Street and the Brink's-trucks-lined Diamond District.

Even Great-Aunt Ruta would've been encouraging me: *Go get this man!* Probably adding, *Though, you might get hit by a bus.* I wished there was a bus. No buses. If there were, they'd be stuck buses. Taxis were honking but not moving. I pressed on, weaving among window gazers, camera snappers, map-reading foreigners, flower-laden messengers, T-shirted camp groups, box-balancing deliverymen, package-toting shoppers, and joggers; while sidestepping hot-dog carts and scaffolding. My chest hurt. My legs hurt. I now knew why Nike doesn't make tap shoes; they're not meant for running. I ran past the public library. Lord & Taylor at Thirty-Ninth. I passed more GNC vitamin stores and Duane Reade drugstores than the entire population of Manhattan could possibly need. I'd catch my breath and curse under it at red lights. Tap-tap-tapping. My heart pound-pound-pounding. I scurried around a FedEx man, barely missed tumbling over a rolling suitcase. The smell wafting out of the vents from the Heartland Brewery almost did knock me off my feet.

Plenty of women who watched *Sleepless in Seattle* might have said, "Meg! Am I seeing this straight? Give up Bill Pullman, who had much better hair than Tom Hanks and probably as good a job—although for the life of us, despite how many times we've all seen the movie, can anyone tell us what Bill Pullman's job was?—but, honest to God, Meg, you want to toss your entire future out that fancy restaurant's view-of-the-whole-big-sparkling-city window *just in case* Tom Hanks—whom you've never exchanged a single word with—*happens* to fly from Seattle and be hanging out in New York on Valentine's Day? *Meg, are you off your rocker?*" But she went for it. Nora made her go for it. Wrote that script and said you can't settle for the wrong man; how can you *not* run toward love no matter how crazy romantic a fairy tale this story might seem?

What Nora didn't mention was the long ticket line at the Empire State Building. How did Meg get up to that observation deck so fast? I checked my watch; it was ten after three. I scanned the lobby. It was crowded, festive and *beautiful* with its gray-and-lilac terrazzo floors, gold- and aluminum-leaf murals of sunbursts and stars, its ceiling murals of gears and wheels and cogs. It takes your breath away, which in my case was easy. I was clammy, sticky, outfitted like a cat; my hair a disaster and my makeup melting. But I made it through the security line. A woman in a leotard doesn't have a lot of secrets. My handbag made it through the scanner. I forgot my skirt and shoes; I'd left them with the Rockettes. Maybe they'd go on tour together. Had I missed Cameron? Was he able to do it, get on the elevator and step off on that rooftop? He was determined. Determination counts. He might do it. I waited in line for my ticket, still hoping to spot him, invoking Zeus, Buddha, Jesus, Moses, anyone who'd help, hoping that I'd turn and find him right there, yet hoping he'd done it, he'd made it to the observation deck. Cameron. Who'd observed so much in me. The line crawled. Oh, how it crawled. A man ahead of me said to the woman with him, "I told you to buy the tickets online!" "What am I, your secretary?" she said. While they squabbled, a family behind me argued in a language I didn't recognize, but I'm sure the wife was saying, "I told you to buy the tickets online!" A boy with a small backpack and a teddy bear stared up at me. Finally it was my turn. Twenty-five dollars for a ticket—unless I wanted to pay the express price of $47.50 and move to the front of the elevator line. I handed over my charge card: "Express." I signed the receipt. The woman behind the register looked at me, looked at my leotard, gave me my ticket, and said, "I know *you'll* have fun."

I hurried to the elevators, smug that I could cut ahead for my extra twenty-two bucks. The doors were about to close on a filled car. I scooted in, made room for myself. I was late, too late, but I had to get up there. I paid $47.50 dammit!— get this elevator up there! The doors closed. Then opened. The elevator operator said, "Sorry, folks. We seem stalled a moment." The doors closed and opened again. And there, in the lobby, standing by himself, looking nervous and scared and delicious in a crisp, new Cincinnati Reds cap, was Cameron Duncan. Staring toward the elevator. I smiled at him. He smiled back. I stepped off the elevator as the doors closed behind me. I hadn't realized before that music was playing in the lobby. Well, I heard music. Jimmy Durante.

I walked up to Cameron. My Cameron. "Nice cap," I said.

"Nice leotard," he said. He glanced skyward, shrugged, smiled that sweet, crooked grin of his, now rueful, embarrassed. "I'm never getting up there."

"So, you never get up there. I like it down here."

He took my hand. "I love it down here."

"Let's stay here."

And before he kissed me, he said, "Yes, this is a good place to start."

Acknowledgments

Major amounts of gratitude go to Joyce Hunt, Debi Feinman, Dolores Barnett, Joan Black, Sybil Sage, Chrissy Cross, and Gina Bogin for their cheerleading skills, and to the beautiful Charlotte Arthur, who saves me from anachronisms. To Kathy Sagan for saying I should do this, Gail Hochman for agreeing, and Vivien Yellin for insisting. And to my fabulous Gallery gals: Tricia Boczowski, Elana Cohen, and the two Jens: Bergstrom and Robinson. And of course, thanks go to Mr. Simon and Mr. Schuster, my imaginary boyfriends.

What Nora Knew
Linda Yellin

Molly Hallberg is a divorced writer living in New York City. For the past four years, Molly has been on staff at *EyeSpy,* an online entertainment magazine, getting all the wacky assignments. She's jumped out of airplanes, snuck vibrators through security scanners, and tested kegel-squeezing panties. What she really wants is her own column and to publish her literary essays. Her latest assignment is to write about romance "in the style of Nora Ephron," and she strikes out big-time. A self-professed cynic, Molly's no good at love—she's dating a chiropractor who's comfortable, but safe—and she won't acknowledge the one man who can go one-on-one with her. But with insights from Nora Ephron's iconic comedies, Molly learns to open her heart and find her own fairy-tale ending.

1. The epigraph at the beginning of the book is a quote from Nora Ephron. "There's no one who's more romantic than a cynic." Do you agree? Why do you think the author chose this quote?

2. "Deep-down love, deep-in-the-ventricles-of-your-heart love, was something that happened to other people,

make-believe people in fairy tales and movies," (p. 9) says Molly. Do you think she really believes this? How does her divorce affect how she understands love and romance? Does her relationship with Russell prove or disprove this belief? In what way does Cameron change this thinking?

3. Setting is an important part of Nora Ephron's movies, from the rain-drenched houseboats in *Sleepless in Seattle* to the infamous "I'll have what she's having" scene in Katz's deli in New York in *When Harry Met Sally.* How does the geography of New York influence this story? Could it have been set anywhere else?

4. While discussing *Sleepless in Seattle*, Molly tells Cameron "we know Meg will end up with Tom. But it's not about who she's going to end up with. We still want to keep watching. We're mesmerized by the journey." (p. 91) Would you say the same is true of this story? Why or why not?

5. "Happy couples create romantic narratives; they tell meet-cute stories worthy of a romantic comedy." (p. 236) Do you think this is true? How much of an influence do you think movies have on what we look for in romance? Have they conditioned us to expect the grand gesture (p. 290) in our own romances? How does it affect us to compare our own lives to the stories we see on the big screen?

6. Discuss the role of technology in the romantic lives of the characters. How do online dating, Twitter, Facebook, and Pinterest play into the story? What do you make of the fact that Molly writes for an online magazine? Does

technology help the characters find love? Stand in the way? How would this story be different if it had been written before the advent of these technologies? Consider Nora Ephron's movie *You've Got Mail*, about how email brings two people together, which was an updated version of *The Shop Around the Corner*, about two lovers who communicated by letter.

7. "The thing is, why are sex scenes necessary?" (p. 118) Molly believes keeping the details of what happens in the bedroom off screen (and off the page) is better than describing these acts in detail. Do you agree? How does it change the story to keep the bedroom scenes off the page? What is gained and what is lost by not showing the details?

8. Molly breaks up with Russell while waiting in line for a terrible movie he wants to see. Throughout the story, his thirst for Nicolas Cage movies is at odds with her love of Nora Ephron movies. In a book so deeply rooted in film references, what else does their differing tastes in movies say about them? What does it say that Cameron takes Molly to see *Sleepless in Seattle*? Can you judge a couple's compatibility by their taste in movies?

9. Cameron insists that elements of his book aren't stolen from other writers, they're homages to other writers. Do you think the same is true of Nora's movies, in the way *Sleepless in Seattle* is a take on *An Affair to Remember* and *When Harry Met Sally* nods to *Casablanca*? Do you see this book as a take on Nora Ephron's movies? An hom-

age to her? What allusions to her movies did you like? Not like?

10. Do you believe in love at first sight? Why or why not?

11. Molly dreams of having her own column and, eventually, publishing a book of her essays. Through the course of the story, she does get both a column and an agent, but both opportunities come because Cameron has pulled strings for her. Is this a weakness, a sign that she needs a man's help to get ahead no matter what she thinks? Or does this come across instead as a type of modern chivalry, a sign that shows how much he cares for her? How do you interpret his interventions in her career?

12. Through most of the story, Molly is something of a cynic about love, but she admits, "I wanted to feel cherished. I wanted to feel adored . . . I wanted someone to *get* me and then love what he got. Most of all, I wanted to believe, re-believe, that was possible." (p. 211) Do you think she gets this at the end? Why or why not? Does her transformation from cynic to romantic feel believable?

13. "How do we know they ended up happy?" Molly says of Tom Hanks and Meg Ryan of *Sleepless in Seattle*. "We never saw a sequel." (p. 150) Do you think Molly and Cameron end up happy? What makes you think that?

Enhance Your Book Club

1. Pick one of the movies Nora Ephron wrote (you can find a list at imdb.com) and watch it together. Or take it a

step further and watch *An Affair to Remember* (referenced in *Sleepless in Seattle*), *Casablanca* (referenced in *When Harry Met Sally*) or *The Shop Around the Corner* (like in *You've Got Mail*). Make lots of popcorn.

2. Mike Bing is Cameron Duncan's literary alter ago, and while he shares some of Cameron's quirks, he has a more glamorous job and love life, and is an idealized version of the writer. Imagine what your own literary alter ego would be like. What would she do, and how would she act? Share your thoughts with the group.

3. Nora Ephron's last full-length screenplay was *Julie & Julia*, about a woman who cooks through every recipe in Julia Child's *The Art of French Cooking*. Make your next meeting a French-themed dinner, creating recipes from the cookbook (don't forget the butter!) and drinking French wine.

4. In addition to her screenplays, Nora Ephron was known for her essays and journalistic writing. Check out some of her non-fiction, including *Crazy Salad: Some Things About Women*, *I Feel Bad About My Neck: And Other Thoughts on Being a Woman*, or *I Remember Nothing: And Other Reflections*.

An Interview with Linda Yellin

Your novel is filled with subtle references to Nora Ephron's movies. Or what some people might call *stealing*. What are some of those references?

Well, the description of Cameron is a description of Tom Hanks, and Molly is blond like Meg Ryan. The scene with Cameron and Molly sitting back to back in a café is in the same setting as the scene between Tom Hanks and Meg Ryan in *You've Got Mail*. And the montage when Cameron and Molly walk together follows the same route as Tom and Meg's in *You've Got Mail*. Molly sees a boy with a teddy bear in the lobby of the Empire State Building; that's a shout-out to Jonah and his teddy bear in *Sleepless in Seattle*, as well as the Jimmy Durante music Molly hears. And Arnold and Shirley are the names of the hamsters in *Heartburn*. There are other references, but they're so subtle even I don't remember them.

Did you have to do research for the story?

Yes. Anything that takes place in Long Island, I had to call my friend Suzi in Merrick. Plus I watched all the Nora Ephron movies. Except *Silkwood*. I've never seen *Silkwood*. It sounds depressing.

Isn't that what Kristine says in the book?

She stole that from me.

What was the most interesting thing you learned?

That Nora went into the family business; her parents were also Hollywood screenwriters.

Did you ever consider going into your family's business?

No. I had zero interest in manufacturing dog bowls.

Everyone falls in love in the book. Who's your favorite couple?

It's a toss-up between Arnold and Shirley or Joyce and Irwin.

Aren't Joyce and Irwin turtles?

Correct.

Doesn't that give the edge to Arnold and Shirley?

That depends on how you feel about turtles.

Who's your favorite character in the novel?

Emily. She's so divinely intrusive, and her workplace demeanor reminds me of my first job as a catalog copywriter at Sears. The copywriters all sat in cubicles, and we devoted far more of our workdays to pranks than to writing about toasters and washing machines. For reasons that now escape me, I had a rubber figurine of the Pillsbury Doughboy as well as a plastic donkey on my bookshelf. My buddies Mike and Jim were always sneaking into my cube and arranging the Doughboy and donkey into obscene positions.

Emily doesn't do that.

Only because Molly does not have a plastic donkey. Otherwise, I'm sure Emily would.

How did you come up with the names for your characters?

I asked for volunteers on Facebook. It just goes to show how trusting some people are. I could have been writing a book packed with murderers and terrorists and naming all those murderers and terrorists after my Facebook friends, but nobody seemed to care. Except for one woman who stipulated that I wouldn't use her name for any French schoolgirls. I don't know why. But it wasn't a problem because there are no French schoolgirls in the book.

Molly says she's terrible at writing sex scenes. Do you have the same problem?

Yes, and thank goodness. I avoid them. All my husband needs is me going, "Honey, that little thing you just did with your tongue—how do you spell that?"

Molly seems to cover a lot of unusual assignments. Sneaking vibrators through security. Wearing kegel underpants. Oddly enough, you seem to have covered many of these same magazine assignments in your own career.

Yes. But I have never posed nude.

Why not?

Nobody's ever asked.

Let's play a game. Pick one: Billy Crystal or Tom Hanks?

It's a draw.

Bill Pullman or Greg Kinnear?

What's the difference?

Bruno Kirby or Rob Reiner?

Definitely Rob Reiner. I've been crushing on him for years.

Carrie Fisher or Rosie O'Donnell?

Carrie. Mainly because her mom is Debbie Reynolds.

Meg Ryan or Meg Ryan?

Meg Ryan.

What's the best way to get to know the real Linda Yellin?

Go to LindaYellin.com. Or spend eight weeks with me in summer camp. Preferably in Wisconsin.

Molly says in the novel that writers are always asked about their process. What's your writing process?

There tend to be two camps. Neither of which is in Wisconsin. The first is writers who make thorough story outlines. The second is all the writers who believe that, if there's no surprise for the author, there's no surprise for the reader. They start with a premise and a few characters and see where it takes them. I fall somewhere in-between. I make a rough list of possible scenes that might create a story flow. But no roman numerals are involved.

When Harry Met Sally was made in 1989. *Sleepless in Seattle* in 1993. *You've Got Mail* was 1998. Why do you think Nora Ephron's movies are still so beloved even decades after she made them?

Who doesn't love a love story? And her characters are totally endearing. You can't help but root for everyone to end up happy. But the movies aren't just romantic; they're filled with all that witty banter and repartee. So even though you're sitting there crying at the end, you feel sophisticated.

Did you ever meet Nora Ephron?

No. When I first moved to New York in 1996, we lived in the same apartment building, this big kinda famous courtyard building on the Upper West Side, but I never ran into her. All sorts of celebrities lived in the building and I never ran into any of them. Cyndi Lauper. Bob Balaban. But every morning I'd watch Rosie O'Donnell through my bedroom window when her limo picked her up for work.

You spied on her?

That's one way to put it. I'd prefer to say I *observed* her. Spying would be if I broke into her apartment and hid behind her dining room curtains.

So, Linda, having written this novel, is there any way you feel you're at all similar to Nora Ephron?

Yes. I have a long, skinny face. Other than that, I remain forever in her awe. She was a genius.